For Little Black D

Thanks for picking up this Little Black Dress book, one of the great new titles from our series of fun, page-turning romance novels. Lucky you — you're about to have a fantastic romantic read that we know you won't be able to put down!

Why don't you make your Little Black Dress experience even better by logging on to

www.littleblackdressbooks.com

where you can:

- ♥ Enter our **monthly competitions** to win **gorgeous** prizes
- ♥ Get **hot-off-the-press** news about our latest titles
- ♥ Read **exclusive** preview chapters both from your **favourite** authors and from brilliant new writing talent
- ♥ Buy **up-and-coming** books online
- ♥ Sign up for an essential slice of romance via our **fortnightly email** newsletter

We love nothing more than to curl up and indulge in an addictive romance, and so we're delighted to welcome you into the Little Black Dress club!

With love from,

The *little black dress* team

Five interesting things about Anne Dunlop:

1. I helped with the sheep farming in Ireland when I was growing up. Nowadays I prefer my lamb served in a stew, with mint sauce.

2. In a karate competition I once fought the coach of the British team. He punched me on the nose; I kicked him in the head. I won a full point off him and a big hug afterwards.

3. I can say 'Tea or coffee?' in a dozen languages. I'm also pretty fluent in 'Chicken or fish?' and 'Please fasten your seat belt.'

4. In Africa I learned that shining a torch into the eyes of a lion will make it run away. I have never had an opportunity to try this.

5. I am a huge fan of the cloak-like black *abaya* worn by women in the Middle East. I wear one whenever I can, with my pyjamas under it, on the school run.

The Revenge of
Lady Muck

Anne Dunlop

little
black
dress

First published in 2010
by LITTLE BLACK DRESS
An imprint of HEADLINE PUBLISHING GROUP

A LITTLE BLACK DRESS paperback

1

Cataloguing in Publication Data is available from the British Library

ISBN 978 0 7553 5121 3

Typeset in Transit511BT by Avon DataSet Ltd,
Bidford-on-Avon, Warwickshire

Printed and bound in Great Britain by
Clays Ltd, St Ives plc

Headline's policy is to use papers that are natural, renewable and
recyclable products and made from wood grown in sustainable forests.
The logging and manufacturing processes are expected to conform to the
environmental regulations of the country of origin.

HEADLINE PUBLISHING GROUP
An Hachette UK Company
338 Euston Road
London NW1 3BH

www.littleblackdressbooks.com
www.headline.co.uk
www.hachette.co.uk

For Lesley

Prologue

Sarah Gordon lived in the shadow of four up front, funny, cynical sisters who were perfectly wonderful at everything. When she was growing up, Sarah spent a ridiculous amount of time comparing herself unfavourably to Laura, Helen, Daisy and Jennifer.

'I wish I had Laura's confidence,' 'I wish I had Helen's charisma,' 'I wish I had brains like Daisy,' 'I wish I could ride like Jennifer.'

Sarah's sisters couldn't see what all the fuss was about. They said, 'We wish we were tall, slender and blonde, with a flawless complexion and big breasts and boys queueing up to ask us out!'

Sarah was stricken. 'Is that really all I've got going for me? A pretty face? Blond hair? Big tits?'

Of course Mummy didn't understand. She said, 'Darling Sarah, what more could any girl ask for?'

Daddy didn't understand either. He said, 'Blondes have more fun. Gentlemen prefer blondes. Wasn't your mother a blonde when I married her?'

Even her sisters tried to help. 'All the boys fancy you!'

But Sarah couldn't enjoy it. Self-conscious and shy, she hid herself away in the kitchen, with her generous breasts safely enveloped in an apron, her blond hair pulled back off her face and her back to the world, up to her elbows in the sink as she washed the dishes. Soon a pattern was established. When Mummy had a Tupperwear party or the clergyman visited, Sarah's sisters crowded in, mad for the chat, while Sarah hid in the kitchen and made everyone cups of tea.

The Gordons lived at Derryrose, a rambling old farm in rural South Derry, bordered on one side by mountains, with a freshwater lake in the distance, and Derryrose village less than a mile away. The view from the upstairs windows was of green fields and purple heather, a silver lake and sometimes blue sky. The farm had been in the family forever, but this was the first generation to have no son to inherit, so all five daughters helped out with the farming to a greater or lesser degree. Daisy, in particular, loved country life, but Sarah preferred to remain indoors. She helped Mummy with the housework and kept her grand-mother company; Gran Gran read romantic novels to her about blushing virgins and handsome princes and the final chapter was always a wedding scene . . .

When she got older, Sarah's favourite hobby was flicking through bridal magazines and cutting out pictures of fairytale frocks, trimmed with diamonds and pearls, crowned with a tiara and framed with an acre of floating veil. She stuck them into a scrapbook with photographs of extravagant bouquets, elegant wedding cakes, satin shoes and ornate engagement rings.

'You've no photos of the husband!' said her lusty sisters, for when they thought of marriage they immediately thought of sex.

'I've not yet met my handsome prince,' said Sarah and her pretty, unkissed lips trembled.

'Our Sarah's a very impractical girl,' said Laura, Helen, Daisy and Jennifer. 'Her head's in the clouds, she's out of touch with reality, she's a daydream believer. Unless Prince Charming rides up on a white horse, wearing his crown, there'll never be a man good enough to take her.'

'Sometimes I don't think I belong to this family,' Sarah told her mother.

'I know you'll not thank me for saying it, but you're the picture of me when I was your age,' Mummy replied.

Sarah met Ian Flemming at a church party when she was sixteen and every Friday night, regular as clock-work, Ian came courting. Sometimes he brought Mummy a bar of chocolate, and she flirted with him while Sarah stood patiently waiting, dressed up in her very best outfit, with her legs shaved and her teeth brushed and her make-up immaculate; she looked a bit like a doll.

'Your mother is a lovely woman,' said Ian. He'd take her to the seaside for ice cream or to the Chinese restaurant for sweet and sour pork, and when he left her home he didn't stop his car in a pool of dark shadow in the farmyard. He never licked his lips and whispered, 'Make a bad boy out of me.' Instead, on her eighteenth birthday, he asked her to marry him.

'Why are you getting married so young?' asked her sisters when Sarah modestly showed them a diamond as big as the Ritz. They'd only just escaped from the wetlands and gone to live among the bright city lights, to university in Dublin. Sarah didn't have their sense of adventure.

'Oh, we're not getting married until I finish my teacher training, and we can afford to buy a fridge and a washing machine and a dishwasher,' she told them.

'And his 'n' her matching pyjamas?' they sneered.

But Sarah was blissfully content. She stopped going out with trainee teachers. She told them: 'Ian wouldn't like it.' Instead, she stayed in her room in the halls of residence, dreaming innocent dreams of a brand-new house in the town where Ian would do the gardening and she would keep her double-glazed windows spotless. They would have endless supplies of hot water and a daughter called Rosemary and dainty lace curtains so the neighbours couldn't see in.

*

Sarah's sisters came home at the weekend from Dublin with love bites and hangovers and broken romances. They discussed in exhaustive detail their experiences of shifting and sex.

Helen especially had an abundance of boyfriends, and always a story to tell: 'So there we were on his bicycle, I was sitting on the crossbar, and his hand was groping around inside my bra as we freewheeled down the hill from the college. "I can't find your breasts," he said. "Your hands are so cold you've shrunk them," I told him.'

Screeches of unladylike laughter ricocheted throughout the farmhouse.

'You girls are disgusting!' said Sarah as she polished her lovely diamond and thought beautiful thoughts about Ian who hoovered out his Twin Cam Corolla every Friday night before he came courting.

Helen said, 'Ah, but then it started to snow. I could feel snowflakes on my eyes and in my mouth when he kissed me . . . we lay under the tree in the garden – it forms almost a canopy even in winter. I could feel snowflakes melting on my naked skin, and everything around us was still and silent under the blanket of snow . . .'

'Which boyfriend was that?' asked Sarah, for Helen changed her boyfriends as often as she changed her socks.

'Oh, he's not a boyfriend! He's just a frog who

offered to hand rear my breasts.' Helen replied. 'I'm a lucky lucky girl to have met my handsome prince without ever having to kiss a frog!' Sarah said with solemn piety.

Every weekend her sisters threw their jeans and boots and student jumpers to one side. They bathed in perfumed water and exfoliated with porridge oats. They made face packs with mashed up cucumber and squeezed lemon juice into their fair hair to encourage natural highlights. They plucked eyebrows and painted fingernails and wriggled into tight, provocative frocks and went 'on the pull' to the local disco.

'The competition is fierce. It's a cattle market out there,' they said, but they weren't complaining.

'Come with us, Sarah!' they said, but, of course, she wouldn't go. On Saturday night she went to bed early, to look fresh and feel well rested for church on Sunday. She always sat in a pew at the front and smiled shyly at Ian who'd be singing his heart out in the choir to impress her. 'Ian wouldn't like it,' she said.

Kind Helen said, 'I know you think we're shallow, and you're absolutely right, we *are* shallow! But these are the best years of our lives, the freedom years between school and marriage, and you are wearing a handbrake called "Ian's engagement ring". I hope he's worth it.'

Sarah's life changed for ever when philandering Helen fell in love, irrevocably. He was a young man from her university, his name was Richard Knight, and officially they were just good friends. Sarah met him only once, on a Christmas shopping trip to Dublin. He called with another friend, Elisabeth; they were going, all three, to the theatre. He was just like every other young man who came calling, looking for Helen, except it was impossible to ignore the vibration between them. They couldn't stop touching each other – tiny subtle touches; they didn't even realise they were doing it. Toes and elbows touching, she brushed invisible dust from his shoulder; he stroked a strand of hair from her cheek. She looked as if recently she'd been covered in passionate kisses.

Sarah was frankly bewildered. She whispered, 'Your eyes are shining like stars and he isn't even your boyfriend!'

Helen couldn't care less. 'I've been hit by a thunderbolt! When we're together it's like his body is talking to my body. And my body answers . . .'

All the way home to Derryrose Sarah tried to imagine Ian's body talking to her body, and her body answering. She couldn't think of a thing their bodies might say to each other.

Mummy said, '*Of course* it's all right to sleep with the man you're engaged to! I strongly recommend it! After you're married you're going to have to sleep with him every night for the rest of your life. So much less hassle to find out now whether or not you're suited. Look at my friend Ruth Paisley. She thought Johnny was just shy till she married him. Then she realised the only thing that turned Johnny on were pipe band competitions. What was she supposed to do? Dress up in a kilt every night and blow into his bagpipes?'

Mummy went with Sarah to old Dr Hennessey for her first prescription of contraceptive pills, which she swallowed carefully and conscientiously for the recommended full three months before she brought up the subject of sexual intercourse with Ian.

Ian said, 'Your mother is a lovely woman. If your mother says it's all right . . .' And he'd rubbed himself, clumsy and excited, against her.

Sarah still shuddered when she thought about those first unhappy attempts at lovemaking. Ian had stayed over at the halls of residence in the teacher training college. She'd got him a special pass. He'd brought roses and chocolates and worn his best boxer shorts; she had scented candles and a bottle of baby oil, though she wasn't sure what to do with it.

They both wanted so much for the first time to be perfect. Instead, it was painful and messy and embarrassing. And it was so uncomfortable squashed underneath him.

'Couldn't you have told him to shift his weight off you?' said Helen when Sarah tentatively confided that all was not well in the bedroom department. The anxiety had brought her out in a rash; she wondered if maybe she was allergic to Ian. 'Or maybe you could get on top of him?'

Sarah said, with desperation, 'But I've unblocked toilets with more enjoyable prodding and poking!'

Helen shrugged. 'All right, so he's crap in bed, there's a lot of it around. There's no need to dwell on it. Why don't you get that book *The Joy of Sex* and learn together what buttons to push, how to relax, how to come?'

'I wish I could,' said Sarah sadly but already she'd lost all her sexual confidence and the thought of trying again with Ian and a book of illustrated diagrams gave her a seasick feeling. Her disappointment was crushing. She broke off her engagement.

It was decision she never regretted; not even when Richard proposed to Elisabeth and broke Helen's heart in a hundred pieces; not even when Ian found a very fine replacement and got married with indecent haste.

Sarah firmly believed there were worse things in life than living at home with a box full of wedding memorabilia stuffed into the back of her wardrobe.

Daisy Gordon and Johnboy Jackson were neighbours in the Irish sense of the meaning; their farms shared a boundary hedge. But they didn't fall in love until Daisy borrowed Johnboy's drilling machine when she was starting her PhD in organic potato farming. She told him, 'It's for my field trials. I'm going to have drills of organic potatoes randomly scattered all over the farm.'

'But how can you protect organic potatoes from blight unless you spray them with chemicals?' he asked her. Blight was the curse of Irish potato farming: it was airborne and uncontrollable; once it attacked the potatoes they became mushy, black and inedible.

Daisy said, 'Oh, I'm not focusing on blight! I'm more concerned with integrated plant management. I'm going to be matching the variety of potato to the soil type, and taking into consideration sunlight levels and fertilisation.'

Johnboy scoffed, 'I've never heard of anything so mad. I'll have to come and see for myself.'

One thing led to another and the next they knew, Johnboy was presenting himself in Derryrose's parlour, scrubbed and blushing, with his sister Alexandra at his elbow for moral support, to formally ask Daisy's permission to court her.

Now they were getting married and their engagement announcement was splashed across every farming supplement in every national newspaper. Their wedding photograph was booked for the cover of *Agriculture Ireland*. This was the 'Wedding of the Year'. Daisy Gordon from Derryrose marries Johnboy Jackson of Muff; an alliance by marriage of the two biggest farms in South Derry. Johnboy's mother could hardly sleep with the excitement. Daisy was formally invited to Muff to discuss the wedding arrangements.

'I wish you were coming with me, Sarah! I feel so much braver when I'm with you!' Daisy stared at her anxious reflection in the cloudy old mirror above the tiled fireplace. She was plump and pretty, the picture of health, with luminous skin and sparkling eyes; she was also a bag of nerves. All morning since she'd come in from the milking she'd been soaking in perfumed bath water and scrubbing at her hard-working hands with a Brillo pad and bleach. Now she was brushing her thick, bouncing hair and taking deep, calming breaths. She was trying to think only beautiful thoughts. She so desperately wanted the wedding-plans lunch to go smoothly and for everyone to be friends.

Again she said, 'I wish you were coming with me, Sarah! I know you could explain what sort of wedding I want so much better than I could myself!'

Sarah was dressed in jeans and a T-shirt, her hair pulled back with a scarf. She'd been out for a walk to pull lilac from the hedges around Derryrose; it was a gift for Mrs Jackson. She said, 'But you know exactly what you want! You don't need me to speak for you.'

Daisy's voice was querulous. 'And you know what Mrs Jackson is like – she's very, very scary! When she was my teacher at Derryrose Primary School she shouted so much, and whacked me so often, for the most trivial of misdemeanours. I still break into a sweat at the sound of her commanding voice . . .'

Sarah wrapped the lilac in damp newspaper. She handed the bunch to Daisy. 'Johnboy won't allow her to bully you,' she said, 'and isn't Mummy going?'

Daisy was impatient. 'Yes, of course Mummy's coming. She has to come. She's the mother of bride. But you know Mrs Jackson makes no secret of the fact she thinks Mummy is light in the head! Oh, I wish you were coming! Mrs Jackson likes you. She's always saying, "I saw Sarah at church on Sunday. She was wearing the loveliest trouser suit . . ."'

Sarah was very gentle. She said, 'I can't come with you. I haven't been invited.'

Honk! Honk! Mummy's old wreck of a car pulled up in a skid of gravel. She had to keep revving and honking or the car would splutter and die. Then they'd be late for the lunch and Mrs Jackson would be sniffy.

Daisy said, 'There's Mummy! Time to go! "Once more unto the breach . . ." Do you think I look sluttish in lipstick? Do you think I'm too fat for this frock?'

Sarah said firmly, 'You look lovely, but you're very nervous . . .'

Daisy waved to her mother from the bedroom window, then grabbed her cardigan and was gone, down the narrow back stairs, at breakneck speed.

'Good luck!' shouted Sarah, adding, more quietly, 'You're going to need it.'

Sarah lifted Daisy's wet towel and threw it over the banisters down into the tiled hall below. She tidied the sticks of Daisy's make-up into a wicker basket. She arranged Daisy's shoes in pairs in the bottom of the old-fashioned wardrobe and carefully hung up the outfits Daisy had tried on and discarded before deciding to wear her wrap-over dress.

'Untidy slut!' she said with affection.

She'd shared a bedroom with Daisy for years, since Gran Gran's sister, Great-aunt Maisie, had come seeking sanctuary at Derryrose after burning down her own house. The first few weeks had been volatile. Sarah would scream, 'Pick your dirty knickers up off the bedroom floor', and Daisy would shrilly answer her, 'Pick them up yourself!' Things had got so inflamed a line was drawn in chalk along the floorboards to divide the room in two and rolled-up towels were put down the middle of the double bed.

Sarah would brush and dust only her side of the room and smooth out only her side of the sheets in the morning.

Meanwhile, on Daisy's side, dust and detritus accumulated: half-drunk cups of coffee, half-eaten pieces of toast, mouldy apple cores. Daisy was shameless. She said, 'If it doesn't bother me, why should it bother you?'

Mummy had tolerated their adolescent posturing much longer than most mothers would – she'd called it 'artistic expression' until the morning she went into the bedroom to open the window and a mouse popped its head out from under Daisy's pillow. Then she'd freaked out and insisted one of her daughters move out of the bedroom and share with Jennifer.

'You've got to be joking,' said Sarah, for Jennifer was the smash-and-grab sister – there was one in every family – she liked to pick fights and steal clothes and she never, ever cleaned up after herself.

'Better the devil you know,' Daisy had agreed and so, with great determination and positive thinking on both sides, she and Sarah had managed for years to share the bedroom without any more unladylike, unkind slagging each other off. The fact they still shared a bedroom even though they were now the only two living in the farmhouse said more about Daisy and Sarah than it did about the size of the house they were living in.

*

Sarah ate a solitary lunch of soft-poached eggs and a salad. She read through Monday's lesson plan. This was her first year teaching in Derryrose Primary School and they'd told her at her teacher training college the first year would be the most challenging while she found her feet and learned for herself the dark arts of primary school teaching. Always be prepared, they'd told her. Always have a back-up strategy. Always have your lesson plan learned . . .

Once she had her lesson plan learned, Sarah kept busy all afternoon scrubbing and polishing at Derryrose even though the ramshackle farmhouse sat up a long lane, surrounded by green fields and only the postman called on a regular basis. She washed the windows inside and out and wiped the sills with a damp cloth. She vigorously chopped at firewood with an axe, loaded it into a wheelbarrow, wheeled it to the scullery door and carried it into the kitchen to feed the Aga. She hoovered out the inside of her car. She organised fridge magnets alphabetically and baked a chocolate cake.

She waited with expectant dread for Daisy to return from the wedding-plans lunch. She hoped Daisy wouldn't return in tears for everyone knew Mrs Jackson was a militant traditionalist who would insist the happy couple have a big splash of a formal white wedding. Everyone also knew she was an overbearing battleaxe who, when crossed, had been known to bellow: 'Don't you know who you're talking to?'

It wouldn't be the first time Sarah's shoulder had been cried on since Johnboy came courting with a dozen duck eggs.

Derryrose farmhouse was sparkling and Sarah was icing the chocolate cake when Daisy burst into the kitchen and dramatically announced: 'Mrs Jackson wants lilies and Pachelbel's *Canon* played slowly as I glide up the aisle – imagine me gliding! I'll have to practise!'

Sarah wiped her hands on her apron. She said, 'But that sounds more like a funeral than a wedding. And not to your taste at all! Could you not have said "No, Mrs Jackson"?'

Daisy shook her head sadly. She didn't do confrontation. She couldn't say 'boo' to a goose. 'I don't really care. I don't have *strong feelings* about it. My wedding day is only one day in the rest of my life with Johnboy and I'd rather not fight with his mother.'

She buttered herself a large piece of soda bread and stuffed the whole thing into her mouth.

Sarah said, 'I thought you were going to tell her you wanted an informal country wedding with a bouquet of flowers pulled out of the hedge, and a ceilidh in the hay barn afterwards . . .'

Daisy said, 'I tried to tell her but she held up her hand like a policewoman directing traffic and said in her commanding voice, "Just a moment please. There will be time for you to speak later. First, I think I ought to tell you I'm expecting great things at this wedding. It is the Wedding of the Year, after all, and it's going to be splashed across all the newspapers. It might even be televised for *Good Evening, Ireland!*" '

'*Good Evening, Ireland* – are you serious?'

Daisy began to foam at the mouth. Her voice had an edge of hysteria. She said, 'I don't like to say bad things about my prospective mother-in-law, but the woman has delusions of grandeur! *Good Evening, Ireland* – have you ever heard worse? Can you imagine Johnboy and me on the television? I would die of fright!'

Sarah was very soothing. She said in the softest of voices, 'What an exhausting lunch party! I think you need a little lie down! Go up to bed and have a sleep. I'll bring you a cup of tea before you go out to the milking . . .'

2

O nce Daisy was safely in bed, with the pink satin
curtains quietly drawn and her lovely frock hung
up in the wardrobe, Sarah pulled on her wellies and
walked down the lane to her parents' brown and white
bungalow which they called their love nest but which
had actually been built as a retirement home.

Traditionally in Ireland there was only ever one
house on a farm, even a farm as big as Derryrose. And
in this one house all generations of the farming family
lived together – there was Granny in the corner,
Mammy in the kitchen and Baby in the playpen, or, in
the case of the Derryrose Gordons, five daughters in
the playpen and Gran Gran had her own sitting room.
Mummy had cheerfully tolerated her role as Mammy
in the kitchen, but dreaded the day when she would
become Granny in the corner.

So when Johnboy had started courting Daisy she
campaigned for a second house on the farm. She'd
said, 'In these modern times a young married couple
expects to have their own space.'

Daddy had liked the idea of Daisy and Johnboy getting married, living together at Derryrose and taking over the farm when he died. Already Daisy milked his cows, organised the day-to-day management of the farm and juggled the accounts in addition to studying for her PhD. She was better than any son and he wasn't afraid to admit it. To Mummy's delight, he'd bucked tradition and built himself and his wife a brown and white bungalow, full of *all mod cons*. And when Johnboy proposed to Daisy he gave them the farmhouse as their wedding present.

It was a sunny, bright afternoon; sparkling, fresh and breezy. This was what Sarah loved most about living in rural Ireland – the clean smell of the countryside after a shower of rain. It was what she'd missed in the city when she was training to be a teacher. For three years she'd lived in an ugly white room, in an anonymous hall of residence, week in, week out, patiently tolerating litter, traffic fumes and harsh city voices. But she had never really settled. Every Friday night, while her friends were getting dressed up to go out on the town, she'd come home on the bus and the first thing she'd do was to run a bath to wash the city away.

'There's no place like home!' murmured Sarah as she knocked on the back door of the bungalow.

'Come in, come in,' shouted Mummy from where she was reclining in her pretty cream sitting room, on her cream leather sofa, with a chilled, folded facecloth on her forehead. A large glass of Andrews Liver Salts fizzed quietly on a table beside her.

'Pass me my drink, will you, darling?'

It was hard to believe, when you looked at Mummy, that she had five fully grown-daughters and three grandchildren. Today she was dressed in faded jeans, a skin-tight T-shirt and vertiginous platform sandals. With her chandelier earrings and luxurious blond hair, and her fondness for heavy, musky perfume, all heads always turned in her direction when she made an entrance into a room. In poor lighting, from behind, she might have been Sarah's artistic older sister.

'How was the lunch party?' Sarah asked.

Mummy sipped her drink through a straw. 'The Jacksons have a thousand sheep, two chicken houses and three hundred acres of early potatoes blowing in the wind. They're the richest farmers in the country. Yet Eva served us plastic food from plastic bags for lunch! I have just eaten something called a Turkey Twizzler and a portion of unidentifiable vegetables called "wedges". I don't know how I managed to swallow. Not only will I be constipated for a week, but my friend Ruth also says processed food causes cellulite,' she said.

'Oh dear,' said Sarah noncommittally.

'She didn't even have peppermint tea to aid digestion afterwards. It's probably too late now to save me, but I'm hoping these liver salts will flush the impurities out of my body. Then I'm going for a brisk walk to try to dislodge the saturated fat that is lining my stomach. Do you want to come with me?'

'Of course I'll come with you. But first, please tell me exactly what happened at the wedding-plans lunch. Daisy is in a state of near hysteria. She's barely coherent. She's ranting on about Pachelbel's *Canon*, *Good Evening, Ireland* and delusions of grandeur. I had to put her to bed. I'm wondering if I should sedate her.'

Mummy pointed to a bottle-green outfit, in a flowing, old-fashioned crêpe de Chine, with a matching hat and gloves, lying over the back of the sofa.

'You can sedate me, too, while you're at it. Not only has Eva presented me with an enormous list of things she expects me to organise for the wedding, but she has also given me that Mother-of-the-Bride outfit to wear. As if I would be seen dead in anything she likes! She says she bought it for Alexandra's wedding last summer. In fact, she bought three different outfits for Alexandra's wedding, and when she tried them on, Alexandra said, "I like you best in the peach, Mother", so Eva wore peach, and that green monstrosity has been hanging in her wardrobe ever since. It has shoulder pads and a built-in girdle. I felt armour-plated when I put it on.'

Sarah was severe. 'But even I can see from here it's at least two sizes too big on you! There's no way you can wear it!'

Naked desperation suddenly flashed from Mummy's eyes.

'What on earth made Eva think I was as fat as she is? I blame those gel fillet inserts I was wearing in my bra and my knickers! My friend Ruth told me it was the fashion, at the moment, to have a big round bottom! She told me *voluptuous* and *boho* were the buzz words this season . . . so much for *voluptuous* and *boho* – I'm never wearing them again.'

Sarah read through the wedding list. At the top was '**The Wedding of the Year**' in bold type, underlined, then a list of crazy razzmatazz: two hundred wedding guests, Cinderella carriage for the bride, lilies and Pachelbel's *Canon* at the church, champagne reception in Belfast Castle, a string quartet to play during dinner . . .

'She thinks it's a royal wedding,' said Mummy.

Sarah sat down beside her mother. She took her manicured hand and gave it a little shake. Gently she said, 'Could you not have told her, "This may come as surprise to you, Eva, but I'm perfectly capable of organising my own daughter's wedding. Didn't I manage to get Laura married off and Jennifer as well, without your most excellent interference?" '

From under her navy-blue eyelashes Mummy peeped at her beautiful, upright daughter – so elegant, aloof and not a hair out of place. Sarah always made everything seem so simple, for she lived her life in black and white. The only grey area in Sarah was her clear grey eyes.

'I tried to, I really did. I even opened my mouth, but the words wouldn't come out. Oh, why do I find it so difficult to stand up to Eva?'

'Because you feel sorry for her,' said Sarah.

Sarah didn't usually meddle. Growing up with four volatile sisters she'd learned early in life to mind her own business or risk cat fights and quarrels of biblical intensity. The Wedding of the Year was Daisy's wedding, nothing to do with her. She had been asked only to be a bridesmaid and her duties were to look decorative and make tea when well-wishers called to the house with presents. So what came out of Sarah's mouth next was as unexpected as it was unrehearsed.

She said, 'Would you like me to organise Daisy's wedding?'

Warm relief was written all over Mummy's face. 'Oh my darling, would you? I know it's a horrible imposition, especially after what happened with Ian . . . But Eva likes you so much she might actually listen to what you have to say! Unlike me – she treats me like an imbecile just because I stayed at home rearing children and she was a teacher for thirty years . . .'

Sarah folded the wedding list neatly and slipped it into the hip pocket of her jeans. She said, 'I'll just pop over to Muff and have a word with Mrs Jackson before we go for our walk. Will we walk to the windswept graveyard up the side of the mountain?'

Mummy closed her eyes and snuggled down on the sofa. She said, 'Yes, darling, that's a brilliant idea, but let's not go walking until after *Star Struck* – Barney O'Connor has got through to the final and there's a phone-in vote on the show. It's the least I can do, to vote for him when he played his fiddle so beautifully at Laura's wedding, and Jennifer's . . .'

Suddenly Sarah felt very tired. Truth be told, she wasn't at all looking forward to Daisy's wedding for she knew her own broken engagement would be raked up and gluttonously picked over by the well-wishers. Already she could hear their nudge-nudge-wink-wink whispers – 'The tall one was jilted, don't you remember? Yes, just before her wedding. There was such a scandal about it! They were going to sue him for breach of promise . . .' She had even, at one stage, wildly hoped she might not have to be a bridesmaid, and that she might fade quietly into the background, for Daisy wanted only two bridesmaids and she had four sisters to choose from. Sarah had even suggested she choose Laura or Jennifer, but Daisy had not wanted Laura or Jennifer. She'd said, 'You're my best friend, Sarah, I need you there beside me.'

Sarah kissed her mother. 'Bye-Bye. Wish me luck.'

Mummy said, 'Oh, I know you'll be fine! Eva *adores* you! A little birdie told me she's the reason you got the job at Derryrose Primary School! Alexandra didn't want to work with you, but Eva insisted. You can hardly blame Alexandra – she's bound to feel threatened, poor thing.'

Sarah frowned. 'Where did you hear Alexandra didn't want to work with me?'

'The beauty parlour. Where else? Alexandra told my friend Ruth, last year when she was in Curl Up and Dye having her moustache electrolysed before she married Ian.'

Daisy was asleep on top of the bed. She'd been up half the night, worrying about potato blight, and back up at six for the milking. And what with a morning of emotional anxiety preceding the wedding-plans lunch and an afternoon of comfort eating afterwards . . .

'Wake up,' said Sarah softly, 'I've brought you a cup of tea.'

She arranged a small tray with a teapot and cup on the table beside Daisy's bed. Then she pulled back the pink satin curtains and allowed mellow afternoon sunlight to flood into their bedroom. Dazed, Daisy sat up and looked around her. Her face was creased with sleep; she looked young and very vulnerable. No one could ever have guessed she was Sarah's older sister.

'Thanks for tea,' she said. 'Did you bring me a piece of your chocolate cake?'

Sarah shook her head. 'Sorry! I need that chocolate cake for business not pleasure. I'll bake us another one later, if you like.'

Daisy watched as Sarah pulled off her jeans and

changed into one of her trouser suits – this one was a soft brown pinstripe, she wore it with a blouse of antique white lace. She slipped her feet into gladiator sandals and lovingly wound the long sliver straps round and round her tanned calf muscles. She brushed her blond hair till it gleamed and twisted it into a tidy chignon. She skilfully applied the prescribed amount of make-up and squirted herself with a businesslike perfume.

'How do I look?' asked Sarah, for though tall and blonde and beautiful she rarely looked in the mirror except to criticise her hair which she thought too fluffy and her eyes which she thought too dark.

Daisy said, 'You're a vision of loveliness. Where are you going?'

'I'm going to do battle with Mrs Jackson,' Sarah said. 'I'm going to tell her the Wedding of Year will be a simple country wedding – just the way the bride wants it. I'm taking the chocolate cake with me. To soften the impact of the blow.'

Daisy solemnly regarded her most favourite sister. All her life Sarah had championed her, in small, discreet, practical ways. Even when they were children she'd packed Daisy's school bag and polished her shoes and reminded her to brush her teeth every day.

'You're the best sister anybody could ever have. What would I do without you?' she asked.

'Sure, you'd do the same for me,' said Sarah.

S arah drove into the farmyard at Muff and parked. What a fancy place this was with big modern buildings and everything freshly painted and the yard swept; a professional operation and as tidy as a stud farm. Old John Jackson, God rest his soul, had always treated farming as a business, and there was an air of industrious efficiency about the place that was not usually found on Irish farms. Even now, on Sunday afternoon, Sarah knew she would find Johnboy busy at something – counting animals, or oiling machinery, cleaning out water drinkers, building stone walls. He never sat down.

Sarah stepped carefully out of the car and removed the chocolate cake from the passenger seat. She had deliberately parked well away from Muff's modest dwelling house for she knew Mrs Jackson was a woman of great formality who did not suffer casual callers lightly. Even the clergyman had once had the front door slammed in his face when he'd arrived without an invitation.

'Cooee! Johnboy!' she shouted.

Johnboy's head appeared in the middle of a potato field where he was bent over double, inspecting his plants. He waved and Sarah waved back.

'Hello, there,' he shouted. 'It's lovely weather for potato blight.'

'And here I was thinking a man on the brink of marriage might be thinking about his fiancée . . .'

'But I am thinking about Daisy! If she doesn't spray soon with Bordeaux Mixture she's going to lose her entire crop to blight.'

He vaulted the five-bar gate at the edge of the potato field and dropped lightly on to the tarmac lane. He was a jovial little man, but even he had sensed the uncomfortable atmosphere at the wedding plans lunch.

He said, 'I'm guessing you've been sent to poison my mother with that chocolate cake!'

Sarah laughed. She was very fond of Johnboy and could not understand why some people thought he wasn't good enough for Daisy. Since their engagement, Daisy's intellectual (and unmarried) university friends had sneered at his lack of academic qualifications and her father's idle (impoverished) relatives had made unkind jokes about his work ethic: 'Daisy is marrying a boiler-suit farmer. How *could* she?'

But when you thought about how many unhappy marriages there were in the world and the husband and wife with nothing in common, it was possible to forgive Johnboy for anything, even for having Eva as a mother.

'Of course I've not come to poison your mother! But I am here to have a little chat with her. Please will you walk up to the house with me, and tell her I'm here? I'd rather not barge in unannounced.'

'Delighted to be of service,' said Johnboy. 'May I carry your cake?'

They walked together up the tarmac lane to the dwelling house at Muff. It was bleak and pebble-dashed with ugly plastic windows; neat as a doll's house. An aseptic garden surrounded it; there wasn't was a blade of grass out of place. The flowers grew with military precision and weeds did not dare push through the polished gravel. Even the wind seemed to blow with more restraint and less joy through the tidy privet hedge. Sarah thought it looked very forlorn and it pleased her to think that Johnboy would not be carrying Daisy over so austere a threshold. Instead, Daisy would be carrying Johnboy over the threshold of Derryrose.

After the wedding Sarah would be moving into the brown and white bungalow with her parents. Already she'd packed most of her work clothes and play clothes and exercise clothes; her work shoes and play shoes and exercise shoes; her make-up and toiletries and perfumed talc; though the official moving date was not until the wedding day.

*

Eva was lying flat out on the sofa in the Good Room. She was watching *Little House on the Prairie* on the television. Since John's death, six months before, she'd developed a particular affection for the 'good old days' when life was simple and youngsters were biddable. And, of course, Pa Ingalls was pretty darned gorgeous. Last week he'd injured his ribs and spent most of the episode sitting bare-chested in the doctor's surgery, his broken, tanned, muscular torso artistically wrapped in bandages . . .

Johnboy stuck his head round the door.

'Wake up, Mother! You have a visitor!'

Eva heaved herself into a sitting position and stuck her feet into her shoes. She smoothed down her hair and plumped up the cushions behind her. She wondered who on earth it could be, calling at such an unsociable hour – in rural Ireland Sunday afternoon was always reserved for a sleep on the sofa.

She folded her hands and her ankles and was regally upright when Sarah was ushered in bearing her chocolate cake.

'Good afternoon, Mrs Jackson.'

'Good afternoon, Sarah. Won't you please take a seat?'

Sarah set the cake down and sat in an armchair. From her handbag she removed the list of wedding plans – bold type, underlined. There was a pleasant smile on her lips and a look of steely good manners on her face. This was the expression she always adopted when confronted by yet another over-zealous parent, barging into her classroom with a list of affronted complaints.

In her very best teacher's voice she said: 'First, I must apologise for the impromptu nature of this interview. It is my personal preference to schedule appointments with people. But given the serious nature of the list I have just received, I think we have something very urgent and immediate to discuss.'

The silence in the Good Room was as loud as a crash of cymbals. Johnboy held his breath. Eva could not have looked more surprised if Sarah had pulled a gun from her handbag and threatened to shoot her with it. The tension was terrific. Sarah continued to sit ramrod straight and unyielding. She had said her bit. Now it was Eva's turn.

Then Eva started to laugh. She laughed and laughed until she almost choked.

Johnboy became alarmed. 'Are you all right, Mother? Will I get you a glass of water?'

Eva wiped tears from her eyes with her handkerchief. She said, 'Yes, I'd love a glass of water. Or maybe a cup of tea. Will you take a cup of tea with me? Johnboy, love, make us two cups of tea.'

She dismissed him, bemused, to kitchen. Then she said, 'Oh Sarah, you're such a laugh. Those are the exact words I taught you to say when you took over from me at the primary school!' Sarah's ramrod posture relaxed very slightly and she allowed her eyes to twinkle. 'I learned the rules of engagement from the very best.'

'And do those opening lines still work?'

'Every single time.'

Eva Jackson had been the headmistress at Derryrose Primary School right up until her husband John became ill. Then she'd taken early retirement, and the board of governors had advertised for a new teacher at the school. There had been a hundred applications; many of the applicants had years of experience. Sarah Gordon from Derryrose had made the shortlist only because she was an old girl. Yet out of a hundred applicants, Sarah had got the job.

'What a lovely, sensible girl, she's by far the most suitable candidate,' said Eva after the interview.

Johnboy brought in a teapot, two cups, a milk jug, sugar, side plates, napkins and a knife. He said, 'I won't take a piece of cake, thanks. I'm rushing out now to the Farmer's Club barbecue. Bye-bye, Mother. I'll be home about ten.'

Eva said, 'Phone me if you need a lift. Please remember two pints maximum is the drink driving law in this country . . .'

'Yes, Mother,' said Johnboy and he winked at Sarah.

'Bye-bye, Johnboy,' she said.

Then he was gone, hairy and squat, in jeans and dealer boots and a Farmers' Club T-shirt which said something cryptic and obscene about men being men and sheep being scared.

Sarah said softly, 'You're going to miss him when he gets married and moves to Derryrose.'

'Only the first day,' said Eva.

She poured the tea and said, 'I apologise for writing that list. I know it's a horrible breach of etiquette. I know it's the bride's family who traditionally organises a wedding. But, in my defence, this is the Wedding of the Year and your sisters' weddings were informal in the extreme . . .'

Sarah noticed Mrs Jackson's hand was shaking slightly as she sipped her tea. Gently she said, 'Nobody wants you to feel uncomfortable at Johnboy's wedding. My goodness – you *are* the mother of the bridegroom! What I propose is that we go step by step through your list. I'm sure we'll agree on some things and we can agree to disagree on others.'

A sense of relief washed over Eva and all the fight seeped out of her. Her hard old face melted and she smiled. 'Yes, let's go through the list together. And if there's anything at all you need help with, please just ask! I have so much time on my hands now John is dead and I don't have to dance attendance on him. My friends at the Widows' Group are also eager to offer their assistance. They're such a talented bunch of ladies! Phyllis has been arranging flowers for years, and Mary Murphy bakes delicious cakes . . .'

They had a lovely discussion about the wedding

arrangements. They agreed on certain refinements.
There would be no lilies, no Pachelbel's *Canon* and no
Cinderella carriage. The wedding flowers would be
wild flowers pulled out of the hedges around
Derryrose. The wedding reception would be held in
the hay barn at Derryrose.

Sarah said, 'Is there anything in particular you
would like to include in the wedding arrangements?'

Eva filled up their cups with more tea. 'I'd really
like two hundred guests to fill up the church so there
are no empty pews. Empty pews look so sad at a
wedding. I'd like to invite all the farmers in the South
Derry area – Johnboy knows most of them since he
became President of the Farmers' Club . . .'

Sarah nodded. 'And Daisy knows most of them too!
What an excellent idea – why don't I go to their
barbecue now and invite them?'

It wasn't as if she had anything else planned for
the rest of Sunday. At Derryrose Daisy was milking the
cows – if Sarah went home now she would be as alone
as she had been all afternoon. A scenic drive down to
the Farmers' Club barbecue in Lisglasson village
would help pass the time until *Star Struck* was finished
and she and her mother could go walking together to
the windswept graveyard up the side of the mountain.

Eva looked worried.

'I'm not sure I like the sound of that. The Farmers'
Club is a bastion of misogyny. Women are not welcome
except to make tea and babies! And you know what

farmers are like after a couple of pints – they've not an ounce of common sense. Why don't we phone Johnboy and ask him to do it? It is his wedding, after all!'

Sarah stood up and straightened her shoulders. She shook cake crumbs from her trouser suit. She said, 'I'm not afraid of a bunch of farmers.'

Mrs Jackson was suddenly wistful. 'Of course you're not afraid – you're not afraid of anything! There are not many young women who could organise a beloved sister's wedding, after such a disappointment suffered in your own love life, my dear. A broken engagement is still a bereavement – though maybe not quite so sad as a death . . .'

Once Sarah had gone, Eva took down from the piano a framed photograph of her dead husband. 'I'm so glad Sarah is going to be organising the wedding, John. She's such a safe pair of hands. I was quite right to trust my instincts and recommend her for my teaching job, even though she had no experience and her mother is Jenny Gordon and insanity runs in the family . . .'

Eva had a habit of talking to John when she was alone in the Good Room at Muff. Of course she knew he was dead, she wasn't mad or anything, it was just that she'd always talked to him about everything, and she found it hard to stop, just because he was dead.

At five o'clock Alexandra and her husband Ian swept into Muff for high tea. What a lovely young couple they were: Alexandra was headmistress at Derryrose Primary School and Ian, an accountant, was heir to his father's fitted-bathroom empire.

Eva was delighted to see them. She said, 'Come in, come in, my darling Sandra, and bring that big, handsome hunk of a husband with you.'

She ushered them into the Good Room and fussed about with china teacups. The remains of Sarah's most excellent chocolate cake sat in splendour on the occasional table. Ian licked his lips in anticipation. He had a shocking sweet tooth for a man.

'What a magnificent chocolate cake!'

Alexandra eased herself on to the sofa. She was expecting a baby; she wasn't finding it a beautiful experience. She was bloated and swollen and her haemorrhoids were killing her.

'I've had to sit on a cushion for a week. There's something *pressing* . . .'

Eva clucked with sympathy. She poured tea and handed it round. Alexandra and Ian politely sipped, baby fingers delicately elevated as Eva recounted her adventures at the wedding-plans lunch.

'After those stories Ian told me about Laura Gordon's wedding – the dancing on tables and the falling off chairs, and Jenny in a dress of plunging pink lace with her breasts hanging out – well, I was afraid to hold my tongue and say nothing . . .'

Alexandra said sharply, 'You were perfectly right to speak up. Daisy is arty-farty. Johnboy says she's given names to all her cows. The next thing we know, she'll be wanting to get married in a field of cows.'

Eva beamed. If she'd been a dog, she'd have wagged her tail. She said, 'I'm happy to say the wedding is now in safe hands.' And she told them her wonderful news.

'Well, thank goodness for Sarah Gordon,' said Alexandra, and her voice was sarcastic and bitter.

'Sarah to the rescue . . . what would we do without Sarah?'

Gently Ian stroked his wife's arm. 'Hush, darling . . . you'll upset yourself and the baby. Breathe in – one, two, three. Breathe out – one, two, three. Think beautiful thoughts . . .'

Alexandra slapped his hand away. 'Don't touch me! It's making my flesh crawl.'

Ian tried not to feel hurt and offended for he knew his wife was only suffering from the furious hormones of pregnancy. He'd read all about them, those hormones, in *The Dark Side: A Loving Husband's Guide to Navigating Nine Eggshell Months*. 'Stop the breathing. You're breathing too loud. Can't you stop it?'

The clock struck six. Ian cleared his throat. 'It's been lovely to visit you, but we've really got to go! The Farmers' Club has asked us to sing at their summer barbecue. Chop-chop, Alexandra, and drink up your tea, I don't want to keep them waiting.'

Alexandra regarded her husband with a cynical eye and snuggled down deeper into the sofa.

'Go on without me. I'm not a barbecue sort of girl. And if I know the Farmers' Club, as well I might, since my brother is its president, they'll be throwing the sausages and burgers at each other instead of eating them.'

'But aren't you singing too?' asked Eva for Mrs and Mrs Ian Flemming were a much celebrated gospel singing double act in South Derry. Their photograph was often splashed across the society pages of the local newspaper. 'Mrs and Mrs Ian Flemming who sang at the wedding of X and Y', 'Mrs and Mrs Ian Flemming who sang at the funeral of Z' . . . It was unthinkable that one might perform without the other.

Alexandra shook her head. She was suffering so horribly from heartburn, chances were she might belch or break wind in the middle of a high note. 'I can't face it until after the baby is born. Ian is going to sing without me.'

Ian explained: 'My pregnancy book, *The Dark Side*, recommends I find myself a new hobby or revisit an old hobby – or, in this case, rework an existing hobby, to help me to maintain a sense of perspective during the challenging months of Alexandra's pregnancy and to help me empathise with the hormonal upheavals she is experiencing.' He bent over to kiss his young wife 'Goodbye.'

She said, 'Don't kiss me. You're making me nauseous.'

Eva walked slowly with Alexandra down the back lane to her brand new house, just recently built on the edge of the farm. She waited with her while she organised a tray of self-help remedies to prevent and manage her pregnancy sickness through the night.

Dr Hennessey had assured Alexandra at the beginning of her pregnancy that the unbearable nausea she was suffering would ease off after the first trimester, and she would bloom. But it had not happened. If anything, her nausea had increased in line with her length of gestation. At three months' pregnant she'd thrown up on average three times a day. Now she was seven months' pregnant and she vomited every hour. And nothing stopped it – nothing! She had surfed every website and read every book, tried every quack remedy going. She had even tried grasping her tongue with a piece of her clothing and pulling when the urge came upon her to vomit – it was a recommendation from a reputable website – but all it had achieved was to hurt her tongue and the vomit had splashed all over her face instead of into the toilet bowl.

On the tray beside Alexandra's bed was a glass of cold water with a tablespoonful of cider vinegar and some honey dissolved in it. There was a packet of ginger snap biscuits. There was a bowl of salted mixed nuts and milk in a thermos flask. Chewing gum. Ritz crackers. Lemon peel for sniffing.

Alexandra was depressed and exhausted. She said, 'I can't believe the relentlessness of this nausea! So much for mind over matter and the power of positive thinking! Those relaxation techniques they taught me at the antenatal classes are useless.'

Eva was very encouraging. 'But something is working! You're still fit to teach, your baby is growing . . . Just take it one day at a time.'

'Easy for you to say – you've never thrown up in your life, not even when Johnboy fell off the roof of the boiler house and broke his leg and the bone was poking through the skin and Daddy fainted at the sight of it.'

Eva carefully dripped lavender oil on a cold face cloth, to fold and place on her daughter's forehead; she dripped lavender oil on the terry cloth cover of a hot-water bottle; this Alexandra tucked under her arm.

'Can I help you with anything else?' asked Eva.

'Open the bedroom window, if you don't mind. A cool air helps with the nausea. And sorry, but I've forgotten my bangles. They're sitting on the sink in the bathroom. I would be very much obliged if you'd fetch them for me . . .'

Eva trotted off to fetch the plastic bangles. 'What do these do?'

'Stop nausea by applying pressure to my inner wrist. They're used by sailors with sea sickness problems. I've no idea if they're working or not.'

Once Alexandra was comfortable, her mother switched off the bedroom light and tiptoed quietly down the stairs. She'd just make herself a quick cup of tea and drink it in front of *Star Struck* – Barney O'Connor was a past pupil at Derryrose Primary School, and she was willing him to win at the final in London. Then she'd slip back upstairs and check one last time on Alexandra before she walked back to Muff.

Ian got out of his car and looked up the higgledy-piggledy street. Lisglasson village was only three miles from busy and bustling Derryrose, yet it might have been three hundred miles and thirty years, so quiet and picturesque were the straggle of houses and shops. At the top of the street, looking down, was the entrance to Lisglasson Estate, a grand old place built by the first Lord Glass in 1732, or so it was carved on the magnificent stone gateposts attached to a pair of old gates. Today the village street was crammed full of tractors, pick-ups and mud-splattered Landrovers: the boys were back in town.

The Farmers' Club met once a week during the long, dark Irish winter in the local pub. Every Friday night the hen-pecked and the lonely, family men and bachelors, clattered into The Lisglasson, many of them still in their wellies, for an evening of liquid refreshment and *craic*. For some of the mountainy men who lived in isolated dwelling houses, it was the only bit of socialising they got all week. This barbecue was their last gathering before the long, brutal hours of summer when they'd be harvesting crops and kicking hay, dodging the unpredictable weather and always watching for rain. If the sun made an appearance at all, they took the wife and wee children to the seaside. They wouldn't meet up again until after the harvest was in.

Ian's natural self-confidence faltered when he smelt the aroma of animal excrement floating up from the wheels of the abandoned vehicles. He was a townie boy, born and bred, and he always felt squeamish with the farmers. Unless you were born to it, could it ever be possible to feel comfortable with men who stuck their hands up ewes' bottoms at lambing, who fondled cows' breasts at milking time, who assisted the boar in the pig-breeding house?

Outside the pub, on the street, a forty-gallon drum was filled with fire and belching smoke. A catering committee of farmers was boat racing pints and casually supervising the cremation of burgers and sausages. One of them, a man of brutish proportions, was making obscene gestures with the two-pronged barbecuing fork. Another had his head stuck into the flames; he was lighting a cigarette.

'Smell that!' he shouted. 'I've just singed my eyebrows!'

From the bowels of the pub came unearthly shrieking, raucous applause and the exuberant stamping of steel toe-capped dealer boots on a flagstone floor. Willie Simpson was tuning in his karaoke machine.

'One, two, one two, can everybody hear me?' bellowed Willie.

A flush of panic washed over Ian. His breath became shallow and rapid. The dark lenses of his spectacles steamed up. His lips began to tremble. Until this moment it had never occurred to him that he might not have the nerve to sing at the Farmers' Club barbecue without his formidable wife by his side to support him. Until now he had not quite realised just how much he depended on Alexandra for her encyclopaedic knowledge of farming and her talent for talking to farmers. She understood their mysterious vocabulary; she knew their wives, and their children and their ancestors back three or four generations. She could work a room of farmers better than any career politician.

'Look, everybody! It's the entertainment arrived!'

Johnboy broke away from the boat-racing farmers and came up the street to greet him. 'Hello, there. How's she cutting? And where's that big breeding sow of a sister of mine? I was just telling the lads she's in mighty condition. Getting bigger every day. And crosser. She can turn on you and attack faster than a sow with a litter of wee pigs . . .'

Ian stared uncomprehendingly into his brother-in-law's open, friendly face.

He said, 'Alexandra's condition is very delicate. I'm sorry to announce that she doesn't feel well enough to sing tonight.'

'Shame!' said Johnboy. 'I was really looking forward to hearing "Psalm 119 for Two Voices". Just as well, then, that we've got the karaoke machine to keep us entertained! Now, what do you want? Hot dog or burger?'

Ian said, 'I'll have a burger, please. But no ketchup, if you don't mind.'

The pregnancy book had recommended he find himself a new hobby and a solo career in singing had seemed like the obvious choice. But in his heart Ian knew this wasn't a suitable venue to launch it. Much wiser and safer to wait till the next time Mr and Mrs Ian Flemming were asked to sing at a wedding or funeral. Then he'd push himself forward as a solo alternative – a congregation was a captive audience, and in church he couldn't be pelted with bread rolls.

5

Sarah sat serene and detached on a barstool, inside the pub, quietly looking about her. She didn't usually frequent this pub, for she taught in South Derry's Bible belt and though not averse to the odd little drinkie she had never, in public, been known to drink anything stronger than an espresso.

The farmers watched Sarah watching them. They nudged each other and whispered, 'I wonder if she's blonde *all over* . . .'

They had napkins tied round their faces like bandits. Empty glasses were piled high on the tables, and a dozen or so pints of Guinness were lined up along the bar, gently settling. Willie's karaoke machine was squashed in between the darts board and the toilet. Sarah hoped the darts had been confiscated.

She chose not to hear what the farmers were whispering about. She tried not to feel intimidated, for weren't they just like a class of boisterous children and she knew from her teaching experience if they smelt fear off her she was done for . . .

'What can I get you to drink?' asked Willie.

His mad red hair was gelled up and there was an earring in his ear. He worked part-time as a barman in the Lisglasson and the rest of the time in Johnboy's chicken houses. He was the partner of Sarah's sister, Laura, and aspired to becoming a writer. Laura was helping with *Confessions of a Chicken Farmer* and there was always an abundance of eggs in their kitchen.

'Unfertilised!' said Willie. This was his favourite chicken-farmer joke.

Sarah said, 'I'll have a soda water and lime, please. Is this the full collection of farmers? Will I make my announcement now?'

Willie shook his head. 'Hold fire, the dairy farmers aren't here yet. They're always the last to arrive. Still milking their cows, I'm thinking. Give them another half-hour.'

Sarah sipped her drink and tried not to feel impatient for hadn't her own entire childhood been overshadowed by the demands of her father's milking cows, morning and evening, every day of the year, even Christmas Day? They'd never once gone away on a holiday.

'Can I offer you a complimentary Orgasm?' asked Willie.

Sarah shook her head. 'Tempting, but I think it might send me to sleep.'

What a long day it had been, and emotionally draining, first with Daisy, then Mummy, then Mrs Jackson. This was her last little job. Then she was going home to strip off her pinstripe trouser suit and release her feet from the grip of the gladiator sandals. She'd walk to the windswept graveyard with Mummy, then she'd run a bath. Burn some candles. Relax. It might even be warm enough to open the window in the ancient old bathroom at Derryrose. Perhaps tonight she wouldn't have to switch on the electric bar heater, and to worry about splashing it with water and getting herself electrocuted. Oh gosh, but she could hardly wait to move into her parents' brown and white love nest; Mummy had a fancy fitted bathroom in polished chrome and white marble, with under-floor heating and Jacuzzi jets.

Johnboy brought her a hotdog. 'It's the least I can do to say "thank you" for reining in my mother. She's a hard-pulling old mare when she gets the bit between her teeth.'

Sarah smiled. 'Your mother and I speak the same language, we understand each other.'

She bit into her hotdog and chewed. The sausage was burnt black. She tried not to think about carcinogens. The generous lashing of bright yellow mustard burnt her lips and stained her teeth. She tried not to think about e-numbers. Gamely she ate the whole nasty thing while Johnboy watched with approval. She tried not to think about food poisoning.

Austin Morris came into the pub, fair-haired and smiling and smelling of cows. Sarah knew him by reputation. He'd once proposed to her sister Helen with the immortal line: 'The life a dairy farmer is very lonely', and then wondered afterwards why she wouldn't marry him.

'Willie! The dairy farmers are finally here! Can I make my announcement now?'

'Certainly, sweetheart,' said Willie and he came out from behind the bar and took the microphone from the karaoke machine.

'A moment of your time, please gentlemen. This lady has something to say.'

It was only when Sarah stood up to speak that she noticed Rupert Glass leaning lightly against the white-washed wall at the back of the pub. Dark and handsome, Byronesque, he lived in the game keeper's cottage on the edge of the vast Lisglasson estates that had been in his family for centuries. Sarah drove past his gingerbread house every day on her way to and from school but she knew him only by reputation, for he presented *Good Evening, Ireland* on the television and spent much of his week in the city.

The Farmers' Club was the last place she'd ever have expected to see him, for he was a fastidious city slicker, and on television always wore a formal three-piece dark suit. She wondered if perhaps he was covering the barbecue for the local interest slot on his programme and if that was why he was dressed like a farmer in a soft, checked shirt with the sleeves rolled up and the points of the collar frayed. She looked around for cameras or a microphone but there was no sign of either. The presenter of *Good Evening, Ireland* was having his day of rest, just like everyone else; he was chatting to Michael Temple, a farmer from the foot of the mountain.

Rupert looked up from his pint and straight into Sarah's grey eyes. And suddenly it seemed as if they were the only two people in the pub. Even the noise seemed to fade. Sarah's insides defrosted and a fire flared up in her stomach. Her heart was singing though no noise was coming out. She had heard he was charismatic and that women often fainted in front of him. Or pulled off their knickers and threw them, or offered him sexual favours. Until this moment she'd been faintly disgusted by the lack of propriety in modern young women, but now she understood! There was something about him, something special . . . even when he was dressed like a farmer.

Willie handed Sarah the microphone and she took it as if in a dream. She knew her mouth was hanging open, she hoped she wasn't drooling. She knew there were a hundred farmers looking at her, waiting to hear what she had to say, but she was aware only of Rupert's dark eyes. Shamelessly she spoke to him: 'My name is Sarah Gordon. I live at Derryrose. I teach in Derryrose Primary School. I'm twenty-three. I'm young, free and single. My telephone number is—'

Willie poked her gently and whispered, 'You're supposed to be talking about Johnboy and Daisy, not about yourself.'

Sarah faltered and blushed. What on earth had she been saying? It was so difficult to think clearly when her guts were in turmoil and Rupert's eyes, like caressing hands, were running appreciatively over the top of her trouser suit.

I wish I wasn't wearing a trouser suit. I wish I hadn't scraped back my hair. I wish I was wearing Mummy's chandelier earrings, with rings on my fingers and bells on my toes, she thought.

She tried again. 'I've come to invite you all to the Wedding of the Year. Not my wedding, of course, I'm not getting married – yet – not that I wouldn't rule it out if the right man came along—'

Willie nudged her again.

In a rush she finished her announcement. 'Please give me your name and address, if you'd like to come to the wedding of the year.'

Rupert set down his pint and approached her. A funny light-headed liquid feeling swelled like a bubble inside her. She knew she was grinning like an idiot. He was smiling too. He opened his mouth to speak, but just at that moment Ian leapt out of nowhere and plonked himself between Sarah and Rupert. He was brandishing one of his Mr and Mrs Ian Flemming business cards.

'Hello, there, Sarah!' he said.

He was even fatter than she remembered, so fat that she couldn't see round him. His lips puckered up in a familiar way and, instinctively, she knew he was going to kiss her. She ducked – just in time to see dark, handsome Rupert swerve away from her and walk towards the bar, taking with him the funny light-headed liquid feeling and leaving behind only a void. Furious with disappointment she turned on Ian.

'What are you doing here? You're not even a farmer . . .'

But Ian was impervious to her contempt. He was having a Eureka Moment. He was thinking: *What better place to kick start my solo career than the Wedding of the Year? I'll be among friends and family; everyone will be kind. And from what Eva was hinting this afternoon,* Good Evening, Ireland *is going to cover the happy event. This is a golden opportunity, a once-in-a-lifetime chance, to publicise my talents to a countrywide audience!*

Ian's eyes were burning and his palms were damp with excitement. He was smiling broadly. He said, 'And you're not a farmer either! We shall have to stick together, you and me, two non-farmers in a sea of farmers – safety in numbers, don't you think? Can you hold this little business card of mine while I buy you a drink?'

Without pausing for her to answer he clicked his fingers at Willie.

'Barman! We'll have two soda waters with lime.'

Sarah watched Rupert's retreating back with a sinking feeling of resignation. Tempting though it was, she could not be rude to Ian. There was too much history between them. She had once loved him, for goodness' sake! Pity she'd never really liked him.

When Willie got home from the Farmers' Club barbecue he found Laura heavily asleep.

'Push over, Fatty,' he whispered and he rolled her over to the back of the bed, stripped off his beer-stained clothes, and jumped in beside her. He thrust his cold feet under her bottom and his hand began its evening wander beneath her nightdress.

'I'm feeling very pleased with myself. I think I'll get a job as a matchmaker,' he said.

'Why's that?'

'Rupert Glass was at the barbecue and he couldn't take his eyes off your Sarah. I've been telling you for months they're perfect for each other.'

Laura smiled in her sleep. 'From what I know of that fellow's reputation, Sarah is the only woman left, under the age of a hundred and fifty, who has not yet been bedded by him . . .'

Willie found what he was looking for under Laura's nightdress, and with practised ease he rolled his fingers forward and backwards while Laura began to jerk and shudder, to gasp and grow hot and cold. She bit hard on the pillow to stop herself screaming, for the twins were sleeping close by and once they woke up they might stay awake for the rest of the night.

Afterwards she murmured, 'What was Sarah doing

at the Farmers' Club barbecue? I thought it was a men-only event?'

Willie chuckled.

'It *is* a men-only event and there's a very good reason for that – some of those mountainy farmers don't see a woman from one weekend to the next. Just as well your Sarah is so scary, or they might have kidnapped her and carried her away! Do you know they call her Lady Muck, though not to her face, of course?'

Laura laughed. 'So there was more than Rupert Glass eyeing up Sarah? Not that she even noticed! Sometimes I think she's frigid. Sometimes I think she doesn't belong to our family at all.'

Willie said, 'Ah, but the difference was Sarah was looking at Rupert. And I'd go so far as to say her nipples were hard in the frumpy blouse she was wearing.'

Alexandra woke gingerly. The seasick feeling of nausea was upon her and she hesitated to raise her head. All her fastidious night-time preparations ensured only a decent night's sleep; now she had, with Ian's help, a regular ritual in the morning. He brought her milky tea and salty crackers to eat. He eased her slowly into a sitting position. He held the cup to her mouth for she suffered from carpal tunnel syndrome and her wrists were numb and her hands too weak to hold the cup by herself. Then Ian ran her a bath of tepid water and helped her into it. He gently brushed her teeth, and sponged her all over with perfume-free soap. He helped her back out again and dried her. He rubbed stretch-mark cream into her belly and breasts. Gently he helped her to dress. Sometimes on good days they managed it without a break for retching in the bathroom.

Alexandra could see the digital clock from her horizontal position. It was ten to eight, which was ten minutes later than Ian usually brought her tea. If he didn't immediately come with it, she was going to be late for school. Where was he with her tea?

She shouted, 'What's keeping you with my tea?'

There was no answer. Maybe he was using the bathroom at the other end of the house. She'd give it another minute, then she'd shout again. The minute passed, then another.

Alexandra became anxious. Perhaps he had fainted in the kitchen? Perhaps he'd had a heart attack? She was constantly nagging him about his weight gain, at least two stones since their wedding. He said it was because he was happy . . .

Alexandra could lie no longer. She raised herself slowly on her numb wrists and hauled herself into a sitting position. 'Where are you?' she shouted.

She struggled out of the bed, taking deep, calm breaths like she'd been taught at the antenatal classes, and slowly and gently the dizziness cleared and she was able to walk to the kitchen. She flicked the switch on the kettle and shouted again, 'Where are you?'

Their house, The Meadows, brand new, barely finished, and fitted with top-of-the-line designer everything was very, very quiet.

She tried to call him again. 'Where are you, Ian Flemming? I need you!'

And suddenly there he was, dressed in the most extraordinary outfit. He was wearing skin-tight clothing, with stripes. And fingerless gloves. And a helmet with some sort of a rear-view mirror attached to it. And special dark glasses which looked like swimming goggles. With a bit of imagination, he might have passed for an overweight superhero.

'What the hell are you wearing?' she said and a bubble of laughter, the first since the start of her pregnancy, forced its way out of her mouth.

Ian looked moderately offended. 'We've already discussed this. I can't believe you've forgotten. Flemming's Fitted Bathrooms have bought each of their staff members a road bike. We've instigated a cycle-to-work policy. It's our company's small way of reducing the carbon footprint. We got a special deal on the bikes.'

Alexandra narrowed her eyes and tried not to frown. Yes, of course she remembered the conversation, but that was months ago. Last summer, in fact, about the time they got married and she clearly remembered Ian saying, 'Over my dead body. My father is losing his marbles if he thinks he's ever going to get me to perch my arse on that uncomfortable thing.'

The bike had been gently gathering dust at the back of the garage ever since.

She said, 'What has suddenly stimulated your interest in cycling to work?'

'You're always telling me I ought to lose weight and take more exercise.'

'But it's raining outside!' said Alexandra.

'My cycling glasses have interchangeable lenses. I've

just inserted the lenses for "wet conditions" this morning. I shall be perfectly safe. Please don't worry about me. It's only five miles to work. Most of it downhill.'

She would be a supportive wife if it killed her. This crazy notion would soon go off him, once he'd got soaked a few times. She smiled and said, 'Good luck. I'm proud of you.'

He preened a bit in his silly outfit, which was obviously much too tight on him. She worried moderately if the Lycra would split at the first bit of exertion, the first uphill climb. She was actually considering driving behind him to check he was going to be all right when he said,

'Sarah says the first couple of days will be the worst, until my thigh muscles get used to the effort. She says after a while I'll feel the pain, but it won't hurt me. She says she cycles a lot in the gym . . .'

A cold hand clutched Alexandra's heart.

'Sarah who? Sarah Gordon? When were you talking to Sarah Gordon?'

'Last night at the Farmers' Club barbecue. She asked me if I'd like to sing at Daisy's and Johnboy's wedding. I said I would be delighted.'

Alexandra was suddenly furious with herself for allowing Ian to go to the barbecue unchaperoned.

She said, 'Well, I hope you told Sarah the bride will have to phone the help-line number on our business card and arrange an appointment with you in the Music Room and formally book you and *pay* you.'

She knew she sounded outrageous, manic, hormonal and mad to be demanding money for singing at her very own brother's wedding, but Ian didn't seem to notice. He answered quite agreeably. He said, 'Daisy has phoned me already. She's coming over this evening. I think she's going to ask me to sing "In a Country Churchyard" – she told me Chris de Burgh was her favourite singer. I'll just check if we have the music so that when she comes I can sing her a sketch of it . . .'

He bounced exuberantly out of the kitchen like a testosterone-fuelled little boy. She shouted after him, 'What time is Daisy coming?'

'In the evening after she's milked her cows. I know you have an antenatal class – Pain Relief in Labour, isn't it? I'll join you there, after I've met with Daisy.'

Alexandra clamped her lips shut to stop shouting out, 'Is Sarah coming with her?'

No, she wouldn't say it. She wouldn't even think it. She was happily married to Ian and they were expecting a baby together. It was nice for him to bump into Sarah occasionally; she was an old flame, it was natural. And jealousy was such an ugly emotion, sexual jealousy even worse. It ate away at your heart and your guts, scrambled your brains, interrupted your sleep . . .

If Alexandra had been allowed to choose, she would not have chosen Sarah to teach with her in Derryrose Primary School. If Alexandra had been allowed to choose, Sarah's first teaching post would have been on a leper colony with the very real chance that she might contract leprosy and her pretty face rot and fall off.

Failing that, she'd have chosen for Sarah a teaching job in Outer Mongolia, or the Empty Quarter in Saudi Arabia – or some other desolate hole with no telephone, Internet linkage, or any other method of communicating with the outside world.

When Eva had chosen Sarah to replace her in Derryrose Primary School, Alexandra had shamelessly tried to talk her out of it.

She'd said, 'I honestly don't think I'd feel very comfortable working alongside Sarah, not if she's anything like her older sisters. You've no idea how unfriendly they were when I was at university with them. They never once invited me over for tea! I know Johnboy insists they're misunderstood but *I* think they're terrible snobs!'

Eva had nodded sagely.

'I understand exactly what you're saying and I would not employ one of those Gordon girls either. But Sarah is not a bit like her sisters. Really, if it wasn't for the striking resemblance of mother and five daughters, no one would ever believe she belongs to the same family.'

So Sarah had got the job and now they'd been teaching together for almost a year. And so far Alexandra had managed to keep their working relationship exclusively formal. She always called Sarah Ms Gordon, and expected Sarah always to address her as Mrs Jackson-Flemming. And she'd made it clear from the very first day that the staff room was not intended for Sarah – except for her to make herself a cup of tea. She refused to approve a common kitty, and she never engaged Sarah in conversation.

It did make the days rather lonely, but Alexandra was determined not to become too friendly with Sarah, for the next thing to happen would be an invitation to a dinner party at Derryrose, and she and Ian would have to go because Johnboy was courting Daisy. Then they'd have to return the invitation. And before you knew it, Sarah would be going everywhere with Alexandra and Ian, there would be three people in their marriage, and when the baby was born there'd be four, and she would be left holding the baby while Ian confided in Sarah that his wife didn't understand him any more . . .

7

Sarah's car pulled into the school car park at 8.35 a.m. Already a crowd of parents and children had gathered, though the school doors didn't open until 8.50, and Alexandra in her role as headmistress was very firm about time-keeping.

'They'd leave their children off here before eight o'clock, if they could get away with it, especially those who are commuting to Belfast and trying to miss rush-hour traffic. Mums and dads must learn we do not provide a babysitting service at Derryrose Primary School!'

Sarah could not be so brutal. Most of the children standing in the rain every morning, with bare legs and runny noses and ankle socks getting soaked, waiting for the school door to open, were not the offspring of wealthy commuters because the wealthy offspring were sitting in a car with the heater running and the windows steamed up. These were the village children from the council estate and they'd walked to school with younger brothers and sisters hanging on to a pushchair. Or they were the mountainy children who had come by bus and the bus didn't wait until the school door opened. They were wet and cold through no fault of their own; Sarah worried that the more delicate among them might catch pneumonia.

Quickly, she unlocked the door and the crowd surged forward into the tiled cloakroom to take off their wet coats and shoes and warm up cold hands on the radiator.

Sarah slipped past them into her classroom. If Alexandra was running late she would not notice this deliberate bending of school rules; there would be no vicious email later to Sarah's class computer reminding her that the school door did not open in the morning until 8.50 a.m. – for security and insurance reasons – and kindly requesting she lead by example.

The assembly bell went. Alexandra still hadn't arrived and there was no one in the junior classroom, supervising the younger children, just one of the mums, Emma Flood, who was conscientious and kind and had one happy girl in Sarah's class and three terrified little boys in Alexandra's class. The school year was almost over, and the youngest one, Sebastian, was still howling every morning, 'Please don't leave me, Mammy.'

'No sign of the big, bad wolf,' said Emma as they marched the children into the hall for their morning sing-song and pep talk. Sarah's ears were strained for the sound of Alexandra in the corridor – her laboured tread and heavy breathing. The work was really too much for her in her heavily pregnant condition, bobbing up and down all day, fetching and carrying and very hands on with the sand play and water play and puppet theatre and Lego.

She said, 'I'm sure she won't be much longer. Maybe she's been held up in traffic.'

She'd suggested they swap for the last term of school – the senior classroom almost ran itself, and Alexandra could have rested more, but Alexandra wouldn't hear of it. She'd sent a sharp little email:

> Thank you so much for your offer but I wouldn't dream of allowing you into my classroom to confuse the children with your teaching methods . . .

Alexandra finally arrived as the children were singing 'All Things Bright and Beautiful' – badly out of key, because Sarah and Emma could not hold a note, and neither was prepared to play the piano. A couple of older boys were blowing into recorders, some younger children were clapping. It was chaotic and fun and everyone was warm again after their soaking at the school door.

Emma discreetly nudged Sarah.

'There she is. With a face like a slapped arse, as usual . . .'

A couple of times in the middle of the day, when the classroom was quiet and the children were working, Sarah thought about Rupert. He had gone to

Derryrose Primary School, the same as everyone else in the village; his photo was up on a wall in the hall. Mrs Jackson had taught him, and scolded him and praised him, same as everyone else.

She was too young to remember him but Laura, her oldest sister, had been to one of his birthday parties and she'd come home with fantastical stories of magicians and jugglers and face painting. And Rupert, dressed up like Little Lord Fauntleroy in velvet britches and a frilly shirt, had led a white pony round the lawn with his guests taking turns to ride on it.

At lunchtime, when the children were running mad in the playground, Sarah sat down at her class computer and googled *Good Evening, Ireland*.

Oh gosh – there he was on the Home Page, in his very formal swanky suit, with his dark hair swept back off his forehead, shaking hands with the President of the United States.

Then she googled 'Rupert Glass, TV presenter', and the list of publications where he was recently featured was endless, for he was the darling of the tabloid newspapers and hardly a week went by but he was splashed across their pages with yet another voluptuous, partially dressed starlet clinging to his arm.

One headline screamed that more young Irish women dreamed of marrying Rupert than even the film star Colin Farrell or the rugby hero Brian O'Driscoll. On Valentine's Day a tabloid had run a full-page spread of Ireland's most eligible bachelorettes –

supermodels, actresses, singers – and asked Rupert to pick which one he liked best. At Christmas there'd been a feature: 'Who do you most want to kiss under the mistletoe?' and Rupert had won again – the President's wife said she wanted him wrapped up in a ribbon, *and nothing else*, as a present from Santa Claus.

A bell rang for the end of lunch and the children crowded back into the classroom. Sarah closed down the computer, took a deep breath, and returned to reality.

'Please put that apple core in the bin, Colin Simpson. Don't be a litter lout. Line up in a tidy row, children, shortest on the left, tallest on the right, I want to make sure everyone has clean hands before we start our needlework.'

There was no harm in looking. No harm at all . . .

At four o'clock Sarah left Derryrose Primary School. She was contracted to stay until four, even though the children had been gone for an hour. In theory, this gave her paid teaching time to schedule meetings with parents and to catch up on marking and lesson planning, so she didn't have to take work home with her, but in practice, Sarah preferred to pull on a pair of industrial-strength rubber gloves and to scrub, scrub, scrub at the classroom. There was an official school cleaning lady, but her job description was 'a lick and a polish'; it did not cover scrubbing desks to remove paint and felt-tip pen or bleaching the toilet bowl in the senior boys' bathroom.

'It isn't healthy to keep things too clean,' said the cleaning lady when she discovered Sarah scrubbing the back of the toilet bowl. 'Children need dirt to develop immunity to it.'

Once the classroom was sparkling Sarah checked her emails again. She had heard absolutely nothing from Alexandra all day. Not even a text message to say thanks for holding the fort in the morning or a brief explanation for her lateness. Of course, the headmistress did not have to explain herself to the junior teacher and, of course, Alexandra never spoke to Sarah unless it was absolutely necessary; they had never once had any degree of personal chit-chat – Sarah only knew that Alexandra was pregnant because Johnboy had told her and her belly was growing bigger and bigger since after the Easter holidays.

But even so . . . until today there had always been a deluge of work-related communication through text messaging and by email. Today there was not even the usual reminder that school stationery request forms must be 'submitted by Tuesday' for countersigning by the headmistress. There was no follow-up to Sarah's suggestion of a cake sale at School Sports Day. There was not even Alexandra's weekly 'Point to Ponder' that Sarah was supposed to incorporate into the daily running of the classroom. Last week's Point to Ponder had been: 'Dominick Dunne has just won the Hennessey Award for literature – that's a very prestigious award and a lot of money too! Mr Dunne was born in a house at the foot of the mountain, and when he was a wee boy he walked four miles to this school every day. His most famous poem is: "Late Again".'

Sarah hesitated briefly at the door of the junior classroom. Alexandra was still in there, sitting hunched up over her computer. She could not possibly leave the school until she had said something to diffuse the frigid atmosphere between them.

'Good bye until tomorrow, Mrs Jackson-Flemming.'

Alexandra did not acknowledge her. She remained hunched up in front of her computer.

Sarah always went to the gym on Monday after school. On Mondays, Wednesdays and Fridays she went to the gym; on Tuesdays, Thursdays and Saturdays she went swimming. Sunday was rest day. It wasn't so difficult when you were disciplined. And, frankly, there was nothing else to do at four o'clock in the afternoon in rural Ireland, especially when it was raining, for most people were still at work. She changed out of her trouser suit into a stretchy top and clipped on her little pink iPod. She wriggled into tight Lycra leggings and pulled her hair into a ponytail. On the treadmill she ran with a long, loping style and listened to Nirvana. She didn't notice the admiring glances from a man lifting weights in the corner, for by nature she was a modest girl who rarely flaunted her fabulous figure, and didn't expect attention when she did.

She tried to relax and allow the tension of the day to evaporate but Alexandra's puerile silence had upset her. Again. She knew, of course, what was wrong with Alexandra. It was the same problem over and over. Alexandra did not like it when Sarah spoke to Ian Flemming and she did not like it when Ian Flemming spoke to Sarah. Even the most innocent and unavoidable of conversations – at the door of the church, for example, 'Good morning, Sarah, how are you?' followed by, 'Good morning, Ian, I'm well', – was enough to send Alexandra into a sulk where she might remain for a week.

The fact that Sarah and Ian had spent a whole evening together at the Farmers' Club barbecue without Alexandra's supervision meant she might sulk for a month with Sarah. In fact, she might never speak to her again! And the atmosphere in the primary school would become heavy enough to cut with a knife. And the aspirational parents who were on the board of governors would start talking about 'personality clashes' and 'the importance of a tranquil learning environment' and at the end of the school year – her probationary year – Sarah would be cast out. She would have to leave Derryrose, and her friends and family and all she loved, and seek work somewhere else. The thought of leaving Derryrose made Sarah feel physically sick. A sweat broke out on her forehead and it was nothing to do with the exertion of the exercise . . .

When Sarah got home, the first thing she noticed was Helen's red sports car; she'd bought it on whim the day she moved out of the farmhouse; it was as frivolous and fast as Helen herself. A month ago Helen had gone to live in a villa by the sea. She'd said, 'Of course I'm sad to be leaving, but this villa's much closer to work. Five minutes by car instead of an hour. That long commute was breaking my heart . . .'

Sarah parked at the scullery door and lifted a box of groceries out of the boot of her car. She could hear Helen's favourite song coming from the house – 'It Should Have Been Me' – playing at full blast. Right up until a month ago this song had greeted Sarah every evening when she came home from work. With added raucous laughter if Helen was entertaining one of her fan club of farmer boyfriends; she had one for every night of the week who wined her and dined her and took her for spins to the beauty spot by the Lough shore.

'Of course I don't *need* a man!' Helen would laugh,

'Nobody *needs* a man . . . But don't you think they can sometimes be useful? Help fill up the empty hours . . .'

Sarah had missed Helen horribly since she'd moved out; Derryrose felt empty without her. Some days she even forgot she was gone, and made her pots of lemon tea which sat fragrant and stewing on the edge of the Aga. Always she hoped she might come back home. Helen was very firm about that. 'I've got no home to come home back to! The farmhouse belongs to Daisy now! And anyway, the beach at my villa is full of surfers in skin-tight wetsuits. What's not to like about leaving?'

Helen was sitting at the kitchen table drinking lemon tea and sorting through her post and her messages. When Sarah came into the kitchen she looked up from her sorting and smiled. She was immaculately groomed as always, with lashings of lipstick, a platinum bob, and glamorous designer frames on her spectacles. She had a prestigious management job, and a sharp, sexy wardrobe to match it. On first introduction it was impossible to believe her father was a farmer and that when she was growing up she had always helped with the farming.

Sarah said, 'Hello, stranger! Why didn't you tell me you were coming? I'd have missed the gym and rolled out a red carpet . . .'

Helen said, 'I didn't know myself until four this afternoon! I was in the middle of a conference call when Mummy phoned and insisted I drop all and drive here to help you organise the Wedding of the Year. Despite the fact that you and I both have demanding, stressful jobs and our mother is a lady of leisure! She really has the most enviable talent for delegation.'

When they were growing up, it was always Helen who'd pushed the boundaries, and gone head to head with Mummy. Every day there'd been rows, slammed doors, raised voices and furious bad-tempered weeping. They'd never seen eye to eye on anything and their volatile relationship had not mellowed with age.

Sarah set down the armful of copy books on the edge of the table. She switched off the music and switched on the television. She flicked the channel to *Good Evening, Ireland*. Then she carried her gym bag through to the laundry room, put her gym gear into the laundry basket, lifted a boiler suit and two pairs of jeans out of the washing machine, and fastidiously shook out the creases. She carried them back into the kitchen and said: 'What have you been roped in to do?'

Helen said, 'It seems our mother wants Daisy to wear her antique white satin wedding dress as Laura and Jennifer did. But Daisy is never going to fit into it, not even with ribs removed . . . I've been nominated to do the alterations since I always got an A in needlework at school.'

Sarah unhooked a rope and lowered the kitchen maid ceiling-mounted clothes airer from its cosy position above the Aga. Quickly and neatly she removed underpants, vests, socks, stockings and brassieres and sorted them into two piles – one for herself and one for Daisy. She hung the damp jeans and boiler suit over the wooden slats and hoisted the clothes airer back up to the ceiling.

She said, 'Mummy's Sixties style of dress most certainly will not suit Daisy. A girl with her voluptuous charms should wear a frock that gives her a figure. Do you want to take a look through my bridal scrapbook for ideas? There are loads of photos of wedding dresses – there might even be a section, "Fairytale Frocks for the Fuller Figure". It's so long ago now I can hardly remember.'

'Your bridal scrapbook!' said Helen in awe. 'I always wondered if you'd kept it. I think if it had been me, I might have been tempted to throw it into the Aga. And throw Ian Flemming in after it!'

Sarah said mildly, 'It's in a drawer in my bedroom. I'll get it for you now while I'm taking this underwear up to the hot press.'

Helen trotted out of the kitchen and down the tiled hall to their grandmother's sitting room; Gran Gran had been dead seven years, but the room was just as she'd left it; not a thing had been touched or tampered with. The wallpaper had large green swirls, and the shag-pile carpet had large green swirls. The curtains were dark forest-green, heavily tasselled.

The furniture was plastic. When Helen had lived in the farmhouse, this was where, on Sunday afternoons, she had entertained her fan club of farmers, who came in a gang, safety in numbers, to see her. On rainy days they'd pushed back the sofas and played Musical Statues with Daisy banging out hymns on the piano. In better weather they'd gone outside to the garden and run three-legged races, using fishnet stockings to tie their legs together.

Helen opened a drinks cabinet made of teak and smoked glass. She removed a bottle of Cointreau, a bottle of gin and an elegant stainless-steel cocktail shaker and carried them up to the scullery. Gran Gran had been an accomplished old dear. She'd taught Daisy to play the piano, Sarah to tie a bow tie and Helen how to make a White Lady. She squeezed out the rest of the lemon she'd used to make lemon tea and strained it into the cocktail shaker, applied liberal but accurate dosages of Cointreau and gin, and shook it all together with ice. When Sarah reappeared with the bridal scrapbook under her arm she poured two White Ladies into two glasses; one she handed to Sarah.

'Cheers!' said Helen.

Then together they flicked through the romantic pages of fairytale frocks, trimmed with diamonds and pearls, floating veils, extravagant bouquets, elegant wedding cakes, satin shoes and ornate engagement rings.

Suddenly Helen exclaimed with a laugh, 'Oh my

goodness! Here's a photo of Laura's wedding – she looks so pretty in Mummy's dress. And so happy! And so thin!' She pointed to a formal group shot of a beautiful bride flanked by her four sisters in bridesmaid dresses of heavy navy-blue satin. 'Wasn't it evil of Mummy to make us wear her old bridesmaid dresses? There's not an inch of our flesh showing – we look like nuns at a picnic!'

Sarah sipped her drink. She said, 'Mine smelt of moth balls, and gave me a rash round my neck.'

Helen laughed. 'I said to her at the time, "These are horrible dresses, Mummy", and she said, "You don't think I'm going to allow you to upstage your sister's wedding by dressing like a tart?" '

For years Helen's taste in provocative clothing had caused bitter rows with Mummy – almost as many rows as Helen's fondness for the drink and her inability to commit to less than six boyfriends at a time. For years there'd been endless preaching by Mummy about 'a young lady's good reputation' – and how easy it was to lose it, and how once it was lost no decent man would go near you with a barge pole . . .

Right up until a month ago Helen had laughed at her mother's speeches and said, 'You're showing your age, Mummy dearest! No one cares about "good reputations" any more.' Then, a month ago, Richard had married sober, well-dressed Elisabeth. And Mummy had said: 'I told you so, Helen.' And Helen had packed her bags and moved out of Derryrose farmhouse. Softly, Sarah said, 'I don't think you dress like a tart. And Daisy doesn't think so either.'

Helen eyes twinkled through her heavy-framed spectacles. She said, 'I'm glad you think that way, Sarah. You'll be happy to know, then, that Daisy does not want us to wear the navy-blue bridesmaid dresses at her wedding! She says I can choose what we're going to wear! Isn't that very adventurous of her?'

Sarah began to make dinner. On Monday it was Thai Chicken Curry. She plopped garlic and green curry paste into a pot on the Aga and added two tins of coconut milk. While the flavours were gently warming together she chopped up four chicken breasts.

'You'll join us for dinner, won't you, Helen?'

Helen sniffed the delicious aroma. 'If it's Monday night's Thai Chicken Curry, I might! Will I peel the potatoes for boiling? Or steep the basmati rice? Top and tail the green beans? Blanch the broccoli?'

Sarah shook her head. 'No thanks. No need. Everything's already prepared. It's all sitting out in the pantry. I'd be very much obliged, though, if you'd mark my class's homework for me – twenty-five versions of "My Big Mistake". They're in that tidy pile of copy books the end of the table. Give marks for punctuation, grammar and spelling . . .'

Helen said, 'What about imagination?'

'No marks for imagination. This is a piece of reportage. We've been learning in school that no one is perfect and everyone makes mistakes. You make the mistake, you learn from it, you move on . . . It's in the personal development section of the new curriculum.'

Helen began to read and the kitchen descended to silence but for the comforting chatter of *Good Evening, Ireland* in the background. Before long she was thinking again about her own big mistake. What had she learned from it? Nothing. Would she do it again? In a heartbeat . . .

She looked up from her reading and said, 'What was your last big mistake, Sarah?'

Promptly Sarah answered, 'Not telling Ian Flemming "No thank you, Ian, we don't want you to sing at Daisy's wedding." I *so* wish I'd said "No thank you, Ian", but he cornered me when I was feeling vulnerable – at the Farmers' Club barbecue of all places! I couldn't get away! And he talked and talked about wedding music – as if I wanted to talk about weddings with him!'

Helen pulled the wrapper off a Bounty Bar and stuffed it into her mouth. She'd become addicted to Bounty Bars since leaving Derryrose and striking out on her own, she who had never had a sweet tooth. She listened quietly and didn't interrupt.

Sarah said, 'He still does that terrible thing with the blinking when he's talking to me. Do you remember how we used to giggle about it? And he's still wearing tinted glass in his spectacles – it makes him look so *seedy*.'

Helen took off her own designer spectacles and folded them carefully into their box. She knew better than most the terrific advantages of hiding one's eyes from public attention. For without the protection of heavy spectacles her carefully made-up sharp little face was as soft and winsome as that of an angel. And her eyes had been crying forever.

She said, 'My goodness, Sarah, it's not like you to say unkind things about anybody! And especially not a man you were once engaged to. Such passionate bad-mouthing of the bold Ian can only be described as provocative. Are you quite sure you're over him?'

Sarah was very emphatic. 'Of course I'm over Ian! How I wish I'd never been under him!'

Helen laughed. For such an elegant little thing she had a guttural laugh which promised much and delivered more. Really, she needed a sign on her back that said: 'Danger! Don't jump in unless you can swim.'

She said, 'Then why are you so worked up about seeing him at the Farmers' Club barbecue?'

The Thai Chicken Curry came to the boil and Sarah transferred it into an oven-proof dish and slipped it into the simmering oven. Fastidiously, she wiped at a splash of coconut milk on the hot surface of the Aga. She watched *Good Evening, Ireland* out of the corner of her eye. Last night he'd been wearing a soft, checked shirt with the points of the collar frayed. And faded jeans and earth warrior sandals. She had noticed most particularly that he had beautiful feet. What would Rupert Glass have said to her, if Ian hadn't jumped in first? He might have offered to buy her a drink. She might have asked for an Orgasm. It made her feel quite weak just thinking about it. When she closed her eyes she saw him. When she opened her eyes she saw him. She couldn't get him out of her head.

Softly, she said, 'There was a man in the pub last night. He had beautiful feet. He was beautiful . . . we smiled at each other . . . he was coming over in my direction to talk to me when Ian appeared out of nowhere, with his idiot business card "Mr and Mrs Ian Flemming, By Appointment Only" and his insistence that he sing at Daisy's wedding . . . I couldn't shake him off. The man with the beautiful feet swerved away and didn't come to talk to me after all.'

Unexpected tears welled in Helen's eyes. So this was what was eating at Sarah; an itch that couldn't be scratched, an itch as old as time. Not the regret of losing an old lover, but the thwarted frustration of missing her chance with a new one. It was an itch Helen could well understand – the bittersweet aftertaste of missed opportunity.

She took a large gulp of her White Lady and said, 'So you've finally met someone you fancy and just like the poisoned dwarf in a fairytale, Ian Flemming got in the way. No wonder you're so upset with him! Oh well, chin up! All is not lost – perhaps we can still find the prince? I know for a fact that there aren't many princes who drink in the Lisglasson! I don't suppose you found out his name?'

'Rupert Glass,' said Sarah and she observed with a tickle of amusement the amazed expression on Helen's face.

Helen said, 'You're such a tease, sometimes, Sarah! Why didn't you tell me immediately you'd caught the eye of Rupert Glass! It's not as if I don't know who he is! Isn't he on the TV every night, presenting *Good Evening, Ireland*? Isn't he on the TV right now as we speak? Oh, that's why you switched it on! I wondered! You never usually watch it.'

Together they turned to look at the small portable black-and-white television sitting high up on the dresser with a metal coat hanger stuck into its back. Through the snow storm of poor reception they could easily recognise Rupert: urbane and professional; handsome; dressed in his trademark three-piece suit with his hair swept severely back, like the hero of a film made in the Thirties. He was interviewing a small, stout woman, breathless, with swollen legs, whose dog had been diagnosed with diabetes.

'You wouldn't believe it, but the symptoms of diabetes in my wee Fluffy are exactly the same symptoms as are suffered by human beings.'

Rupert's face was inscrutable. It was one of his biggest interviewing talents that no one could ever guess what he was actually thinking – no matter how surreal the subject matter, Rupert always remained posh, polite and professional.

'And for the information of the viewers, Mrs Smith, how does diabetes present itself in human beings and dogs?'

'A terrible thirst, Fluffy suffered from a terrible thirst. He drank water out of the toilet bowl and he drank the bathwater once I got out of it. And he peed all over the house. Excuse my language, but my house was stinking with dog pee.'

'How is Fluffy's condition being treated, Mrs Smith?'

'With diet and exercise and insulin injections . . . just like human beings. My poor, wee Fluffy is on injections every day for the rest of his life, morning and night before I feed him.'

Sarah couldn't stop smiling at the serious and polite expression on Rupert's face. It was exactly the same expression she wore when she was cornered by aspirational parents who came to share with her their personal opinions on how to make Derryrose Primary School a better school than it already was . . .

She set the table for three with bamboo placemats and water glasses. She put a plastic orchid in a pretty vase at the centre. It was her ambition to one day visit Thailand, the Land of Smiles and fake watches.

She said, 'I know you'll find this hard to believe, but Rupert Glass doesn't look a bit like that in the flesh.

He's taller and thinner. And softer . . . and his hair is dark brown, not black. It was flopping forward on to his forehead last night . . .'

Helen was impatient. 'I'm sure he was only gorgeous . . . He looks like a man who visits the beauty parlour on a regular basis – I think they call that "metrosexual", don't they? The *important* question is what are you going to do about this instant and immediate attraction?'

Sarah sighed, shrugged and said softly, 'You mean am I going to start chasing after him, like every other woman in Ireland? No, I most certainly am not! Rupert Glass would never look at me – a plain little school teacher from the village! He's a celebrity! His life is nothing like mine. It's all Botox and posing in the limelight. And being stalked by paparazzi. . . . But I really do wish he was a normal man, for I honestly think I was hit by a thunderbolt when he smiled in my direction last night!'

Helen was suddenly furious. She said, 'But he is just a normal man! All men are normal men! I think you're discriminating unfairly against him because he works in the media and other women find him attractive! He's still a normal man.'

They turned again to the television. Rupert was now interviewing a young Ulster footballer, Markie McBride, who had just been signed for one million pounds to the English team Manchester United.

'Following in the footsteps of the great George

Best! Congratulations, young man!' said Rupert and, on air, he asked Markie for his autograph. It was this common touch which made Rupert such a hit with the viewing public. Everyone knew he was football mad and had once been selected to play for the Manchester United Junior Squad. And that his old-fashioned father had refused to allow him to go because he said footballers were unmanly the way they hugged each other and kissed, after they scored a goal. So Rupert had got a job in television instead.

Helen said, 'I happen to know Rupert Glass coaches the village boys most Saturdays on the pitch at Lisglasson . . . That autograph will be for them.'

Sarah took the basmati rice off the heat and left it in the saucepan to fluff up. She lifted the casserole dish, full of the Thai Chicken Curry, out of the Aga.

She said, 'You're very well informed about Rupert Glass's movements . . .'

'I met him that summer I was going out with Austin Morris,' Helen replied. 'Do you remember that terrible summer, the one after I left university when I was convinced the only way to get over Richard Knight was to find myself someone else? As if Austin Morris and his hundred dairy cows could ever be adequate compensation for Richard! There are some men you can never get over . . . anyway, Austin used to help Rupert with the football coaching on a Saturday morning and I used to go to Lisglasson pitch to watch Austin helping Rupert. I got to know him quite well, for we always went for a drink together afterwards to the Lisglasson.'

'What's Rupert like?' asked Sarah. She was almost afraid to ask.

Helen said, 'Well, he's terribly posh, of course. But I rather liked him. You know, I have a soft spot for toffs . . .' And suddenly her face was very sad.

Rupert Glass was not just a toff – he was an
aristocrat. He was the youngest child of Lord
Laurence Glass, tenth Baron Glass of Lisglasson in the
County of Derry, and there was great rejoicing at his
birth, fireworks in the village, and free drinks in the
pub, for he had four older sisters and his parents had
almost given up hope of a son.

'I'm so sorry, Laurence,' Lady Glass had apologised
when Prudence, Genevieve, Antonia and Sylvia were
born, though they were lusty and healthy, with dimples
and chubby legs; any other parent would have been so
proud of them . . .

'You must try harder, old girl!' Laurence said, for a
son was the only thing he truly expected from his wife.

Finally, Little Lord Rupert was delivered to the
world and for the rest of her life Lady Glass loved to
recount, at posh dinner parties, to posh friends, the
desperate measures she'd resorted to and the
degrading techniques she'd learned to get him.

'Not that the girls were even my fault! The doctor

on Harley Street told us the sex of a baby is determined by its father – it's a medical fact that there are
two types of sperm, male and female, and from our
breeding results it was clear that Laurence's female
sperm were simply better swimmers that his male
sperm!

'Such a relief, I must tell you, for I was starting to
think Laurence might *steal* a male child from the
village, and try to pass it off as his own. He denies it, of
course . . .'

Instead, Lord Laurence was advised to dine on red
meat and salty food to increase the vigour of his male
sperm swimmers. Every two hours his wife took her
temperature – her *vaginal* temperature – and when the
thermometer said she was 'optimum' she douched with
a foul-smelling herbal concoction guaranteed to kill
fast-swimming females . . .

'Once my vaginal environment was favourable only
to male sperm, I whistled for Laurence and we
copulated. The doctor told us standing up was the best
position to use to try for a male conception and, let me
tell you, it's quite tricky until you get the hang of it!
Laurence is so much shorter than me he had to stand
on the library step ladder. After ejaculation I lay on my
back, waving my legs in the air, *et voilà* – we have a
son!'

With such an inauspicious and unromantic start to
his life, it was little wonder Lord Rupert Glass was
now thirty-three and unmarried.

Little Lord Rupert's life was mapped out for him from the moment he was born and the midwife said, 'It's a boy!'. It was the same life his father had lived, and his father before him, and his father before that. It was the same life his sons would be expected to live. There are no alternative lifestyle choices among the upper classes in Ireland.

His earliest years were spent at home, in Lisglasson. From a distance, Lisglasson was breathtaking, Palladian and very beautiful; the reality of living there was also breathtaking, but in a different way, for the attic was under siege to a plague of rats, there was no central heating, no running drinking water, and some of the rooms had no electricity. But for the antique wallpaper and a few threadbare carpets, some useless sideboards, and a dim corridor hung with dirty oil paintings of long-forgotten ancestors, the Gordons kept their dairy cows in better housing conditions at Derryrose.

Little Lord Rupert lived in isolated splendour, the youngest child of five. His mother did not mix with her neighbours so he had no friends in the village. His sisters had no friends either, but at least they had each other and, anyway, they were hearty, unimaginative girls who slept with their dogs and lived for their ponies. Little Lord Rupert had a nanny and a tutor and permanent drip at the end of his nose. It was Nanny's job to wipe his nose and the tutor's job to teach him to 'talk posh', so that when he was sent to an approved prep school at the age of eight, his parents would not have to fork out for elocution lessons. After prep school he'd go to a public school, after public school into the Army, or maybe the Church or the City. The choice was up to him. Some choice. Then he'd select a suitable young woman, trained from birth like his mother and sisters to tolerate the isolation and boredom of aristocratic rural splendour, for better or for worse, but, more likely, for worse. She would bear him a son and the life cycle of the Irish aristocrat would start all over again.

Little Lord Rupert was skinny and delicate, but only on the outside. On the inside, he had pluck and, from a very early age, he'd known his own mind clearly. He knew he did not want to be educated at home by an effeminate tutor with garish bow ties and an affected accent. He knew it was not cool to have Nanny trailing after him, wiping his nose and boxing his ears and making him eat up all his spinach.

So he'd developed a talent for escaping out of the draughty old house when Nanny's back was turned, and sprinting down the avenue, out of the magnificent gates with 1732 inscribed on the stone gateposts, into the higgledy-piggledy village where the local boys, his neighbours, were kicking a ball to each other and wrestling.

From the earliest age, Little Lord Rupert practised his famous powers of articulate persuasion: 'Please, Father, don't send me to prep school. I am only a little boy. Please allow me to go to the village school so I can make friends with my neighbours.'

Lord Laurence might never have agreed if all his lovely money hadn't gone – mismanaged and squandered and spent. What little was left was being saved for his son's public school fees; his name had been down since birth at the school his father had attended, and his grandfather, a Glass boy for every generation right back to the days when the Battle of Waterloo was won and lost on the school playing fields.

Little Lord Rupert explained to his father: 'I'm heir to Lisglasson and heir to an aristocratic title. I don't *need* to attend an expensive prep school to find a place for myself in the world.'

So Lord Laurence had sacked the tutor and his son was allowed to join the ranks of the great unwashed in the village school. He sat beside Michael Temple, a shy boy who smelt of cows. They became the best of friends.

This was a unique opportunity for Little Lord Rupert to learn how the other half lived, without actually having to live it himself, for, regardless of what school he went to, nothing could change the fact that he belonged to the unique world of the Irish aristocrat – a world where the male of the species drinks port after dinner, passed clockwise, and the female prefers to sleep with her dog.

*

After school, Rupert got a job in television in a position so humble it did not have a job description. And he might have remained there, Little Lord Nobody, if those hadn't been the turbulent days of civil unrest in Northern Ireland with bombs going off every five minutes and riots and fires and fear. The News Room in Belfast was a hive of activity; there were never enough reporters to go round.

'We need a man on the scene at City Hall . . .'

'Hand me a microphone, I'll go!' said Rupert and he'd plunged into a career no one could ever have anticipated for him.

'Good Evening, Ireland, and just behind me is a hostage-taking situation . . .'

His gorgeous toff's voice and public school polish had reassured the anxious viewers that evening. The situation was horribly tense – a terrified politician had been doused in petrol, his captors were brandishing a list of demands and a blow torch. But the people of Ireland did not panic. They knew things couldn't be half as bad as they looked if Rupert Glass from the television wasn't wearing protective clothing.

Rupert said afterwards, 'Of course I felt frightened, but stiff upper lip and all that . . .'

Through the remainder of the civil unrest, even when entering the most dangerous areas, Rupert was always immaculate in a three-piece suit, starched shirt and beautifully polished handmade shoes. He carried a silver cigarette case and offered cigarettes to those he was hoping to interview. On wet days he wore a belted mackintosh. Jealous colleagues joked that a bullet-proof vest might have tossed his hair.

'Oh Rupert, darling, do be careful!' said his mother. Part of her was very proud of her little boy, the face of *Good Evening, Ireland* and so reassuringly familiar there was even a mural painted of him on a terraced wall in Belfast, alongside tribal slogans and emblems. But already he had scars all over his body from flying glass, and a burn on his back from a petrol bomb, and she worried that one day his luck would run out, that he'd be in the wrong place at the wrong time, caught up in the line of fire, and that she'd switch on the television to discover Rupert *was* the news on *Good Evening, Ireland* . . .

And all that awful effort she'd gone to, to have him, would be wasted, since he showed no interest in marrying and producing an heir to the family titles; he didn't even have a steady girlfriend.

'Stop fussing, Mother! There'll be plenty of time for lovemaking after a ceasefire.'

And it certainly seemed to be the case, once peace descended and the streets of Belfast became safe again. Fashionable restaurants opened; there were charity balls, rock concerts and theatre performances. And Rupert in the thick of it, tricked out in a bow tie and tails, always with a different photogenic, shapely starlet on his arm each night. 'Happy now, Mother?' asked Rupert.

Lady Glass refused to be teased, for it was quite obvious that Rupert had no intention of committing himself to any one of the ambitious young women who hung tight to his arm, pouting and flirting while he interviewed world leaders and movie stars. They were delicious to look at and delightful to hold, but they were also hoping to be discovered themselves . . .

'Those girls are not suitable at all!' said his mother.

By 'not suitable' she meant they were not the daughters of her aristocratic friends, and the friends of her aristocratic daughters. Lady Glass wanted Rupert to marry a girl with a dynastic family tree and a solid breeding pedigree – a girl she could boast about at the wedding – so she insisted her only son accept all upper-class invitations to county house weekends, twenty-first birthday parties, school reunions and society weddings. She insisted he be chivalrous and sexy with every suitable girl he met. If one slipped into bed with him in the middle of the night she insisted he do his gentlemanly best to show her a good time.

After Rupert turned thirty, she insisted he enter into a 'special understanding' with the oldest daughter of Charlie Churchill-Knox – little Angela, who was heavy and hirsute; she'd been on the shelf for years.

'I'm not insisting you marry her! I'm simply suggesting you ought always to have a suitable girl on standby. Your father and I are very tolerant, but we expect you to be married by the time you're thirty-five. If you don't find yourself a suitable girl to marry before you turn thirty-five, we will insist you marry Angela.'

Rupert liked Angela well enough, but was it too much to ask that he might actually be sexually attracted to the woman he was expected to marry?

'Angela looks just like a horse! And she's so horribly *jolly hockey sticks*.'

'You're far too fussy,' said Lady Glass, which was probably true and probably the reason why Ireland's most eligible bachelor spent every Saturday morning coaching junior football.

H elen was always practical when it came to attracting a man's attention. It was something she had a real talent for.

'Sarah, I don't see why you can't just happen to be jogging past Lisglasson football pitch next Saturday in your most sexy sports gear. You don't even have to look at Rupert. Trust me, when he sees you jogging past looking amazing he's going to be the one doing the looking. And, of course, all the little boys whom you teach will be able to tell him your name . . .'

Sarah took Helen's advice. What did she have to lose? Even if Rupert Glass didn't notice her, only she and Helen would know about it. And one thing about Helen was that she was very discreet, tactful and supportive. She would never make Sarah feel like a loser if she didn't get lucky with Rupert. Helen's motto was: 'You win some, you lose some, but you're never a loser until you quit trying.'

Sarah laid out all her sports clothes neatly across the bed and chose what she considered to be the most sexy outfit among them – a tight, green stretchy vest top, with the shoulders cut away, and a cunning zip from breastbone to chin; short, skin-tight leggings, in white, and a pair of hot-pink running shorts.

She'd bought this eye-catching gear on special offer in a sports shop in Belfast. The girl at the till, a dumpy little thing, had told her: 'Everybody tries on that stuff but nobody can get it to fit properly. It's made for an unnatural body shape. That's why it's going so cheap.'

When Sarah tried on the top in the privacy of the changing room cubicle she could immediately see it had been made for her 'unnatural' body shape. The cut-away style accentuated her broad and well-toned shoulders and arms yet the plunging zipped neckline gave the illusion of generous breasts and a tiny waist – hey presto, an hourglass figure!

She'd wriggled into the leggings. Perfect again for a girl who had no superfluous fat and whose buttocks were toned and tight, thanks to her disciplined exercise regime. Really there was no need for the jaunty pink shorts, except she liked the colour; Sarah had no embarrassing areas that needed clever disguising.

The girl from the till knocked on the cubicle door.

'Are you all right in there? Do you need any help? Most people who try on that sports top almost strangle themselves trying to get it off again . . .'

Sarah had stepped out of the cubicle.

'Thank you for your concern, but the top fits me well! What do you think?'

The girl was so shocked she crossed herself. 'Well, I never did! Are you one of those Gladiators you see on the TV on a Saturday night?'

On Saturday morning the weather was fine. Sarah felt optimistic. She ironed her pink pompom socks and washed her hair to make it shine. She applied some subtle, sweat-proof make-up.

'You're looking lovely,' said Daisy when Sarah jogged down the stairs and into the kitchen.

Sarah replied gaily, 'The summer is here! I'm determined to try some open-air jogging. It's so much more refreshing to breathe in healthy fresh air when I'm running, not that recycled stuff at the gym . . .'

It was also much harder to run on the road than it was to run on a treadmill. There was no give in the road, and the pounding hurt her ankles and feet. Also she had to jump up on to the verge every time a tractor roared past.

The run from the farmhouse to the football pitch was the toughest two miles of her life, and her sweat-proof make-up had melted by the time she got there, to find the place deserted. Well, that wasn't strictly true. There were a couple of little boys kicking a ball to each other, one of them being Colin Simpson. But Rupert wasn't there. She walked slowly home.

*

On Monday at school she asked Colin Simpson, 'How was your weekend?'

'Best of my life,' said Colin and he told her with relish and much detail about a football game he'd watched on the television on Saturday night. The rest of the class joined in. Sarah hardly listened. Something about a World Cup qualifier and how Northern Ireland had snatched victory from the jaws of defeat in the closing moments of the game.

She said, 'So they won, did they? Northern Ireland, I mean.'

Colin was truly shocked. 'You didn't watch the game? Northern Ireland played Spain – Spain is the best team in the world. They're really brilliant. They're tipped to win the World Cup. Or they were until Markie McBride scored a goal against them. Coach says it was a titanic victory of David over Goliath . . .'

Her ears pricked up. 'Coach?'

'That's what Coach said on the TV – he was the commentator. There was no football practice this week because Coach is in Spain with the Northern Ireland team. What's the matter, Ms Gordon, have you never heard of the football World Cup?'

'Of course I've heard of the football World Cup,' said Sarah but, in truth, she knew hardly anything about it, for it was not her idea of entertainment to watch a game of football on the television. The game had been on in the parlour at Derryrose on Saturday night; Johnboy and Daisy had watched it, and Laura and Willie; she had preferred to play with Laura's twins in the kitchen, and to carry everyone bottles of beer and packets of crisps when they called to her. She'd even made burgers with minced steak and grated onion, and lashings of tomato ketchup, and had carried them in, to a fanfare of applause, at half-time. And all the time Rupert Glass was on the television and she hadn't even realised.

Colin said, 'Beating Spain on Saturday night means Northern Ireland has qualified for the World Cup in South Africa next year! There's a gala reception planned for the team in the Europa Hotel. My big brother is trying to get tickets. He says it will be a night to remember . . .'

Sarah refused to be deterred. On Friday afternoon she surreptitiously confirmed with Colin that the football training was taking place at Lisglasson pitch on Saturday morning.

'Certainly is, Ms Gordon. I've got a new Northern Ireland strip to wear. My big brother bought it for me. I'm Number 9 – McBride.'

So off she set again in her skin-tight running gear, with her hair washed and floating like a banner behind her, but no make-up this week, except lipstick. She wasn't half a mile down the road when her mother's old car drove up beside her, coughing and belching.

'Cooee, Sarah, where are you going?'

'Just jogging, Mummy,' said Sarah.

'Oh, let me come with you!' said Mummy. She screeched to a halt and jumped out. She was dressed in extraordinary running clothes, there were diamante sparkles on the vest and her shorts were so tight they might have been shrink-wrapped on to her bottom.

'I saw you out running last Saturday. I called but I don't think you heard me . . . I've really got to lose some weight before the Wedding of the Year, especially if Eva goes through with her mad plan to get us on the television . . . They say it makes you look ten pounds heavier than you actually are. Where will we go?'

She began to jog on the spot, to touch her toes and do star jumps.

'Will we run to Lisglasson and back?' she suggested.

Sarah loved her mother. She was proud of the fact that Jennifer fought the ageing process with enthusiasm. She often told anyone who would listen her mother was fitter then most women half her age. But at that moment she had a strange and overwhelming urge to run away from her at top speed, screaming: 'Leave me alone, you mad old bat! Go back home and do some knitting. Some gardening! A crossword! And try to remember you're on the wrong side of fifty for flaunting yourself in those skin-tight shorts . . .'

Instead, she said, 'Well, actually, I'm planning to run to the graveyard at the top of the mountain. I love the view from up there . . . Will your car be all right, do you think, parked up on the verge?'

'Of course it will be all right!' said Mummy with confidence. 'Right, let's go!' And she shot ahead at a tremendous pace.

Sarah shouted after her. 'Will I close the driver's door for you?'

She followed Mummy to the end of the road, to where it forked left for Lisglasson and right for the steep mountain path that led to the windswept graveyard. She caught up with her easily and they climbed up, up, up the steep mountain road till the backs of their legs were aching and their lungs were bursting with effort. The last bit was in silence till they reached the remains of a stark windswept graveyard; its dry stone wall was tumbled and sheep grazed among the lopsided headstones. Only then did they stop to admire the view below them of summer mists and church spires and the winking Lough, before walking back down to the wetlands and giving the front of their legs the workout.

'That was great fun,' said Mummy. 'I can't wait to do it again next week.'

For almost a week Sarah thought uncharitable thoughts about her exuberant mother. Then she phoned Helen for advice.

Helen said, 'Well, thank God you had the good sense to turn right at the bottom of the road and not left into Lisglasson. There's no way you can take Mummy with you, if you're hoping to attract Rupert

Glass's attention. She'd spoil your chances completely!
You know she would. She's an incorrigible flirt . . .'

'Oh please don't be mean about Mummy!'

Helen laughed. 'Takes one to know one, they say –
an incorrigible flirt, I mean . . . What you're going to
have to do is to cheat a bit, my lovely Sarah. Tell
Mummy you've decided to run on Saturday afternoon
because you're doing something else on Saturday
morning.'

'Something else, like what?'

'Oh, I don't know. It depends on the weather. If it's
wet, you tell her you're going to clean out the hay barn
for the wedding reception, because you've heard on
the news the weather will be better in the afternoon. If
the weather is good, you tell her you're going to cut the
lawn in Gran Gran's walled garden, where Daisy wants
to have her wedding photos taken, and you've heard on
the news it's going to rain in the afternoon . . . Or
something like that. Make sure you pick something she
won't want to help with, then, in the middle of the
morning, slip away to the village in your car, park up at
the beauty spot by the Lough shore, and go jogging
around the pitches. If Mummy sees you leaving and
asks where you're going, tell her you're going for petrol
for the lawn mower, or to hire a power hose to clean
out the hay barn.'

Sarah gasped with admiration. 'But that's diabolical
in its simplicity, Helen! How did you manage to think
of it so easily?'

Helen sighed. 'Years of practice. I should've got a degree in scheming when I was at university and desperately trying to think of ways to make Richard Knight fall in love with me . . . I find the easy part is making the plan. You're the girl who is going to have to go jogging twice in one day . . .'

'It will be worth it if I meet Rupert.'

On Saturday morning, hot sunshine rained down on South Derry.

Sarah woke at six, just as Daisy got up for the milking. Their bedroom was flooded with sunlight from a crack in the pink satin curtains.

Daisy said, 'It's only a week till my wedding. Do you think I'll get sunshine like this?'

'No harm in hoping!' said Sarah and she jumped straight out of bed and started her day two hours earlier than usual. Today was the day, she was sure of it. Today she was going to see him again. Today he might see her. And the wee boys kicking a football might shout: 'Good morning, Ms Sarah Gordon who teaches us in Derryrose Primary School . . .'

Her tenacity and her devotion were about to be rewarded.

Just after eight o'clock she phoned her mother and said, 'I've been listening to the local weather forecast. They say it might rain in the afternoon, so I'm going to spend the morning cutting the lawn in Gran Gran's garden. Will we go running in the afternoon instead?'

'What a lovely idea,' said Jennifer. 'Do you want to borrow my lawnmower?'

Sarah had finished cutting the grass and was brushing the flagstones on Gran Gran's terrace when Daisy's head popped around the French doors. She said, 'I wondered where you'd got to! I've been calling and calling. The little brown hen has started to lay in the hedge beside the milking parlour. I've fried us both an egg – come and eat!'

Sarah propped up her yard brush against the stone wall and followed Daisy into the house.

'What time is it, Daisy?'

'Ten o'clock.'

In the kitchen, Sarah ate quickly. If it was ten o'clock, it was time to get changed and drive down to Lisglasson football pitch. Football training started at ten and she didn't want to miss Rupert.

Daisy poured a second cup of tea. 'Where are you off to in such a hurry?'

Sarah had thought long and hard about whether she should tell Daisy about her crush on Lord Rupert Glass. It was difficult not to tell Daisy – they shared a bedroom, they were best friends – but in the end she'd decided against it. There was just too great a chance Daisy would tell Johnboy Jackson, who might make it his mortifying mission to corner Rupert in the Lisglasson after a few pints and tell him: 'My friend fancies you . . .' Already she felt humiliated just thinking about it. Helen could say what she liked about Rupert being a normal man – he was not a normal man! He was the most fascinating and desirable and . . .

'I'm just popping down to the village to get petrol for the lawnmower,' said Sarah.

Daisy was not a suspicious person. Nor was she particularly observant. If she'd noticed the lawn was already cut when she'd gone to call Sarah for her egg, she didn't think to remark on it.

She said, 'I don't know where you get all your energy from. It seems to me like you're always busy . . .'

'I'm busy because I'm sexually repressed,' Sarah replied lightly. 'I'm busy because I'm lonely. All my rushing around to work and the shops and the gym and the church, and helping you to organise your wedding – I do it to give myself something to do.'

But Daisy wasn't listening. Already her thoughts were back with the farming. Today there was a little heifer calving out in the Forty Acres and it was not progressing smoothly. And the weather was so glorious she thought perhaps she should start cutting hay . . .

'That's nice,' she said to Sarah.

Sarah parked her car at the beauty spot by the Lough shore. She checked once more that there was no lipstick on her teeth. She sniffed again under her armpits. She warmed up with a few stretches. She could hear exuberant cheering from the football pitch on the edge of the village. She jogged slowly up from the car park, along the bridle path, through a little copse and out to the sunlit football pitch to find every yummy mummy in South Derry standing spread out along its edges. They were watching their wee sons play football. And watching Lord Rupert Glass. And some of them were wearing hardly any clothes at all!

Sarah's heart sank to her trainers. Oh no! There was no way she could suddenly appear in the midst of all those mummies, *just jogging past* . . . It would be really obvious what she was there for and her reputation as a respectable school teacher would be ruined!

She turned to run back down the lane.

'Sarah, Sarah, what are you doing here?'

It was Emma Flood, the lovely mum she liked so much from school – her daughter Catherine was in Sarah's class. Emma was dressed in elegant riding clothes; she was astride a very large horse. She looked impressively arrogant.

Sarah smiled up at her. She said, 'I think I've taken a wrong turning somewhere . . . I think I'm travelling in the wrong direction.'

She ran back down the lane and jumped into her car. Her disappointment was tangible. She'd caught only a glimpse of him on the pitch – he was wearing short shorts, his legs were fantastic – but how on earth could she accidentally on purpose bump into him when he was surrounded by such hoards of yummy mummies? What she needed was a Plan B. 'Or a miracle,' she said aloud.

*

When Sarah got back to the farmhouse she found
Helen sitting at the kitchen table, drinking lemon tea
and writing a very long letter. Four final draft pages
were covered in her illegible spidery handwriting and
screwed-up paper balls of discarded first-draft efforts
were scattered all over the kitchen floor. Sarah had not
seen Helen for almost three weeks, not since she'd
come to Derryrose to take measurements for Daisy's
wedding dress and Sarah's bridesmaid's dress. She
thought Helen looked pale and thin – without make-up
and clever dressing, she lacked her ebullient sparkle.

'You're very pale Helen, are you feeling all right?'
She asked.

Helen rubbed her eyes. 'I'm feeling very tired! Do
you remember that fairytale where the young girl was
set a task to spin straw into gold? That's what it's been
like for me since I received Mummy's royal summons
to alter her wedding dress for Daisy, and to make you
and me two bridesmaid's dresses. Not that I'm complaining about the bridesmaid's dresses, if the
alternative is navy-blue moth-eaten satin! But for the
past three weeks I've been glued to my sewing seat,
sewing and sewing . . . I worked harder than when I
was doing my finals at university. That's why I haven't
been over to collect my post and my messages.
Anyway, the dresses are finished. I've brought them for
a final fitting. I've left them down in Gran Gran's
sitting room.'

She screwed the lid on her fountain pen, shuffled the pages of her letter together and led the way down the tiled hall.

Sarah followed slowly. 'Who are you writing to?'

Helen smiled a dazzling smile which did not reach her eyes.

'Richard. And Elisabeth. They wrote to say thanks for their wedding present, and to tell me their honeymoon was marvellous, except Elisabeth got sunstroke. I'm writing back to say "Hi". There's no point in losing my two best friends just because they happened to marry each other . . .' She pushed open the door to her grandmother's sitting room. The room was flooded with sunlight and smelt strongly of turf, though no fires had been lit since the winter.

Three stunning dresses, one white, two green, were lightly draped over the back of the light brown plastic sofas.

Sarah admired the delicate stitching on the refurbished wedding dress. 'Oh Helen, it's perfect! How did you do it?'

'I inserted an antique white satin tablecloth in panels into the original dress. I was lucky to find one in Oxfam . . .'

Sarah was impressed. 'I honestly can't see where the old dress ends and the tablecloth begins!'

'Well, thank goodness for that! I've had an awful headache sewing those tiny stitches. But where is Daisy to try it on? I promised her I'd be here by lunchtime.'

Sarah said, 'There's a little heifer calving and it isn't going smoothly. She went straight back out after ten o'clock tea to check on her, and I haven't heard tell of her since.'

'In that case, will you try on your dress first and let me see how you look?'

Sarah modestly stripped and, with her back to her sister, slipped into the light-as-air chiffon dress, silver in one light, green in another. It was a dress that could only have been made by Helen; it was flirtatious, provocative and skimpy.

Sarah said, 'Which is the back side? And which is the front? Are these are the dents for my kidneys?'

She twisted self-consciously to inspect her back, which was flawless and smooth and tanned.

Helen nodded. 'You've got it on right. You look great! Aren't you lucky you tan so beautifully? I'm going to have to bath in a bucket of fake tan to get my colour up to your high standard.'

'But this material is almost transparent, Helen! I can't possibly stand at the front of the church with the outline of my nipples showing!'

Helen was sympathetic but firm. 'I'll put on my dress too. We'll have a grand inspection. I promise there's no sign of nipples . . .'

They stood side by side in front of an ornate old mirror which dominated one whole wall, reflecting soft light from the French doors and windows into the sitting room. They made a striking pair of bridesmaids, though the family resemblance was scanty, for Helen's hair was platinum, and her skin was luminescent and lightly freckled. Today her dress felt uncomfortably tight. She was going to have to let it out. Again. She thought perhaps homesickness for Derryrose was making her fat.

Sarah inspected her reflection carefully. Never before had she worn a clinging bias-cut dress; it dipped at the front and back and hugged the athletic contours of her body . . .

'OK, I apologise. You're absolutely right about my nipples not showing! It's just that my bosoms are so large . . .'

Helen spoke lightly. 'You're lucky to have bosoms! I'm almost totally flat. It's such a pity, I think, that chocolate doesn't make your boobs grow bigger – only your waistline! Soon I shall have a fun-size pot belly . . .'

Lunchtime came and went; there was no sign of Daisy. Sarah and Helen dined together on green soup and brown bread. Helen opened a bottle of wine and drank it down in gulps while Sarah recounted her misadventures at the football pitch.

'You have no idea how glamorous those yummy mummies are!' said Sarah. 'Especially the yummy mummies from the new development at the edge of the village . . .'

Helen was unimpressed. 'I'm disappointed in you,

Sarah. To turn and run away because of a few well-dressed women out of Bluebell Orchard! "Faint heart never won fair lady" – or, in this case, I suppose you would say, "Faint heart never won fair lord" . . .

Sarah sighed. 'And I still have to go running with Mummy.'

She changed into fresh running clothes and together they walked down the lane to the brown and white bungalow.

Mummy was sitting at her 'daylight' make-up table, which was artfully positioned beside a large window. Upstairs in her bedroom, she had a 'night-time make-up table' surrounded by blazing light bulbs. She was carefully painting her face.

She said, 'Hello, Helen, you've put on weight! And you're very pale! I suppose you've been out gallivanting with the fish and chip crowd by the seaside . . .'

Helen flashed her teeth. 'Well, actually, Mummy, every day for the past three weeks I've been getting up at the crack of dawn to get the sewing finished to be here at the appointed hour for Daisy to fit on her wedding dress and Sarah to fit on her bridesmaid's dress. Now I've been waiting for over an hour and the bride still hasn't come in from the farm – Sarah says she has a heifer calving.'

Mummy refused to be impressed. She slashed on lipstick and fluffed up her blond hair around her face.

'Welcome to my world . . . thirty years almost, and counting . . . your father has never worn a watch nor been on time in his life. Conventional time means nothing to farmers – there is only seed time, harvest time, milking time and feeding time. He left me standing at the altar, waiting for him the day we got married. He was calving a cow, he told me. And wasn't Jennifer born on the side of the road because your father was too busy milking his cows to take me to the hospital any sooner? And the moral of the story is . . .'

This was Mummy's postscript to all conversations about farming.

'Never marry a farmer,' chorused Sarah and Helen.

Mummy slipped her feet into high wedge sandals and squirted herself with 'Poison'.

'Would you like a squirt, my darlings?'

Sarah frowned. 'But aren't you coming running with me?'

'Oh darling, I'm sorry to disappoint you, but Ruth says she can fit me in for a leg wax if I come immediately . . . Maybe next week?'

They wandered back up the lane and met Daisy sprinting and waving, her thick hair bouncing about her, the sleeves of her boiler suit rolled up to the elbow.

She said, 'I'm sorry to keep you both waiting. It was an emergency! That poor little heifer was in the most terrible pain. The calf was stuck inside her. I had to ask Johnboy to come and help me with the calving jack. Childbirth is so rough, you have no idea, I feel rather faint now the baby is finally born. Oh my goodness, I don't envy Alexandra. She has only a month left to go . . . I hope when my time comes they'll have invented a way to grow babies in test tubes . . .'

Helen was suddenly brisk. 'Can you please come and try on your wedding dress? I know time means nothing to farmers, but I still have an hour's drive back to the coast . . .'

Daisy said, 'Please give me five minutes. I need a quick bath. I'm splashed with unmentionable horrors. Did you get your post and your messages? I left them out on the hall table for you.'

Helen nodded. 'Thanks. I got them,' she said.

13

E va was out with the Widows' Group. They met every Saturday afternoon in one of the member's houses for light refreshment and fellowship and to plan yet another activity. The Wedding of the Year was keeping them busy, and not just Phyllis's sourcing of country flowers to decorate the church. Mary Murphy was experimenting with a new type of edible icing, and Eva had hunted down and persuaded Barney O'Connor – the winner of *Star Struck* – to play with his Ceilidh band at the reception.

Today they were meeting in Phyllis's house, to drink Earl Grey tea and to hear the latest progress report.

Eva was gently boasting: '*Society Wedding* phoned on Tuesday. They're going to send a photographer. They want to know if Daisy will arrive at the church in a carriage, or ride up on the back of a cow!'

Her mobile rang in her handbag. Eva was still getting to grips with her phone, and had a tendency to rush from a room to answer it. But today she was semi-trapped on Phyllis's squashy sofa with a china plate of wee buns on her knee, a china cup full of tea in her hand, and two big, hefty widows hemming her in on both sides.

'Can you help me with the phone, Phyllis dear? It's ringing in my handbag and I can't reach it. I wonder who it can possibly be at this strange hour of a Saturday afternoon?'

Phyllis extracted the phone from Eva's bag. 'Good afternoon. Who's calling, please?'

She covered the receiver with her hand and with a theatrical flourish whispered, 'Eva! It's the producer from *Good Evening, Ireland*!'

Everybody stopped talking. You could have heard a pin drop. Eva's hands started to tremble. Thank goodness she was already seated for suddenly her legs felt weak. All those emails and letters she'd sent, and all the phone calls she'd made, begging *Good Evening, Ireland* to consider Daisy's and Johnboy's wedding for their local interest slot . . . Was her persistence to be finally rewarded, or were they phoning to ask her to stop harassing them?

'Good afternoon. This is Eva Jackson. How can I help you?'

The producer on *Good Evening, Ireland* sounded very young and enthusiastic. 'This is just the sort of feel-good story we're seeking in these dark days of recession,' he said. 'With your approval, we'd like to record the entire wedding ceremony on camera and to interview key characters – the bride, the groom, the

mother of the bride, the mother of the bridegroom . . .
A fly-on-the-wall documentary. Of course, we won't
use all of it on the show, just a few highlighted clips, but
you will be welcome to have the entire unedited version.
Let's call it a wedding present from us to you . . .'

Eva felt herself come over all hot. She actually
thought she was going to faint. She fanned herself with
Phyllis's pleated paper napkin.

She said, 'Well, of course I shall have to consult
with the bride's family. Can I call you back? Can you
give me an hour?'

She switched off her phone. The Widows were
agog.

With a dazzling smile Eva said, 'Phyllis, dear, I've
got to go. That was Hollywood calling!'

Eva's brave face collapsed once she got into the car.
Her hands were still trembling as she opened the glove
compartment and pulled out a small, framed photograph of John. 'I think finally I might have bitten off
more than I can chew, John,' she said. 'I honestly didn't
expect *Good Evening, Ireland* to take such an interest!
I assumed they might have asked me to send in a clip
from a home video. I certainly never dreamed they
would send Rupert Glass to interview the bridal party.
I'm not sure I've got the nerve to be recorded on
camera for posterity!'

She started the car and drove cautiously out of
Phyllis's private housing estate. She was always afraid

a child would run out, after a football or something. It was all very well saying children were road smart, just because they were taught the Green Cross Code at school. If she'd learned anything from thirty years of teaching, it was to expect the unexpected.

She said, 'Of course, Jenny Gordon will love to be on the television! I know that now without even asking her. She'll be pushing herself forward into every shot – making love to the camera. No one will be able to get a word in edgeways. There'll be more of Jenny on the television, than even the bride and groom . . .'

Daisy skipped across the landing from the bathroom to her bedroom wrapped only in an old threadbare bath towel.

'What a yuck bath! The water was freezing.'

Her wedding dress was hanging from the door of the old-fashioned wardrobe. The antique satin gleamed. The dress was exquisite in its simplicity. Framing it were her two bridesmaids, in sexy green chiffon, like something out of a glamorous movie.

Daisy dropped the threadbare towel and walked towards her wedding dress with her mouth hanging open and her hands extended. There were tears in her eyes. 'I'm going to be such a beautiful bride,' she whispered.

Helen said, 'I've sewn a corset into the bodice; I thought that was probably the best way to do it. Once we've got you squeezed in, and I think we might need a shoe horn, the dress should hug you all day. So, if you'd like to put on a pair of knickers . . .'

Two minutes later Daisy was dressed and, for the first time ever in her fresh-air, wash-'n'-go life, she took time out to admire her reflection in the faded full-length mirror on the back of the bedroom door.

Helen fussed like a professional. 'I thought Sarah could pull back your hair into one of her signature chignons, and we'll attach the comb in the veil to the top of the chignon and allow it to flow out behind you . . .'

Quickly Sarah leapt forward and smoothed and pinned Daisy's thick, unruly curls. 'Isn't your face beautiful, now we can see it? It's a perfect oval, and your eyes are huge. You should tie your hair back more often.'

Then Helen said, 'And I thought perhaps Mummy could lend you Gran Gran's chandelier earrings – to set off the simplicity of the dress, and the plainness of the veil. I've borrowed them from her – here, put them on.'

Daisy attached the earrings.

'And I thought perhaps a very simple bouquet . . .'

'Oh Helen, you've thought of everything! Now all I need is a pair of shoes . . .'

Sarah said quietly, 'I have a very nice pair of wedding shoes. I could lend them to you – "For loan. One pair of wedding shoes. Never worn . . ." '

She pulled out the heavy drawer at the bottom of

the old-fashioned wardrobe. This was where she kept her unused wedding memorabilia from her broken engagement to Ian – bridal magazines and an order of service; her wedding shoes, silk stockings, confetti – pristine and still in the packaging. An optimistic, cheerful wedding list that started: 'Bottles of vodka, hundred-pound notes . . .'

They'd had a bit of a laugh with the minister, discussing the need for an order of service. 'So you can look back in years to come, and remember the name of the organist? Or look back in years to come and remember the name of the husband?'

Reverentially Sarah handed the shoebox to Daisy. 'Better than bare feet, don't you think?'

'I can't possibly wear these!' said Daisy for Sarah's unworn wedding shoes were handmade in satin and studded with crystals. There was an elegant five-inch stiletto heel and a long pointed toe. They were a work of art that had cost a whole month's wages. Until now Daisy had not been allowed even to touch them, in case her hands weren't clean enough.

Eva's well-maintained car slipped so silently in to Derryrose farmyard no one heard her pull up.

'Knock, knock,' shouted Eva from the scullery door. She could hear the sound of girlish voices, high-pitched and happy from the bedrooms above. They mustn't have heard her arrive.

She called again, but still no one answered. Eva

hesitated. She had two options as far as she could see – three, if you counted driving away and coming back later, but that wasn't an option because she was bursting to tell Sarah about *Good Evening, Ireland*, and to formally ask her permission for the TV camera to record the wedding.

Her two options were to throw gravel at the bedroom window or to climb the back stairs and call to them again from the landing.

Eva climbed the stairs. Gosh, they were spotlessly clean. Had they only just been hoovered? And the little lattice window on the return was shining. And the skirting boards were dust-free and freshly painted. It reminded her a bit of Muff.

She reached the landing and shouted, 'Knock, Knock. It's Eva Jackson.'

'Don't let her see the dresses!' said Helen in a sudden panic. 'It's unlucky before the wedding.' Also if Eva saw the skimpiness of the chiffon bridesmaid's dresses, she might kick up a fuss – Helen held no illusions about the fierceness of Eva Jackson; she'd been walloped by her too many times for playing 'Catchy Kissy' in the school playground.

'Don't be silly! It's only the bridegroom who's not supposed to see the wedding dress . . . There's no tradition concerning the mother of the bridegroom,' Sarah said. She raised her voice. 'We're in the bedroom, Eva. What a lovely surprise! We weren't expecting you.'

When Eva paused on the threshold, the only person she noticed was Daisy, standing pale and straight in the middle of the bedroom. Daisy's first impulse had been to run when she heard Eva Jackson on the landing. But the heels of Sarah's shoes were so high she was afraid to move in case she fell off them. Her corset was so tight that her shoulders were thrust back and her posture was perfect. Her veil and earrings were so heavy that her chin was tilted at an elegant angle.

Any fleeting concerns Eva ever had about Johnboy marrying a nutty professor evaporated. Softly she said, 'You look like a fairytale princess, Daisy. We'll have to take care at the wedding that Rupert Glass doesn't run off with you himself.'

Sarah and Helen exchanged glances.

'Is Rupert Glass coming to the wedding?' asked Sarah and her voice was unnaturally high.

'He's coming to interview us for *Good Evening, Ireland*! The producer just phoned to ask me! Oh please say it's OK, Sarah. Please say you're happy for Rupert Glass to come to the wedding and interview us.'

'I'm happy for Rupert Glass to come to the wedding and interview us,' said Sarah and she could feel herself faintly blushing. She had asked for a miracle and she had got what she'd asked for. It was a curious feeling.

Rupert Glass was sitting in an empty corner of The Lisglasson. He was slowly sipping at a pint of Guinness and waiting for his friend Michael Temple. Michael usually helped with the football coaching on Saturday morning, and his son Patrick, too, but they'd cancelled at the last minute with a one-word text message: HAY.

It was always the same at this time of year. You made plans to do things with a farmer, simple plans, nothing special, but the weather and the farming got in the way. Even something as innocent as football coaching and a pint with your pal had to play second fiddle: the weather was good, there was hay to be cut, it might be raining tomorrow.

Not for the first time, Rupert wondered if he should actively seek out a girlfriend – a proper girlfriend, not a bit of sex, to help fill up the empty hours of Saturday afternoon when his friends were busy farming. Someone he liked well enough to allow over the threshold of his house and into his private sanctuary; a girl who would kick off her shoes and relax, who would scrutinise the books in his library and flick through his CD collection; who could intelligently discuss the art he had hung on his walls, and admire his cooking skills in the kitchen.

Rupert indulged in this little fantasy for a moment then it was back to reality, for in thirty-three years he had yet to meet a woman who had not bored him to sobs after precisely ten minutes. This was the average length of time it took Rupert to seduce a woman – he had calculated it once, in a fit of frustration, at the age of twenty-eight, when all the other bachelors in the world were settling down and he was still sampling the delicious delights of warm, willing, available women. Not that he was complaining, not really, but sometimes he wondered if he'd been cursed to eat only sweet food all his life and never to sink his teeth into steak.

Michael was very reassuring. 'You've not met the right girl, yet,' he said.

'Easy for you to say, Michael, when you've been blissfully married for nearly twenty years.'

Michael said, 'I was lucky, I suppose, to meet Jane when we were both very young. When you fall in love you can never mistake it for anything else.'

Until the 'right girl' came along, Rupert was making do with the warm, the willing and the available; he preferred them beautiful, also. One lived in Lisglasson village, and they had to be very discreet, for she was married to such a cold fish they honestly didn't know how he would react if he discovered them together.

At the start of the affair she had said, 'It would be awful if he went ballistic, but worse if he didn't care.'

They met on a regular basis at the graveyard on the windswept side of the mountain. She liked to hack out her horse in that direction, and he jogged to keep fit for the television; it made their time together more exciting, in the open air, with the possibility of passers-by seeing them. And he was fond of her. He genuinely was. Even more so, because they both knew their relationship was only sexual; it was going nowhere fast for she was never available when he needed her, like right now when his friend was cutting hay on a quiet Saturday afternoon.

Rupert finished his pint and shuffled the pages of his programme schedule for the following week. He was braced for disappointment for his producer, Young Spunky, and he had wildly different opinions about what made good viewing, and what didn't.

During the turbulent days of civil unrest *Good Evening, Ireland* had been weighty, important and political in focus. There was always something happening – first terror, then ceasefire, then peace talks. Rupert had made his name, and won awards for his intelligent interviewing of grey men in grey suits and gunmen with their faces in shadow.

After peace, the hard-hitting, headline-grabbing stories dried up and *Good Evening, Ireland* had evolved into a magazine-style programme where celebrity interviews carried just as much weight as current affairs. Now Young Spunky had decided to include human interest stories about local people. Much to Rupert's chagrin he was expected to give just as much emphasis to a story about a dog with diabetes as he had once given to the signing of the peace treaties after the civil unrest.

'If the viewers want weighty world affairs, they can switch on to *Sky News* or *BBC 24*,' said Young Spunky.

Of course, Rupert had tried to protest. He was a serious reporter and had the scars to prove it. He said: 'Can't we concentrate on local current affairs? Run a story on the effects on the elderly of cottage hospitals closing, or the crippling price of petrol? Our viewers care about the Health Service and increasing fuel bills . . .'

Young Spunky was not impressed. He'd been born in peaceful, affluent times; he was too young to remember the hard old days of gunfire and ballot boxes and food shortages.

He said, with finality: 'Our viewers want light entertainment when they're eating their dinner after a long day at work.'

The message was clear. Move with the times or get out.

Rupert was not easily intimidated, stiff upper lip and all that; he had always led from the front with his microphone. Now he actively sought out the serious local stories himself; on his webpage at *Good EveningIreland.com* he invited the viewers to post him ideas about serious local issues; he read local newspapers and talked to local people; he listened to what they were saying about their quality of life and their concerns; each week he submitted some of these pieces to camera, and sometimes Young Spunky used them. Last week he had risked life and limb to interview a gang of young hooligans who were terrorising shoppers in a supermarket car park . . .

Today, as he waited for his friends, Rupert thought about the idea for a story that had popped into his head at the football training. Only half the regular intake of boys had turned up; every one of them had city accents, and every mum on the sidelines was a sexy city dresser. The missing boys were the farmers' sons, they were helping with hay.

Would the viewers of *Good Evening, Ireland* be interested in a feature about city families moving out to the country? Why did they do it? What were the benefits? Did they fit in? Did they care? The footballing children had told him they lived in Bluebell Orchard, the expensive and exclusive new development on the edge of Derryrose village. They told him they attended Derryrose Primary School. Perhaps that would be a good place to start with his feature – an interview with the teachers at Derryrose Primary School? Quickly, he made a few pencil notes.

*

'Do you want another pint, Rupert?'

Michael Temple clattered into the pub with his wife Jane, his son Patrick and Patrick's dog Spot. They were taking a break from the haymaking because they knew Rupert was waiting for them, and they didn't like to let him down. They knew they were the reason Rupert still lived in remote Lisglasson as opposed to a penthouse apartment in Belfast. They knew they gave him a much-needed sense of perspective as he struggled with the unwelcome changes in his career; Patrick had particularly enjoyed the story about the dog with diabetes.

Rupert said, 'I'd love another pint. Make yourselves comfortable and I'll get them. What can I get you, Jane?'

'A glass of Guinness,' said Jane.

'And what about you, young Patrick? Fizzy orange or Coca Cola?'

They settled down in to the corner of the pub.

'So, what's up for next week?' asked his friends.

Rupert rustled through the sheets of his programming schedules. He was really hoping his supermarket piece had been included. In an important voice, he read out. 'On Monday, you can expect a bit of culture with your dinner – I'm going to interview the O'Connor brothers who have just won *Star Struck* in London. For those of us who have managed to miss every episode of *Star Struck*, Eoin O'Connor is an Irish dancer, and his brother Barney plays the violin; their double act impressed the viewing public so much they voted for them week after week, even though the judges insisted Irish dancing had gone out of fashion.'

Patrick asked in awe, 'Have you really not seen Eoin O'Connor dance? It's amazing, what he can do with his legs. One week he tapped his ears with his dancing shoes!'

Jane added, 'And his wee brother with the fiddle is a magician. Last week he played "Haste to the Wedding". The studio audience was dancing in the aisles.'

Rupert quickly read through the rest of the schedule.

On Tuesday, he had an interview with geriatric rockers Achilles' Heel, who were re-forming for a valedictory world tour; on Wednesday, he had an interview with the current Miss Northern Ireland who had just spent a week helping out in an orphanage in Romania, thus proving to the sceptical public that she really did love children. On Thursday, he was going to interview a Belfast woman who kept seventeen cats in her terraced house. On Friday night, he was going to a premiere – to see the new James Nesbitt film and to interview the actor. There was no mention of his piece on hoodies in car parks.

Rupert bit back his disappointment. In all his years covering the civil unrest he'd never felt half as nervous interviewing anybody, for the rules of engagement had been clear back then. Now, with widespread drug abuse, broken homes and moral ambivalence, you never really knew what the youth of today might do to you . . .

Instead, Saturday's interview was with Daisy Gordon and Johnboy Jackson, South Derry farmers who were getting married and having a barn dance to celebrate.

'You have got to be joking!' said Rupert and he called his producer to protest.

15

It was that time of year again – the end of the summer term, when the school curriculum was completed, the school exams were over, and teachers and children were killing time till the start of the summer holidays. Yesterday Sarah had taken her class on an excursion to the Wild West Theme Park; today she thought they might go for a nature walk. Not that the country children had anything to learn about birds and flowers and farming practices, they already knew more than she did and weren't afraid to tell her so: 'Hi, Miss, that's not a field of wheat, it's a field of barley!' or 'Hi, Miss, that's not a cow, it's a bull!'

The walk was for the benefit of the city children because, since their arrival in Bluebell Orchard, it sometimes seemed that Derryrose Primary School had been invaded by an alien culture.

'We can't go walking, Miss, it's raining,' said the city children.

'That's hardly rain,' said Sarah. 'It's *soft weather*. Put on your plastic coats and you won't even notice it.

Isn't that the reason you have a coat?'

And out she marched them for a lovely walk, two by two through the village and along the old footpath which ran a straight mile to Rupert Glass's house. He lived in the Gamekeeper's cottage on the edge of the Lisglasson estate – a picturesque folly with ginger-bread facing and mullioned windows, and a very modern extension of glass and metal out the back, joined to the old house by a metal staircase – this much Sarah could see as she strained her neck over the high walls to check for his car before halting her crocodile of children at his gates and elaborately explaining to them what a cattle grid was for, while covertly drinking in the pretty house, the pea gravel and enormous old trees surrounding it. Oh wow, but it was only gorgeous.

'Hi, Miss, Derek has got his foot stuck in the cattle grid.'

They meandered back clutching the necessary nature-walk treasure – limp flowers, interesting stones, ladybirds in a jam jar. One city girl had blisters and even the boys were breathless. They were sitting quietly at their desks, eating sandwiches with the steam gently rising when Alexandra sent her a text message: *Nature Walk in the rain? Where did you go?*

Sarah texted back: *Lisglasson demesne*.

That bit of sulking from Alexandra, the day after the Farmers' Club barbecue, was finally over. Alexandra was communicating again, albeit by text and email and that was all that mattered to Sarah. She hated to work in an unpleasant environment; she hated to think someone hated her.

Another text came through from Alexandra: '*Hope u pointed out Irish Draft mare in Carson's meadow – she's just had a foal, sweet little thing . . .*'

The lunch bell went and the children were filing quietly into the classroom from the toilets when Eva drove into the playground in the Gordons' cream Landrover Defender with a small trailer attached on behind. She pulled up alongside the senior classroom, honked on her horn and shouted: 'Blight warning again! They're spraying. You're going to have to come with me. I've brought you a pair of wellies.'

Sarah opened the classroom window. 'Come with you where?' she asked, for she was in charge of twenty-five children until three o'clock and she was about to take them into the Assembly Hall to teach them how to dance a jig; this week's point to ponder, courtesy of Alexandra – 'Special congratulations to past pupil Eoin O'Connor, joint winner of *Star Struck* with his brother Barney; he has made Irish dancing fashionable again. Such excellent exercise for a wet afternoon!'

Eva said, 'The pig market at the foot of the mountain. Johnboy and Daisy were supposed to go together this morning to choose a fat hog for roasting on a spit at the wedding reception, but the blight warning has sent them spraying. I thought your father might have come with me but Jennifer says he drove off in a cloud of blue smoke an hour ago, and she's hoping he's gone to get the car fixed, but she thinks it more likely he's gone to the hairdresser – he wants a professional haircut, if he's going to be appearing on *Good Evening, Ireland*. Of course we can't be sure where he is, since he refuses to carry a mobile phone. So I'm afraid you're going to have to come with me, to drive this awful old Landrover, and help me choose a pig . . .'

'But I don't know anything about pigs!'

Eva shrugged. 'I don't know anything about pigs either, except that they're a horrible smell. John wanted to buy some years ago when the price for pork was very high, but I couldn't bear the thought of it – the washing on the line would have smelt of pigs and I'd have had to wear a shower cap every time I went outdoors, or my hair would've smelt of pigs . . . John said I'd get used to it – stop smelling it after a while, but I think that would have been even worse if everyone else could smell it but not me . . .'

She raised her voice to the crowd of children avidly listening from their desks in the classroom. 'Is there a Streaghorn in the senior classroom? Identify yourself! If you're one of the pig farming Streaghorns, put your hand up, please.'

'Why a Streaghorn?' asked Sarah.

Eva explained. 'It's in the genes. A Streaghorn will know the perfect pig when he sees it.'

And little Robbie Streaghorn, nicknamed 'Stinky' by the children from Bluebell Orchard, was given his Rudolf moment.

'Robbie, with your extensive knowledge of pigs, will you guide my choice for the wedding reception?'

'Yes, Mrs Jackson, I will.'

'But what about the rest of my class?' asked Sarah.

Eva looked surprised. 'Can't Alexandra mind them for an hour? Go and tell her I said she must take everyone into the assembly hall and teach all of them to dance a jig!'

As Sarah approached the junior classroom she could hear Alexandra roaring: 'Sit up straight when I tell you to. Sit up, boy, sit up', as if she were training a dog. No wonder Sebastian Flood, according to his mother, Emma, wet the bed at night because he was so scared of her.

Sarah knocked on the door and waited for 'Enter!'

Alexandra was sitting in an awkward position. Her left leg was resting on the teacher's desk with a towel draped over it; her right foot was on the floor. She looked close to tears.

Sarah said, 'What's wrong with your leg?'

Alexandra rolled back the towel to reveal bubbling, black varicose veins – her leg was black from ankle to knee. Sarah had never seen worse in her life. She thought she was going to be sick.

Alexandra said, 'I usually wear compression stockings – all day every day – Dr Hennessey prescribed them. Stupid of me not to put them on this morning, but it was so hot and sticky I thought I might faint. Dr Hennessey also told me to elevate my leg when I'm sitting, but the minute I lift it off the floor, that disgusting urchin Sebastian Flood crouches down and tries to see up my skirt. I overheard him talking about me at break time – he's trying to guess what colour knickers I'm wearing. He's only *five*, can you credit it?'

Sarah changed into the wellies – pink with a heel – and jumped into the Landrover beside 'Stinky' Streaghorn and Eva. She started it up and they drove out of the school gates and along the Lough shore to the market yard.

'I've just seen Alexandra's leg,' Sarah said.

'It's all the standing in the classroom,' Eva replied. 'I had terrible veins when I was pregnant with the children. She'll be able to have them operated on, once she's finished breeding.'

'But she's never going to be able to stand all day at the wedding! I thought I might carry out a chair for her, from Gran Gran's sitting room at Derryrose . . .'

Eva was thoughtful. 'There's more than our Alexandra with dodgy legs. Half of Rent a Crowd from the mountain are over eighty, and most of my friends at the Widows' Group. Perhaps we should have a soft-seating area at the back of the hay barn. You're very welcome to my three-piece suite in the Good Room.

I'll get Johnboy to load it on to the hay trailer and drop it over when it stops raining.'

'What an excellent idea. And I'll carry out all the sofas and chairs from the parlour and the sitting room and the dining room at Derryrose . . .'

'Oh, let us help you! The ladies from the Widows' Group and I are going to give the hay barn one last polish on Friday night and help Phyllis with the flower arrangements. Why don't we come a little bit earlier and help you with the chairs?'

The night before she got married, Daisy milked the cows. Her father had offered to do it for her, as had her fiancé, and her sister Helen, but she wanted to do it herself. And she fully intended to milk them the morning of the wedding.

'You've no idea how restful it will be, before all the fussing and beautifying, to stand in the milking parlour, surrounded by girlies who never have to get married, and listen to the gentle chugging of the clusters and the swish of the milk as it fills the glass jars . . .'

'You don't think she's having a nervous breakdown, do you?' Mummy whispered to Sarah. They were standing together in Derryrose's scullery, making sandwiches and arranging teacups for the Widows' Group who were bringing a wedding present for Daisy, and would be expecting a full bells-and-whistles palaver of social niceties after they'd finished polishing the hay barn. Already Sarah could hear their convoy of cars coming up the long lane.

'Daisy is at one with nature. It helps to keep her calm. I think that's a good sign,' Sarah replied.

The Widows drove into the farmyard and parked in neat formation. A forest of blue-rinsed hair got out of the cars – Eva's among them.

'No! No! No! I cannot face her tonight!' screamed Mummy and she climbed out of the scullery window and ran away across the orchard.

Sarah shouted after her: 'They're expecting you to be here, Mummy! You're the mother of the bride!'

'Tell them I'm having a nervous breakdown.'

'Does your mother not have a sofa to share?' asked Eva as they rolled out an ancient and threadbare Persian carpet across one end of the hay barn before arranging the sofas and chairs on the top of it.

Sarah shook her head. 'Mummy has cream leather sofas. She's afraid they might get dirty. She gave me this carpet instead. It's been rolled up in our attic for years.'

The carpet was enormous, and so old that the dark red pattern, with its intricate multiple-connected diamond-shaped medallions, had almost faded away. But it was still beautiful and very stylish; it added an air of Bohemian glamour to the Spartan surroundings of the hay barn.

Once the Widows were finally satisfied with their

flower arrangements, Sarah took them indoors and gave them a guided tour of the wedding presents. She patiently explained that the four framed watercolours displayed on the wall of the dining room were what Daisy had actually asked for – one from each of her sisters.

'They're by Percy French,' Sarah explained. 'Percy French the famous Irish songwriter? Who wrote "The Mountains of Mourne"?'

The ladies from the Widows' Group were not impressed.

'A bit gloomy, aren't they? Bogs and mountains and wet rain – are you quite sure that's what she wanted?'

Then she ushered them into the parlour and offered them tea and sandwiches. The Widows were politely sipping from spotless china and discussing the merits of teabags verses loose tea, when the phone rang.

'Good evening,' he said, and she knew immediately it was him. It was his voice from the television – urbane and professional; a shiver of delicious excitement danced up her spine and her nipples sprang to attention.

'Good evening,' Sarah replied, and she wondered how her voice could sound so normal when her legs were weak and her heart was racing.

'This is Rupert Glass from *Good Evening, Ireland*. Just phoning to confirm Daisy Gordon and Johnboy Jackson are still getting married tomorrow at the

Derryrose Presbyterian church? That's the one on the edge of the village, isn't it?'

'It's the ugly one,' said Sarah. 'With miles of tarmac round it and the headstones lined up in military formation. You know how we Presbyterians praise plainness as a virtue! We're not even allowed to throw confetti over the bride and groom. Reverend Robinson has forbidden it. He says it makes too much of a mess to clean up afterwards . . .'

Why did he have this loquacious effect on her – she who made a fastidious point of never expressing an opinion; who had always restricted her small talk to banal remarks about teabags? In another moment she'd be telling him again she was free and available, a bachelor girl, just as she had the night of the Farmers' Club barbecue. *I think I'm the one having a nervous breakdown, not Mummy*, she thought to herself.

Rupert said noncommittally, 'Thank you, Mrs Gordon, I know the church you mean. I shall see you there tomorrow at twelve.'

'I'm not *Mrs* Gordon,' Sarah told him, but he had already hung up.

16

On the morning of Daisy's wedding, the rain was coming sideways in sheets.

' "Rain before seven, fine before eleven," ' quoted Sarah and she lit a fire in the bedroom fireplace, while the bride was milking the cows. This was where Daisy would be dressing, and Sarah and Helen, too. Mummy was bringing her friend Ruth to help with the make-up and hairdressing.

'I honestly don't think it's going to stop raining!'

The bride was back in from the milking, soaked through and shivering; she sneezed.

'It has to stop some time,' said Sarah, which was optimistic for it rains every day in Ireland, and provided it's not torrential, the Irish carry on regardless. They weren't really asking for much, just for a break in the clouds so Daisy could walk into the church and not get her wedding dress wet or her wedding shoes splattered with muck.

'The weather is something you can't control, Sarah,' said Mummy. She'd arrived, with her entourage, in a crash of summer thunder and a deluge of driving rain. Ruth was shielding her with an umbrella; Kenneth carried her over the puddles.

Mummy's hair was in rollers, her face was slathered with thick cream and from the neck down she was wrapped in tin foil. Ruth had been working on her since seven – scrubbing, filing, polishing, kneading, massaging and conditioning. She was having the full works, the finale of which was a body wrap, guaranteed to remove three inches all over.

They took it in turns to be beautified – the bride, her two bridesmaids and the mother of the bride, though most of the attention was focused on Daisy, who did not bother with beauty parlours and thought herself well-groomed if she remembered to wash her face.

'You're not going to make me look silly, are you Ruth?'

Ruth smoked forty a day and had a fondness for snow-washed jeans and stilettos. But there was very little she didn't know about enhancing the positive and disguising the unsightly. 'I'm going to make you look like a prettier version of you,' she said, and performed on Daisy the waxing and plucking rituals she privately referred to as her 'Virgin Bride' package. This was her favourite type of assignment – to take an unwashed innocent girl with bushy eyebrows and furry legs and transform her into a beautiful swan. And Daisy had such fantastic skin and thick shiny hair to start with . . .

Champagne flowed, a turf fire crackled, Daisy's wedding dress hung from the wardrobe door. This was her wedding day, the start of the rest of her life, a day for dazzle and a toothpaste smile.

'Ahh,' she screamed in anguish as hot wax and coarse hair were ripped from her legs.

'The first time is always the worst,' said Ruth with a grin. 'But it gets easier, the more you do it . . . Wouldn't you say so, Sarah?'

Sarah was twisting and pinning her hair into an effortless chignon. She hesitated briefly before answering. She'd been miles away in a gorgeous day-dream about Rupert and herself getting married, living happily ever after in his gingerbread house with the mullioned windows, and waking up every morning with Rupert in the bed beside her – a vast bed with satin sheets where they'd sleep together naked every night . . .

She said, 'I assume we're still talking about the leg wax?'

Finally the bride was ready and she looked beautiful. It wasn't just thanks to clever hairdressing, make-up or a figure-enhancing wedding dress. Daisy was the happiest girl in the world, her eyes were shining, she couldn't stop smiling – even cynical Ruth, who groomed blushing brides for a living, wiped a tear from the corner of her eye.

Now Daisy and her bridesmaids were stuck in the

farmhouse with not even an umbrella between them for Mummy had pulled rank, as mother of the bride, and taken the only one with her. 'Because everybody's going to be looking at me!'

She'd made a run for it before they could stop her, through the rivers of rain, across the yard, to Ruth's little black sports car.

'See you at the church, girls!'

They were gone. Ruth was wearing sunglasses and a tight T-shirt with the phone number of her beauty parlour, Curl Up and Dye, emblazoned across her chest.

Daisy said, 'Let's give it another five minutes. I'm nearly sure I can see sunshine, over there on the horizon, behind the rainbow . . .'

'I think I can see it too!' said Sarah. She was trying to keep the note of panic out of her voice, to remain calm and optimistic but it was after eleven and the rain wasn't easing off; any more rain and the wedding would be a washout. From the bedroom window she could see a large puddle forming at the door of the hay barn, and the lilac in the lane had its head bowed with rain, drip, drip, drip, in defeat.

Daisy said, 'I know we're already half an hour late, but the bride is supposed to be late, isn't she, Helen?'

Helen's face was green. It was almost the same shade as her bridesmaid's dress. The dress was too tight again; she felt faint. There were beads of sweat on her forehead. She was fanning herself with a letter, picked up at random from the clutter on the dressing table; the handwriting was heart-wrenchingly familiar: 'Mr and Mrs Richard Knight are delighted to accept your kind invitation to the wedding of Daisy and Johnboy . . .'

'What did you say?' she asked.

She'd arrived at the farmhouse that morning with muttered explanations about hangovers and food poisoning and Sarah had bundled her into the car and driven her into the town, in the middle of Daisy's make-up and hairdressing session, for an emergency appointment with young Dr Hennessey – he was an old boyfriend of Helen's, it was the least he could do to give her a quick but thorough examination and pronounce her fit enough to stand at the front of the church during Daisy's marriage service without vomiting or fainting or in some other way making a show of herself.

Daisy frowned. She said, 'You really don't look very well, Helen! What did Anthony Hennessey say is wrong with you?'

'Five-day virus,' said Helen, but not even Ruth's heavy duty foundation, reserved for teenagers cursed with acne, could conceal the words *Emotional Shipwreck* written all over her face. Daisy laughed. 'Dr Hennessey always says five-day virus when he doesn't know what he's talking about!'

Daisy might have stood there for ever, in her handmade white satin wedding dress, staring out of the bedroom window, patiently waiting for a break in the clouds, if Mummy hadn't phoned from the church and said, 'Johnboy's afraid you've changed your mind – he thinks maybe you're jilting him.'

So the bride and her bridesmaids took off their fancy wedding shoes, chucked the special stilettos into a plastic carrier bag, and changed into Wellington boots.

Then Sarah and Helen held a fertiliser bag over Daisy's head and, with her arms full of flowers and her train hitched up over her shoulder, she climbed carefully into the Landrover her father had reversed up to the back door. The Landrover had been power hosed and was gleaming, the inside was hoovered and dusted, and the seats were draped with white satin.

'Don't toss my hair,' said Daddy, who was quite ridiculously proud of his thick black hair: he dyed it with blackberries, fed it special hair food, brushed it a hundred times before bed every night, and used only organic hairspray.

He'd been practising his speech while he waited for them, and trying to remember the name of today's bride, for fate had thrown five daughters at Daddy and it was the same father-of-the-bride speech he'd already used at Laura's and Jennifer's weddings. Daddy was prone to pontificate on sheep diseases but he wasn't a natural orator; by the time all five girls had caught husbands, he'd know his speech off by heart.

'Let's go, Daddy,' said Daisy and she took one last look behind her at Derryrose farmhouse crouching in the rain. The back door was still lying open and the plastic carrier bag of wedding shoes was clearly forgotten in the scullery.

Derryrose Church was festooned with flowers. Everyone had contributed. The children in Sarah's senior classroom had each brought a posy – these were tied to the ends of the pews. Eva had built, with help of her Widows' Group, a charming arch of honeysuckle and dog roses over the altar. And Johnboy had, very thoughtfully, arranged a huge bunch of daisies, in a tall glass vase, on the vestibule table, at the door.

Daisy and her father took up position. Laura's twins stood in front of them; Sarah and Helen stood behind. Helen was making a heroic effort to control her nerves and her nausea but she could see Richard across the posies and the pews; thin with curly brown hair, he was wearing his mouldy old morning coat that fitted him snug as a glove.

'Just as I fit him, snug as a glove,' whispered Helen into her bouquet.

The organist played 'Here Comes the Bride' and a rustle of expectation swelled through the country congregation. All eyes swept to the back of the church as Scarlett and Shaun tripped forward, scattering daisies and rose petals on the flagstone floor.

'Come on! Best foot forward,' murmured Helen, with a pale grin, for though she was as sick as a pig, with barely the strength to carry her bouquet, she was determined to walk with confidence to the front of the church and to act her part well. She stepped forward and fainted dead away. The eyes of the congregation were fixed on Daisy as she swept up the aisle on her father's arm, her eyes shining. Nobody noticed Helen faint except Richard, who slipped out of his pew like a shadow and went swiftly to the back of the church to help Sarah.

'I'll pinch her ear,' said Richard calmly. 'You lift her legs up higher than her head . . .'

Gradually Helen revived. She struggled to stand, though her face was puce and her lip was bleeding. 'I'm so sorry! I can't think what happened . . .'

'I suppose you've not been eating as usual,' said Richard. His voice was harsh but his eyes were frightened. He was still holding her ear, but not pinching it. Sarah, watching quietly, thought, in fact, that he was stroking it with his thumb. And Helen, who was always so self-assured and straight-backed, seemed softer and more yielding at his gentle touch.

'You're probably right. I really ought to eat more. Thank you so much for helping.' She walked away from Richard with her chin up and her head held high.

'All right, then, let's go! "Once more unto the breach . . ." We might catch Daisy before she gets to the top of the aisle . . .'

They swept swiftly past Rent a Crowd, the Widows' Group, Daisy's university friends, Richard's wife and Helen's fan club of farmer boyfriends to the front of the church to where Willie Simpson had the wedding rings safely pinned to his hired morning suit and Laura's little Scarlett had begun, with great concentration, to eat the remainder of the rose petals in her basket.

17

Alexandra and Ian were sitting at the very front of the church, on the groom's side, the right side, with Eva. Eva looked very summery, if perhaps a little overblown, in a dress of startling green with an enormous straw hat, trimmed in green chiffon.

She whispered to Alexandra, 'I got a sneak preview of the bridesmaids' dresses last Saturday, so I rushed out and bought this outfit because I wanted to coordinate with them.'

Alexandra wriggled discreetly and tried to sit on her hands. A haemorrhoid was biting into her bottom. She regretted it bitterly that she hadn't brought her rubber ring into the church. No one would have noticed her sitting on it, no one was looking at her, except the odd scrubbed urchin who pointed and said, 'Look, Mammy, there's our cross teacher from school . . .'

And even if everyone saw, what did she care any more? Her pregnancy ticked all the boxes for awful- ness: nausea, varicose veins, heartburn and haemorrhoids. She was so exhausted every evening she fell asleep dribbling on the sofa in front of *Good Evening, Ireland*. Ian had to wake her up with something nutritious to eat, pasta or soup or mashed potato, or she would never have eaten at all.

It was only her indomitable will that kept her soldiering on; sick as she was, she would not allow a challenging pregnancy to interfere with her upward and onward career in teaching; Alexandra was very proud of the fact she had made headmistress and was not yet thirty.

'Only thirteen more days before the summer holidays,' she'd said to Ian that morning when he'd brought her a cup of tea. 'Only thirteen more days and then I'm going to fall down in a pile on the top of this bed and I'm not going to move until it's time to go to the hospital and deliver the baby . . .'

Ian was already dressed for the wedding, in black leather trousers, black dealer boots and a black shirt with a thin silver line through it. He had a red rose in his button hole.

He said, 'What do you think of my outfit? I bought it last week in Belfast when I went up for the accountancy conference. There was a break for an hour in the middle of the day and I walked up the Dublin Road to look for the music shop that sells backing tracks – I was looking for "In A Country Churchyard" – when I saw this outfit in a shop window. And I just had to have it! It was calling to me! What do you think?'

What did she think?

She thought black was a colour that suited him. She thought he should wear it more often. In fact, she thought he should burn every other outfit he owned and wear nothing but black in future. She thought he looked sexy and fit – thanks to his crazy cycling obsession he was now only half the man he had been. His love handles had disappeared, and his man breasts, and his wobbly tummy. He had lost the fat and gained muscle. She thought women might fancy him when they saw him looking so well – other women, not just her. Other women like Sarah.

Alexandra managed to smile but her tummy was churning. She said, 'I suppose I've seen you looking worse.'

Ian's solo came at the end of the wedding service, after Reverend Robinson had pronounced Daisy and Johnboy man and wife, and said, 'You may kiss the bride.'

This was the cue for Ian to walk to the front of the church so he'd be in position and ready to sing once the bridal party had retired to the minister's room to sign the bridal register. Alexandra chewed her trembling lips; she grasped her order of service. She was suddenly unaccountably nervous for, where gospel singing was concerned, she did not suffer from the blindness of love. She knew Ian had no natural talent. She knew he had no ear. She knew he had an unfortunate habit of starting flat and staying flat the whole way through a piece, without ever realising he was flat. Always before, when they had been Mr and Mrs Ian Flemming, singing at weddings and funerals, she had helped him out with her strong, sweet voice.

Please God, don't let him go flat, or I'll never forgive myself for being too pregnant to sing alongside him.

Ian removed his steel-framed spectacles with dark lenses and handed them to his wife. He walked tall to the front of the church with his shoulders back; he took up position; he smiled. Immediately his whole persona changed. The faintly sinister, faintly comical little accountant was gone. In his place was a handsome beast of a man with a beautiful, strong body and piercing blue eyes. And the way he was standing, in the house of God, with his genital area thrust forward . . .

Eva audibly swallowed, and someone at the back of the church, probably one of the Widows, uttered a little scream of excitement.

Eva whispered to Alexandra, 'Why does he wear the dark glasses? He's really good-looking without them!'

This should have been the most triumphant moment of Alexandra's life. She should have been radiant with pride that she was married to the man whom everyone was looking at. Instead, she thought she was going to be sick. She was so terribly afraid he would muddle it up and that Rent a Crowd and the relatives and Daisy's posh university friends and the

Widows would laugh at him, and ruin his confidence for ever.

I could still get up off my painful arse and walk to the front to sing with him. I could help him with the high notes . . .

Ian flicked the switch on the ghetto blaster, and the sweet opening music of 'In a Country Churchyard' filled the church. Alexandra held her breath. Ian started to sing and suddenly it didn't matter whether or not he was flat, for the congregation joined in and soon everybody was singing.

What a triumph for Ian, the man who always sang flat! It was such a success that the bridal party came scampering out of the minister's room to join in and Reverend Robinson led loud applause at the end, even though clapping was not usually encouraged in Derryrose's Presbyterian church.

The only person who did not join in with the clapping and cat calling was Alexandra. She was huddled into the corner of the pew, and her burning cheeks were buried in her hands. She was thinking horrible, hysterical thoughts. She was thinking Mr and Mrs Ian Flemming was the only glue that held her to Ian, it was the only reason he'd married her, and now he'd found his own voice he would fly, fly away and leave her.

Alexandra had never had any illusions about her place in Ian's life. She knew she was his rebound wife. But she'd loved him so much and for so long, she'd sincerely believed it would be enough that she adored him one hundred per cent, and less important that he did not adore her. He was the only man she had ever wanted, right from the first time she'd seen him, at the grammar school, when she'd asked her brother Johnboy, 'Who is that boy in your class, the one with dark lenses in his spectacles?'

Johnboy had screwed up his nose with distaste. 'Do you mean Ian Flemming? He's from the town. You don't want to be looking at him. He's far too clean to be wholesome.'

But Alexandra could not stop gazing at Ian; she'd drunk him in, from under her eyelashes.

'I like clean and wholesome,' she said.

Ian's girlfriend was Sarah, so much younger, so much prettier than Alexandra. Everyone said it was a 'marrying job'. So Alexandra had thrown herself into her gospel music and tried to forget him. Almost by accident she'd become a well-known gospel singer with an excellent reputation and an extensive repertoire. It was said in South Derry that no wedding or death was complete without Alexandra's omni-presence. She was booked to sing at Ian's wedding when he married Sarah.

The week after Sarah broke off the engagement, Alexandra was singing at a gospel mission. Ian was part of the audience. She'd sung one of her favourites, 'The Old Rugged Cross', and afterwards, when she was leaving, he had offered to carry her guitar.

'Do you think perhaps I could sing with you?' he asked. The words were music to her ears.

'I suppose so,' said Alexandra and, before she had fully realised what was happening, Ian was up at the house every evening, singing. Almost without meaning to they were singing duets; soon Ian was driving her to weddings and funerals; at one wedding somebody said, 'When are you two getting married?'

And Ian had answered, 'When this lovely lady agrees to marry me.'

Their engagement and wedding had passed in a hazy high and Alexandra had tried to ignore the little niggles of doubt – that he'd married her only because she could sing, that he'd married her on the rebound.

Ian had no niggles of doubt. He broke into song at the least provocation. 'Because I'm so happy,' he told her and his lips had found her lips.

That bit of married life was far, far better than she had ever expected for, of course, she'd been a virgin when they married, though not particularly proud of the fact. She was a bit embarrassed, actually, that she'd made it through four years at university, one at teacher training college, and three Mediterranean summers as a Kiddies Rep for a holiday company, yet had never managed to get ravished once. But it hadn't mattered a bit, her gross inexperience and naïvety; it wasn't the point at all, for he had hardly known anything either and they'd had to learn together. 'Practice makes perfect!' they'd said. It was all such fun and so energetic, and *friendly*. They'd christened every room in the house. There'd been an encounter on the stairs when her mother had driven up in her ridiculously quiet car, and *caught them at it*, and an open-air incident in the garden when they were lifting stones to plant a lawn, and Johnboy had driven past on his tractor and beeped. Any lingering niggles of Alexandra's doubt had disappeared. She was prepared for happy ever after . . .

Until she'd woken up one morning with a churning and blamed the ham sandwiches from the church Harvest Festival that Mr and Mrs Ian Flemming had been invited to sing at.

'How come you're not vomiting too?'

Ian held her hair back from her face while she retched into the toilet bowl. 'I didn't eat any sandwiches. I ate only buns . . .'

When the nausea had refused to go away they'd gone together to Dr Hennessey and heard the happy news that Alexandra was expecting a baby.

Alexandra would have given up the singing right at that moment if it had been only her. She'd have called it an 'unforeseen circumstance' and her audiences would've understood. But she'd kept stoically soldiering on for Ian's sake, fulfilling all their singing engagements, because she'd read in her book, *How To Have a Happy Marriage*, that sometimes it was necessary for one partner to sacrifice herself for the greater good of the couple. And Ian did so love to sing! And she did so love Ian!

Right up until the night of the Farmers' Club barbecue, she'd sung though her nausea was suffocating, her varicose veins were bubbling, her heartburn was burning and her haemorrhoids were biting her.

Was that really only a month ago? Now Ian was singing without her. He didn't need her any more. He was going to leave her.

18

The *Good Evening, Ireland* minibus was parked in front of the church. Perched on its roof was Jimmy the cameraman. He was in position to get a crowd-pleasing aerial shot of the crowds of well-wishers shaking hands with the happy couple; it was a picture which told a thousand words. Rupert was standing in front of the *Good Evening, Ireland* minibus. He was wearing a belted mackintosh and holding a large umbrella over his head. Once the crowds eased off around them he was going to briefly interview Mr and Mrs Johnboy Jackson.

The rain was still pouring down but only he seemed to notice it. No one else was carrying an umbrella; hardly anyone was wearing a coat. The well-wishers wore shorts and flip-flops, the invited guests were in summer frocks. With a bit of imagination, if you ignored the shivering goosebumps, this wedding could be taking place in the sun-drenched Mediterranean. Rupert could hear the bride and groom laughing and talking with the crowd.

The groom said, 'My wife's a mare, don't you think?'

The bride said, 'I've only just realised, I'm still wearing my Wellington boots!'

Rupert's face was impassive but out of the corner of his eye, with a sort of horrible fascination, he was watching Ruth Paisley and Mummy in front of the church.

Ruth was saying, 'Stand up straight! And remember, shoulders back, chin up, chest out. I want every woman *of a certain age* looking at you!'

She patted more powder on to Mummy's nose, and stood back to admire the effect. 'You are *so* the Cover Girl I'm looking for, to help me attract a more mature clientele to the salon! Every day we're choked full of young things wanting a leg wax – I rarely have a customer over the age of twenty! I can't believe women *of a certain age* aren't interested in looking younger . . . you've no idea how many of them think blue hair is socially acceptable.'

'Over my dead body,' said Mummy who was still a blonde, though admittedly she was now a blonde out of a bottle.

Ruth was very persuasive. 'Even now, after thirty hard years and five daughters, you're still beautiful. You have the face of a queen, or a goddess . . .'

'Why, thank you!' said Mummy.

So here she was, at her daughter's wedding, all dolled up to the nines, make-up immaculate and hair perfect – posing and pouting at the door of the church. When anyone remarked on how well she was looking, she said, 'I went to Curl Up and Dye. I had the "Mother of the Bride" package – it's on special offer at the moment . . .' while Ruth pressed her business card into their hands.

'Lovely wedding,' said Michael and Michael's wife Jane who'd been invited as part of the Rent a Crowd and were dressed to kill in their Sunday best. Rupert offered his umbrella to Jane.

'Take it, dear lady, you're soaked.'

'Thank you, kind sir. The feathers in my fascinator are indeed water-logged.'

He held the umbrella over her while she shook out the rain from her long dark hair and lit up a cigarette. Michael took off his jacket and hung it gently over her damp shoulders. She kissed him, and her lipstick left a mark on his face which she wiped away with her thumb. He took her hand and kissed the palm and Rupert heard her catch her breath and whisper, 'Naughty boy.' It gave Rupert a funny heartache feeling when he saw Michael and Jane together for this was the sort of relationship he aspired to, never sick-making to watch, just two people who were in love, for better or for worse, while the rest of the world kept on turning around them.

He said, 'Excuse me for interrupting you two lovebirds, but I don't suppose you happen to know those extraordinary middle-aged ladies cavorting at the door of the church?'

Jane nodded. 'I do. The voluptuous blonde is the mother of the bride, Jenny Gordon from Derryrose. I'm surprised you don't know her. She's one of your neighbours . . .'

Rupert's nostrils flared. 'She's also a woman *of a certain age*, and you know I make a fastidious point of avoiding women *of a certain age*!'

Apart from Jane who was married to Michael, Rupert did not socially know any of South Derry's matrons. He actively went out of his way to avoid them, for the next he knew they were inviting him over for dinner and presenting their capable daughters to him with a view to matrimony. And a refusal, no matter how gentle, was never forgiven or forgotten. Rupert had learned this hard lesson in his innocent youth when he'd taken Michael's sister out for a night, and had sown his wild oats all over her, and hadn't called her afterwards.

'I did not *take advantage* of your sister,' said Rupert when Michael had grabbed him by the throat and started squeezing. 'Your sister was all over me, moaning and gasping. She opened her legs when I kissed her. What is a man supposed to think in such a situation?'

That was a long time ago now, when he'd still had to chase after girls, before the girls had started chasing after him; when he'd been skinny and flattered that any girl might want to be with him.

Michael had said, 'What did they teach you at that fancy school your father bankrupted himself to pay for after you went to Derryrose Primary School with me? It strikes me that they taught you about Ancient Greece but nothing relevant to the real world. The fact of the matter is you can do whatever you want with girls who live far away from your home place but a man must never shit on his own doorstep.'

They'd remained the best of friends.

'Jenny Gordon is wealthy, quite bohemian and very eccentric,' Jane said.

Rupert's nostrils continued to flare with distaste. 'How tactful you are, my dear Jane! I spoke briefly on the telephone to Mrs Gordon last night and *I* formed the opinion that, frankly, she was mad. Now I see her in the flesh I conclude my first impression was correct. She is the perfect embodiment of "mutton dressed as lamb". A woman her age should know better. Do you think she realises that the small dark woman in the snow-washed jeans, hovering behind her, is in love with her?'

Jane was used to Rupert's outbursts. She thought them very amusing. Mischievously she said: 'Jenny Gordon is indeed mad, bad and dangerous to know! You'll need all your wits about you when you interview her. She still has two daughters to marry off and I'm told she does not easily take "No" for an answer!'

Rupert wasn't one bit surprised by this information. It was exactly what he'd been expecting to hear. Brassy old boilers *of a certain age* always had unmarried daughters tucked away; he'd been introduced to a few in his time; washed-out, quiet girls, bullied and trampled on by 'Mummy'; they did the flowers and fed the dogs and were treated with benign contempt as unpaid companions . . .

'Thank you for your advice. I most fully intend to hold her at arm's length, and not offer her any encouragement!'

Michael was listening quietly to the frivolous chit-chat between Rupert and Jane. He'd often wondered, in his simple way, why Rupert was so relaxed with his wife, but not with any other woman in South Derry. He had always assumed it was because Rupert was an aristocrat and everybody else wasn't. It had never before occurred to him that it was a sort of desperate self-preservation. Poor bloke felt like a hunted animal. So wasn't it just as well that their daughters Susie, Alice and Cecily were too young to be thinking of marriage, or Rupert might not speak to them either!

'You've met one of Jenny Gordon's shower of daughters already – Sarah,' he said. 'She's standing over there, with the bride and groom. Don't you remember she was at The Lisglasson the night of the Farmers' Club barbecue? She's the one who invited us all to the wedding.'

Rupert looked across the graveyard, beyond the well-wishers, to where Daisy and Johnboy were lost in a kiss, and the photographer from *Society Wedding* was fastidiously positioning the bridal party around them for a group shot. There was a small, fat farmer with unnaturally black hair; – he was wearing white socks with his morning suit – there was a thin, pale-faced bridesmaid with eyes of anguish, and a flower girl and page boy who were dancing with wild abandon, soaked through and mud-splattered, on the top of a grave. And Sarah – standing serene and statuesque, her lightly tanned skin gleaming with rain and her elegant chignon soft around her face . . .

Of course it was her! The tall school-mistressy girl in the pub! Their eyes had met briefly and he'd smiled, tantalised for just a moment, by her commanding voice and exquisite aloofness. She was the size and shape of his favourite fantasises and her trouser suit had excited him. He'd thought: *I bet she's amazing in bed. Unforgettable. The intelligent ones usually are. They know what they want and they know how to ask for it. Perhaps they read books, or ask more questions. Maybe they've just had more practice . . .* He'd even been tempted enough to set down his pint and approach her. Until the funny little fellow who'd sung in the church had jumped in front of him, and he'd remembered, just in time, his best friend's advice to never shit on his own doorstep.

The wedding party moved out to the farm. The
wedding guests crowded into the hay barn. The
ceilidh band played a jig. Rupert removed his belted
mackintosh; Jimmy the cameraman prepared for action
stations. They had a list of things Young Spunky
wanted, and a deadline of three o'clock. Young Spunky
wanted agricultural scenes – cows in a field, a tractor –
then brief interviews with the two bridesmaids, the
mother of the bridegroom and the mother of the bride.
And, finally, a romantic conclusion – the newly-weds
dancing together.

Once this was done he and Jimmy would jump into
the minibus and race back up the motorway, to the
studio in Belfast, where Young Spunky would be
waiting to take their best efforts into his editing suite
to cut and paste them into ten minutes of family-
friendly feel-good television. Rupert would view the
final edit and compose the voiceover links. The show
would go out at six.

Dinner was served and Jimmy was eating a chunk

of the hog roast. He said, 'We're running to a really tight deadline. We've only about half an hour to get the rest of the interviews filmed and a shot of the newly-weds dancing. Can you find yourself an assistant, while I take some footage of the crowd? Young Spunky says I'm to treat the job as if I was working the wedding. I'm thinking he wants to employ me himself when he gets married at the end of the summer!'

Rupert nodded. 'Roger!'

Across the crowds he spotted tall, school-mistressy Sarah. She was deep in conversation with a large stout woman in green. They were helping a heavily pregnant girl find a seat at the front of the stage. Sarah looked like the sort of competent young woman who could round up a bridal party and organise everyone for interview . . .

Rupert composed his features and approached her.

Covertly, Sarah watched him approaching. She'd been watching him since she'd stepped outside the church. Today he didn't look at all like the friendly guy who had smiled at her at the Farmers' Club barbecue. Today he looked older and very formal. Professional. He offered her his hand for shaking.

'Good afternoon. I'm Rupert Glass from *Good Evening, Ireland*.'

Sarah shook his hand. She hoped he didn't sense she was trembling, or maybe women were always trembling when he touched them. Maybe it felt normal to him, a trembling woman's hand . . .

Pull yourself together, Sarah!

'Good afternoon, my lord.'

Rupert smiled in spite of himself. Nobody ever called him 'my lord' – not even the gold-digging aristocratic girls, the friends of his sisters and the sisters of his friends, who were desperate to become 'my lady'.

'Please call me Rupert,' he said.

'Please call me Sarah.'

Quickly, he explained what he wanted. She listened. He liked that about her, the quiet and intelligent way she listened to what he was saying, without interruption, until he was finished. And how she immediately grasped what he was asking of her.

She said, 'Daisy and Johnboy are out in my grandmother's garden, having photographs taken. I should think my mother is with them. Mrs Jackson has gone to fetch a drink for Alexandra. Helen, my sister, the other bridesmaid, is sitting over there . . .' She nodded briefly in the direction of Helen, casually reclining on a striped deckchair, laughing and flirting with her fan club of farmer boyfriends. One was rubbing her feet, another was carrying her drinks. Behind her, like a silent, dark shadow, stood Richard; beside him stood his new wife, haughty and brittle as ice.

Sarah said, 'I shall gather up Helen, and Mrs Jackson too. I'll join you in the walled garden in five minutes. Go out of the hay barn, straight across the farmyard; there's a green-painted door in the high stone wall, behind it is the garden . . .'

Rupert liked her voice. It was calm and confident. He liked her clear, grey eyes. They were also calm and confident. And her smell – it was fresh and unaffected, citrusy. Her hair was a natural blond, cleverly, subtly highlighted; the rain had not ruined her chignon, but rather softened it around her face. Two days ago he had interviewed the current Miss Northern Ireland who had ironed blond hair, a spray tan and acrylic everything else; she was stupid, too, when she opened her mouth. This bridesmaid was far more beautiful, far more enigmatic. He felt a romantic urge to kiss the hand he was holding . . .

She smiled. 'You'll have to let go of my hand if you want me to fetch the bridesmaid and the mother of the bridegroom.'

Once Rupert had walked away, Sarah quickly sat down on a hard chair beside Alexandra. Her body was trembling. Her hand was burning hot where he'd touched her. Her cheeks were blazing. Her breath was coming in short, sharp yelps. She thought she was going to faint. *Be still, my beating heart!*

She shot a sharp glance at Alexandra, who'd had a ringside seat for the encounter. She waited for a sneering remark – 'Dream on, Sarah Gordon! As if Lord Rupert Glass would look at you . . .', but Alexandra was staring silently and fixedly ahead. There were flecks of foam on her lips and she was twisting and twisting at her wedding ring. She looked like she was having some sort of fit.

'Are you feeling all right?' Sarah asked.

Alexandra blinked and shook her head. She took two or three deep breaths. She said, 'Yes, thank you, I've never felt better.'

So Sarah walked over to Helen, and whispered into her ear that Rupert Glass was expecting her in exactly five minutes in Gran Gran's garden. Helen's smile was dazzling. She threw back another drink down her throat, then collapsed into giggles. Apart from her terrible pallor, and the fact that she was not making any effort to talk to her Dublin friends, one might have thought she was having the time of her life.

Sarah held up five fingers and looked fierce. 'Are you listening to me, Helen? Five minutes. Gran Gran's garden.'

Then she walked back to Alexandra. 'Where has your mother gone? I can't see her at the bar.'

But Alexandra had retreated into a strange, staring phase. She might have been muttering 'Fly, fly away', but Sarah couldn't really hear her over the din of the ceilidh band.

Rupert was getting an earful from Jenny Gordon in the garden. He was trying to be as professional as possible but the woman was, quite frankly, mad.

She was saying, 'I never thought I'd see this day and I still can't believe it has happened! Daisy married

– imagine! Do you know she has a first-class degree in Agricultural Science? And that she's doing a PhD in organic potato farming? I told her years ago to hide her brains and flaunt her legs, or she'd never catch a husband. I told her men don't want first-class minds that ignore them! Thank goodness she didn't listen to me! And now she has the qualifications *and* the husband!'

Fascinating as this was, Rupert was not listening to the mother of the bride. His eyes kept wandering away from her face towards the green-painted door in the wall. At least five minutes had passed and Sarah had not yet come. He realised with a pang that he was impatiently waiting to see her again.

Jennifer was impervious to this lack of attention. She simply raised her voice. 'Daisy actually wanted to get married in her boiler suit, in her bare feet, in a field of organic potatoes. Thank goodness Sarah talked her out of it and persuaded her to wear a wedding dress! Sarah organised everything – hasn't she done a marvellous job? My friend Ruth says there's something sick about the way she organised the wedding, when she's not had a boyfriend for years, not since she jilted Ian Flemming . . .'

Before he could stop himself Rupert said, 'I find it very hard to believe that your daughter doesn't have a boyfriend when she is the most—'

He had been going to say 'beautiful girl at the wedding', but stopped himself just in time. This was a

professional interview, he was a professional inter-
viewer. He was here to report on a wedding and the
most beautiful girl at a wedding was always the bride . . .

Then Sarah appeared through the green-painted
door like a ray of glittering sunshine. She seemed to
make everything calmer the moment she walked into
the garden. Even the mad old mother relaxed her
furious grip on his wrist and drew breath before
shouting, 'Cooee, Sarah, come over and say hello to
Rupert. We were just talking about you . . .'

'I'm so sorry I've taken so long,' Sarah said, 'but I can't
find Mrs Jackson anywhere. She seems to have disappeared! On the bright side, though, Helen has gone to
the kitchen to get a drink of water. I'm afraid she's
rather drunk, but I shouldn't worry about that, she's
drunk most of the time, so I don't think it will affect her
ability to talk to the camera. Follow me, please.'

Rupert obediently followed Sarah into the farmhouse, through the green sitting room. What an odd
and awkward shape of a house this was, he thought,
with its large, low rooms running into each other; there
weren't any halls, or corridors.

They were walking through an ancient, sagging
dining room with wedding presents laid out for display,
when they heard the sound of angry, raised voices
coming from the kitchen.

'I don't want to talk to you. And I wish you hadn't
come to the wedding. I'm quite sure you and your wife

have other, far more suitable ways to spend Saturday than slumming it with your common friends from university . . .'

Sarah put her hand on Rupert's arm and they hesitated.

Then a man's voice: 'You never called me.'

'And I don't intend to,' said Helen.

'Why not? Why won't you call me? You can't believe I didn't mean it, what I said to you that night?'

'The night before you married your wife?'

Sarah held her breath. They all knew at Derryrose that something significant had happened to Helen the night before Richard got married. Something that had left her anxious and sad and addicted to Bounty Bars; the straw that broke the camel's back when Jennifer said, 'I told you so'; the reason she'd moved out of the farmhouse and gone to live by the sea.

Richard started to speak again. His voice was soft and low. Unintentionally, Sarah leaned forward, and Rupert leaned forward with her. What they heard him say was so painful, so heartbreaking, it seemed a sin to eavesdrop on it. Silent as mice, they slipped away, hand in hand, back the direction they'd come, towards Gran Gran's sitting room and the garden. Once they were back in the fresh open air, Sarah politely took back her hand and said, 'What a failure I am! I can't find the mother of the bridegroom, and the bridesmaid is otherwise occupied.'

'So there's only you,' Rupert said, and it pleased

him ridiculously that he was going to interview only Sarah.

They sat together in Gran Gran's sitting room, on one of the brown plastic sofas – this one had a sheepskin draped over the back of it. Rupert looked round him with curiosity. The interior decor of this room was astonishing – it was a perfect example of the 1970s. Some touches were exquisite. There was a smoked-glass cabinet full of holiday souvenirs – a Spanish toy bull, a plastic Eiffel Tower, a postcard with a drawing of the London Underground. And scattered around the room were painted pottery ashtrays – 'Greetings from Edinburgh', 'Greetings from Cork' . . . The photographs on the piano were all of a tall, bony woman, dressed in flowing, flowered maxi-dresses; wrapped up in an elegant velvet coat and stepping out of a London taxi; wearing sunglasses in a ferry terminal with the sea in the background; boarding a green Dublin bus . . .

'What extraordinary decor!' Rupert exclaimed. 'It's so out of keeping with the rest of the farmhouse!'

'This was my grandmother's sitting room, her private little kingdom!' Sarah explained. 'I think there were plans drawn up to convert this part of the house into a private apartment for her, with a kitchen and bathroom and bedroom – but Daddy never got round to it.'

He asked her about growing up with Daisy and she told him Daisy was an untidy slut who could not see dirt, but she would hand you the shirt from her back if you asked her for it. She told him Daisy was brilliant but vague; she had once gone to school without socks. She told him Daisy was a wonderful pianist who played Chopin for pleasure and the practising had driven them all half-demented when they were teenagers.

'And what about you?' he asked her.

'I don't play the piano,' she told him.

They chatted about the most curious things that did not seem relevant to the wedding. He asked her about Derryrose Primary School and she explained how they'd been inundated with city children, recently moved to Bluebell Orchard, and how little city girls were so much more *forward* than little country girls – at ten they were wearing make-up and having manicures at Curl Up and Dye, and each one of them had her own mobile phone.

'What about the boys?' he asked her.

'They all love football,' said Sarah. 'It's a universal language.'

It was only when they'd been chatting for ages that she realised the cameraman was gone and Rupert was no longer holding his fluffy microphone to her face.

'I'm so sorry for prattling on,' she said.

He smiled a most enchanting smile. 'That wasn't prattling.'

20

Ian had given his spectacles to Alexandra when he'd got up to sing. Now he desperately needed them back. The particular genetic defect he suffered from had a long and complicated name but the problem was simple enough. The pupils of his eyes did not open and close in relation to the strength of the sunlight, like other people's eyes. Ian's pupils remained permanently dilated. This meant he could see for short periods of time without his dark glasses, but the longer he went without them, the blinder he became.

Ian had been swamped by admirers after his solo at the church. A young couple had asked him to sing 'In a Country Churchyard' at their late summer wedding and another old dear had wanted to chat as they slowly followed Rent a Crowd down the aisle and out of the door into the crowded graveyard. He couldn't see Alexandra anywhere; he was worried she was feeling unwell. He'd gone to their car in the car park to wait for her but the car was already gone. Partial blindness was settling in around the edges of his eyes, and he wondered if maybe he was in the wrong place, and that the car was parked somewhere else. So he'd wandered confused and disorientated, calling for his wife – 'Alexandra, Alexandra, where are you?' – until Johnboy and Daisy had stopped the wedding Landrover beside him and offered him a lift to the farm.

Now he was wandering around the hay barn, still wondering where she could be. The blackness was closing in on all sides, and soon he would have to sit down and wait for her to find him. Ian tried to suppress his instinct to panic. He was in a safe place. People knew him. His wife was here, *somewhere*, with his spectacles. He just had to keep calm till the cavalry arrived.

'Cooee, Ian, come and join us!'

The ladies from the Widows' Group had made themselves comfortable on the sofas and chairs at the back of the hay barn; they were drinking gooseberry wine from sherry glasses and already at least one of them was tipsy. She blew him kisses from a limp, gloved hand. He edged his way towards the kissing sounds.

'Ladies, I don't suppose you know where my wife has disappeared to?'

They shook their heads; a unanimous negative.

'Come, sit with us till you find her,' said Phyllis. Ian gratefully slid down on a sofa. He explained, 'I can't see very well without my spectacles. I can't see where she is.'

Phyllis nodded sympathetically. She also had

terrible eyesight. She said, 'How sad you have to wear spectacles when you're such a pretty boy without them – you have eyes of the most amazing blue . . .'

Then Mrs Murphy asked him, 'How did you manage to lose all the weight, Ian?'

So he'd settled himself for a chat. There were worse ways to wait for his wife. 'I've started cycling to work to reduce the carbon footprint,' he told them. 'It was Dad's idea that Flemming's Fitted Bathrooms buy all our employees road bikes. Top of the line, of course – mine has a built-in computer which tells me my speed, and the distance travelled, and my cadence – that's the number of pedals I do in a minute . . .'

They were fascinated. 'How fast can you go on your bike?'

'Twenty miles an hour on the flat, fifty miles an hour going downhill.'

Now they were impressed. 'But that's nearly as fast as a car!'

Ian smiled. 'It's a marvellous way to keep fit! But I must admit, my bottom hurt a lot at the start until I bought a special seat which is split up the middle to ease the pressure on the perineal area. And, of course, I wear padded shorts . . .'

There is a shape to every Irish wedding, whether it's big or small, formal or informal, urban or rural. First the bride and groom get married in a solemn ceremony. Then they eat their first meal together surrounded by well-wishers and friends. At Daisy's and Johnboy's wedding they'd been treated to a hog roast. Next, there is dancing and the first dance is given great emphasis. In South Derry, the fashion has always been that the engaged couple lead with a traditional waltz; the first dance at every South Derry wedding is always to 'The Blue Danube'.

Jimmy was poised with his camera when Barney O'Connor and his band began to play 'The Blue Danube'. Mr Johnboy Jackson led Mrs Johnboy Jackson into the middle of the dance floor to tremendous applause for their first dance together.

Sarah watched the happy couple take up position and other couples take to the dance floor to join them. This was the great beauty of the traditional waltz, and the tradition of learning the waltz in South Derry: everyone could dance it. Mummy was waltzing with Daddy; Michael was waltzing with Jane; Willie was waltzing with one of Laura's twins; Laura was waltzing with the other. They waved to Sarah. 'Come and join us, Sarah'.

Sarah smiled and shook her head. She could see Rupert looking at her across the dance floor. She thought he looked particularly handsome in his old fashioned suit – a midnight-blue Windsor double-breasted; the jacket had four buttons, the lapel sloped down to the bottom buttons and the sleeves were tapered slightly from shoulder to wrist.

'London cut,' he'd told her proudly when she'd

admired it earlier. 'It gives the pleasing illusion of a big, broad chest! My grandfather wore it when he lunched with Princess Elizabeth, the day she announced her engagement to Philip of Greece, in 1947.'

Sarah walked, tall and straight and without embarrassment, over to him. It was weird that she didn't feel self-conscious or shy. She didn't feel anything at all, except that she knew he would dance with her.

She stopped in front of him. He held out his hand. They walked on to the dance floor together. Of course Sarah had danced with men before, but not as many as you might expect, for she'd always hung out at church parties in her youth, not discos, and there is very little bodily contact during 'The Farmer Wants a Wife', unless you count some farmer falling on you after the vigorous swinging.

Also, as teenagers, when they'd been learning to dance in Gran Gran's sitting room, with Daisy at the piano, banging out Chopin's 'Waltz in A Minor', or Chopin's 'Waltz in C Sharp Major', Sarah, being the tallest Gordon, had always had to take the man's part.

So how did her body know just how to fit into his body? Left hand on his shoulder, right hand in his hand (his hand was warm and dry). Left cheek against his right cheek (his cheek was warm and dry). The rest of her body seemed to melt into his. She had never in her life felt so close to another person. And so comfortable. It was truly as if his body was talking to her body. And her body was answering.

On the edge of the dance floor, beside the bar, Alexandra watched Rupert waltzing with Sarah, and instead of thinking, 'Wow, Rupert and Sarah!', she started to cry thin little tears down her cheeks that nobody else even noticed. *How can I possibly compete for my husband's affections with a woman who is so stunningly beautiful even Lord Rupert Glass is smitten?* She had left Ian behind at the church because she was too frightened to wait for him. She was so afraid he was going to say, 'I'm leaving you, Alexandra. I've found my voice and I'm going to fly away without you.'

If she could prevent it at all, Alexandra was not going to give her husband the chance to say those awful words. He could not say them if he could find her to say them. He could not find her if he could not see her. He could not see her if he was not wearing his spectacles, and he was not wearing his spectacles because she had them in her handbag. She knew she was acting unhinged, keeping his spectacles hidden from him, when she could see him clearly across the hay barn, blind and stumbling and desperate, but she was quite convinced that the minute he found her and put on his spectacles he would utter the dreadful words and then her happy ever after would be all over and, for the rest of her life, her neighbours would nudge, nudge, wink, wink whisper to each other: 'We knew that marriage would never last. He was always in love with Sarah. Alexandra was only ever his rebound wife.'

The trickling tears began to gush. Soon they were spilling out of her eyes. She was so horribly lost inside herself, locked in a vicious circle of paranoia and self-loathing. If only it had been Ian who had done the jilting of Sarah and not the other way round! At least then she'd have known for sure that he had not wanted to marry Sarah. But the fact that Sarah had jilted Ian, just before their wedding, without any official explanation, left unanswered questions about whether or not Ian still had feelings for her. And the fact that Sarah had never had another boyfriend left unanswered questions about whether or not she still had feelings for Ian. If only Sarah would find a new boyfriend!

Alexandra shut her eyes tightly and clasped her hands together. *Please God, let Sarah find herself a new boyfriend. Sooner rather than later.*

21

E va had slipped away for just half an hour to sit in her car, eat Jaffa Cakes, and have a lovely chat with John.

'I'm having a wonderful wedding, John. There are so many old friends to chat to, and so much to chat about! "How are you doing?", "You're looking well!" "Congratulations, I hear you're going to be a glamorous granny . . ." The last time I saw all these people together was at your funeral, John. Rent a Crowd came down from the mountains to pay their last respects. They were dressed in the same formal suits, but without a flower in the button hole, and they wore their funeral faces and it was solemn and sad with hushed voices. All I wanted to do was to shout, "Would you all cheer up! You're making me feel even worse!" '

How strange that the one person who had helped her get through that awful day was Jenny Gordon the flibbertigibbet who'd arrived the morning of the funeral, with her friend Ruth, to fix her hair and her make-up.

'*Everybody* is going to be looking at you, Eva! Of course you want your hair nice! You want John to be proud of you, don't you?'

Eva felt in her handbag for the small framed photograph of John. She clutched it as one would a talisman.

'Jenny tells me they've started an over-fifties promotion at Ruth's beauty parlour in the village. She says I should come along. They start by having a sauna together. Do you remember she took you to the sauna, John? She said it would help you relax. "Healing refreshment", she called it. And then when she got you in there, she slapped at you with birch twigs to improve your circulation. How we laughed about that afterwards . . .'

When she heard the strains of 'The Blue Danube', Eva put away the Jaffa Cakes. She brushed the crumbs off her stunning green dress, and eased herself out of the car. She knew this was the 'first dance' and she wanted to be there to see it. 'I'd better go now, John, and take up position again as the mother of the bridegroom. Speak to you soon, my darling.'

She was wandering back through the orchard in the direction of the hay barn, sniffing the perfumed apple blossom and thinking beautiful thoughts, when she noticed a scrap of green chiffon half hidden behind the trees. She heard the sound of retching sobs. Immediately she thought it was Sarah and rushed forward to help.

'Sarah, dear, what has happened?' she asked.

But it wasn't Sarah, it was Helen, Sarah's flashy, bright, older sister. She was lying, prostrated with weeping, across a wooden love seat built into the hedge at the edge of the orchard.

'Oh, I do beg your pardon, I thought you were Sarah. It was the green chiffon dress. Has something happened, my dear? Can I help you?'

Helen sat up and smiled a watery smile.

'You tried to help me for years, Mrs Jackson, and I wouldn't listen to you. But you were right, you know. You were right. They *are* after only one thing . . .'

'Oh my dear,' said Eva softly.

Eva had been Helen's teacher for seven years at Derryrose Primary School; nine to three, five days a week; it had left its mark on both of them. For seven years she'd scolded Helen for flirting with boys in the classroom. She'd whacked her for playing Catchy Kissy in the playground. She'd warned her that a girl's reputation was the most precious and valuable thing she owned, it was fragile and delicate and easily ruined, and once it was gone no decent man would go near her with a barge pole . . .

Helen had politely listened. She had even agreed with what Eva was saying. 'Yes, of course, Mrs Jackson, you're absolutely right. My mother tells me just the same thing. I will try to be good, I promise.'

Yet the second Eva's back was turned, no boy was safe with Helen. Eva noticed that she seemed to like them all equally – tall, short, dark, fair, clever, stupid, rich, poor.

'I don't know what to say her any more,' Eva confided in John. They'd always discussed her problems at work once Johnboy and Alexandra went to bed. John had a real talent for seeing things from unexpected angles.

'Maybe she's just being friendly,' said John.

'For goodness' sake, John, didn't I see her with my own eyes kissing George Mulholland behind the bike sheds? And the very next minute she was kissing Sam Streaghorn. And straight after that, Austin Morris. It's disgusting, I tell you, disgusting. And it doesn't matter what I say about boys being after only one thing . . .'

John quietly said, 'I think you'll find Helen Gordon is after only one thing, too.'

'What's that?'

'Attention. You've told me her sisters Laura and Jennifer are reckless, bold and confident. You've told me Daisy is very clever, and Sarah is very pretty. What about Helen? Is there nothing special about her? I'm thinking she chases the boys to get someone to pay her attention . . .'

He really had been the wisest of men for all that he was only a farmer, and it was thanks to John's compassionate insight that Eva had stopped whacking Helen and instead encouraged her talent for needlework. She'd praised her. She'd coached her through the eleven-plus and into a grammar-school place. She'd sent her a note of congratulation when she got into university.

Unfortunately, Eva's good influence had not reached as far as Dublin where Helen had slipped back into her old ways, the university version of Catchy Kissy in the playground. For four years Alexandra had carried home sordid details of her sexual exploits and it sometimes seemed to Eva as if Helen had her finger permanently flexed on some sort of self-destruct button.

Eva pressed a paper handkerchief into Helen's hand. Gently she asked, 'Will I fetch your mother?'

Helen dabbed her eyes. She shook her head. She said, 'My mother can't help me. She never could. I'd very much appreciate it if you'd find me Sarah. And please don't tell Daisy I've been crying. I don't want to spoil her wedding day.'

Eva walked briskly back to the hay barn, a woman on a mission. She burst in on a jovial scene. The bride and groom were at the centre of the dance floor, waltzing to 'The Blue Danube'; Daisy was flushed, smiling and happy. Johnboy was frowning with concentration. His lips were moving, he was counting out loud: 'One, two, three, one, two, three.' He caught Eva's eye and winked. She blew him a kiss. Then she turned her attention to Rent a Crowd and the relatives. One of the things she'd learned as a teacher was how to read a room in seconds, so she should have had no problem spotting Sarah.

But, immediately, she noticed Alexandra, weeping bitter tears in front of the stage. And at the far side of the dance floor she saw Ian engulfed and surrounded by drunken widows. He looked sad and strained; he, too, was crying. Eva's heart sank. Weddings were supposed to be happy occasions! Why was everyone crying? There had been fewer tears at John's funeral! Eva turned her attention to the dance floor. She saw Sarah waltzing with Rupert. Eva watched them till the end of the song; she was loath to disturb such a delicious sight! Then everyone stopped dancing and clapped and Eva launched herself forward. But the chunky cameraman was ahead of her. He tapped Rupert on the shoulder, spoke to him urgently and pointed to his watch. Reluctantly, Rupert let go of Sarah. Eva watched him kissing her hand and the look that passed between them. She waited until Rupert was gone before slipping over to Sarah and whispering in her ear, 'Oh Sarah, my dear, your sister Helen is crying in the orchard. She's asking for you. Can you go to her?'

Sarah made her way slowly out to the orchard. That dance with Rupert had done something to her, something she couldn't explain. It had melted something that was frozen; woken up something that was sleeping. Bits of her body were buzzing. It was a curious feeling. Didn't they say dancing was the vertical expression of a horizontal desire? Sarah could understand that now – his body talking to her body and her body answering. And when he had kissed her hand, she had actually felt her knees buckle. If he had asked her, she would have done anything for him, after that kiss on the palm of her hand . . .

22

In the hay barn the ceilidh band broke for a rest, and the bride and groom cut the wedding cake. Johnboy made a speech. He said, 'Now the waltzing is over, this is the happiest day of my life! I'm married to the most wonderful girl in the world. We're going to live happily ever after. Thank you for sharing it with me. And may all our troubles be little ones!'

Eva clapped with everyone else and queued up for a piece of wedding cake. Phyllis and Mary Murphy were cutting generous slices. Mary said, 'I'll give you two pieces, Eva, one to eat and one to put under your pillow to dream of the man you're going to marry . . .'

Phyllis was very merry. 'I don't need to put my piece of cake under my pillow. I just know I'm going to dream of Ian! What a gorgeous man – I've been admiring the muscles in his thighs, that he's got from riding his bicycle. It made me feel quite young again! Your daughter is a very lucky girl!'

Eva took the two pieces of wedding cake, wrapped

up in two paper napkins, and went to sit with Alexandra.

She said, 'Why are you crying, pet? Is it hormones?'

Alexandra wiped her eyes. She knew she must look awful, a huge big fat blob of a pregnant woman with swollen eyes and swollen ankles, dressed in a tent. Was it any wonder her husband didn't love her?

'Because I'm so very unhappy,' she said.

Eva tried not to interfere in Alexandra's marriage, for she firmly believed marriage was a relationship between two people, a delicate thing the rest of the world was not at liberty to understand. An interfering old mother was the last thing any young couple needed as they embarked on married life together. But a fat lot of good non-interference had done for Alexandra. Enough of the non-interference! Eva took her daughter's hand. She gave it a gentle little tug. She said, 'Let's slip away to somewhere quiet and relax for five or ten minutes. It's stopped raining at last. The sun is shining. It's a lovely afternoon. If you want, you can tell me all about it, why you're feeling unhappy. Let's go now when no one is looking. I know the very place . . .'

Reluctantly, Alexandra followed her mother out of the hay barn and into the fragrant orchard. Strong sunlight had broken through the heaped clouds; she could feel its heat on her face. The grass was almost dry. She kicked off her sandals and walked barefoot. Eva set down her handbag on the empty loveseat and said, 'Just sit there, love, for a second. I'll get us some Jaffa Cakes from the car.'

Alexandra felt mildly comforted by the thought of Jaffa Cakes. No one could feel heartbroken while eating a Jaffa Cake. Her mouth filled with saliva at the thought of the delicious orange and black chocolate taste. She opened her mother's handbag to look for a paper handkerchief and found the small, framed photo of John.

'What's this doing in your handbag?' she asked when Eva came back with the Jaffa Cakes.

Eva said, in surprise, 'Don't you think your father should come to the wedding? Now, start from the very beginning, my darling. Tell me what is making you sad.'

Alexandra knew she was not going to tell her mother about Ian. She couldn't. It felt like a guilty secret, her suspicions that her husband didn't love her. That he'd married her on the rebound because Sarah had jilted him. It felt as if she was confessing to wrongdoing, when, in fact, she'd done nothing wrong except grasp with two hands the most wonderful and unexpected opportunity to marry a man she was in love with.

Alexandra took the small, framed photo of John and said, 'I'm crying because I miss Daddy. I do wish he hadn't died.'

Eva nodded briefly. 'The timing wasn't great, I agree, but I don't think he did it on purpose.'

They sat side by side, quietly eating Jaffa Cakes, eyes closed against the hot sun, listening to the drowsy sound of bees in the hedge. Alexandra felt almost happy. It was difficult to feel sad and stressed when warm sun was kissing her body. The last bit of proper sunshine she'd had was her honeymoon the previous year – Ian had taken her to a Greek island and they'd done absolutely nothing for two whole weeks but make love, eat, lie in the sunshine, rub suntan lotion into each other, and bake in the sun.

Eva said brightly, 'I saw the most extraordinary sight during Johnboy's and Daisy's first dance. Sarah was dancing with Lord Rupert Glass, did you see them together, Alexandra?'

Alexandra shook her head. She would not admit it was the sight of Sarah and Rupert which had triggered her tears to start with.

'Pity you missed it,' said Eva. 'They're a very good-looking couple. Well matched, if you know what I mean . . .'

'But he's at least ten years older than her!' said Alexandra.

Eva shrugged. 'Older men suit some women. John was seven years older than me. I noticed Rupert kissing her hand when the dance was over and I think Sarah was blushing. Not that you can tell with Sarah, she's so elegant and serene all the time. Don't you think she'd make a very good wife for Rupert Glass? I do!'

*

Rupert had wanted to shag her. How could he not have wanted to shag her when she had such a beautiful body, and she was so obviously up for it? He'd recognised the clear signals – her burning eyes, her trembling hand, the faint, musky smell of her hair against his cheek when he was dancing with her.

If only his time had not run out and Jimmy had not been there to remind him it was past three o'clock and they needed to leave for Belfast, for his routine in these circumstances rarely varied, and it was always successful. At the end of their waltz he'd have whispered into her ear, 'I want to be alone with you.' She would have whispered back, 'Follow me.' Then she'd have led him out of the hay barn and he'd have followed her lightly tanned, naked back across the yard to the farmhouse. He'd have followed her through the maze of rooms to somewhere quiet and shadowy where they'd have paused to privately touch – all afternoon he had been desperately wanting to dip one hand into the back of her dress and run it over her arse, and to slip the other hand inside the chiffon halter-neck top and for his finger and thumb to grab and pinch at her nipple. All afternoon he had wanted to press himself against her and kiss her neck and the top of her breasts. He had wanted to take off her dress and whatever else was beneath it. He had wanted to kneel in front of her and to bury his face in her belly and to run his mouth down— Jimmy shouted above the roar of the minibus engine: 'You're very quiet, Rupert. What are you thinking about?'

Rupert roused himself from his slump in the passenger seat. He tried to switch off his lascivious thoughts. He shouted, 'I beg your pardon, Jimmy. I didn't mean to ignore you.'

They had never been able to easily chat in the minibus, himself and Jimmy, because the engine made such a terrible noise. Also, Jimmy was reckless behind the wheel and it took all of Rupert's reserves of courage not to scream like a woman every time he overtook on a corner or swung them round on two wheels. It was only on long stretches of straight motorway, such as they were travelling, that they could have any sort of calm and sociable communication.

'So what did you think of the wedding of the year?' asked Rupert.

Jimmy shot his colleague an amused sideways glance. He was expecting more of a sneer at the words 'the wedding of the year', for he knew Rupert hated doing these local feel-good broadcasts and was embarrassed to put his name to them. And Jimmy could hardly blame him, when you thought about the big stories they'd covered, and the extraordinary experiences they'd shared, during the past ten years, especially during the civil unrest. That was when he had started to drive like a mad man – the night a petrol bomb had set fire to Rupert and he'd wrapped him in a curtain out of somebody's bombed, abandoned house, and had furiously driven him to the hospital. The very next day Rupert was back out interviewing the residents of that street; he'd been careful to keep his front side only to the camera to conceal the burns on the back of his head; it had been Jimmy's job to put the bandages on after the broadcast. Then Rupert had spent a fortune, some place in America, having hair plugs inserted into the scarring to grow back the hair that had been burnt off.

'It was a nice wee wedding,' said Jimmy. 'I thought that bridesmaid you were dancing with was very pretty.'

'You noticed her, then?'

'Hard not to notice a lady like that, nothing *common* there. I'd say even your mother might approve of her . . .'

Rupert laughed and braced his feet against the minibus dashboard as Jimmy swerved between an SUV and a horsebox. His camera man had met Lady Glass only once; it was an experience he had never really recovered from.

Afterwards he'd told everyone she was like something out of a horror movie: too much make-up, badly applied, a loud baying voice like a bloodhound, and she stank of gin and body odour! Not even his granny, who had never had hot running water in her house, had ever smelt as bad as that. And to cap it all, the rancid old thing had believed herself to be in all ways superior to Jimmy. She'd taken one look at his bum-fluff moustache, the hump on his back, his black running shoes, the cigarette hanging from his bottom lip, and she'd said in an arrogant voice, 'Who is the common little man you've brought into the house, Rupert darling?'

Rupert was thoughtful. He said, 'I doubt Sarah would approve of my mother.'

'Nice name, *Sarah*,' said Jimmy slyly.

Rupert did not believe in love. And as for love at first sight – no way! Love was a word people used when they meant they were physically attracted – 'I love you, I want to shag you' – he had used it himself a hundred times, maybe five hundred times.

So why was he sitting in the dark of the voiceover studio with Young Spunky's final cut on 'pause' and thinking only of Sarah? And with a little shock of shame he realised it wasn't just her body he was thinking about, though that was amazing enough. He was remembering the crooked tooth at the front of her mouth which gave her symmetrical features an injection of character when she smiled. And her concern for the thin, pale-faced sister who'd had a drunken shouting match with some bloke from her university days who, even though he was married, was still trying to get his leg over. He was thinking of Sarah's clear, grey eyes and how they'd beamed when he was interviewing her. How they'd chatted for ages in the grandmother's extraordinary sitting room and he had not felt bored once. He was thinking this was the first time in his life he had been left wanting more from a woman.

Rupert wasn't sure he liked this feeling. There was a vulnerability to it, a softness, he was unfamiliar with. Quickly he pulled out his mobile and scrolled down the names till he found someone he thought might take his mind off tall blonde marriage material – a quick fix of furious sex to regain his equilibrium.

Jimmy came into the studio. 'I've taken the liberty of running you off your own private movie of that pretty bridesmaid. I forget again what you called her . . .'

Rupert scowled at his colleague. He said, 'You haven't forgotten her name. You know her name is Sarah. Sometimes you and my mother have a lot in common. You're both ruthlessly determined to see me married.'

Jimmy clasped the DVD tightly. His eyes were twinkling with mischief. He said, 'So you don't want this video, then?'

Rupert watched the video of Sarah. It was only five minutes long, so he watched it over and over; Sarah at the front of the church; Sarah in the walled garden; himself dancing with Sarah to 'The Blue Danube'.

Jimmy stuck his head round the door of the voiceover studio. He said, 'I'm going out for a pint. Do you want to come with me?'

Rupert shook his head. 'I've a bit of business to attend to, first. I'll catch up with you later.' Quickly, he composed a letter to the headmistress of Derryrose Primary School, courteously asking her if she'd permit *Good Evening, Ireland* to interview the teachers and the children. He explained he wanted to research a feature about city families relocating to live in the countryside – Why did they do it? What did they think of it? How did they integrate into the local community?

He printed the letter off his computer, signed his name with a flourish, and stuck it into an envelope and addressed it. He'd drop it into the school postbox later, when he was driving up to the windswept graveyard to meet his friend from the village. He had heard the sound of a ceilidh band in the background when he had called her; she had shouted above the noise that she'd be free after eight o'clock.

There was just enough time to grab a quick pint before he drove back to Lisglasson. Rupert whistled a jaunty tune as he pulled on his jacket and walked out of the studio.

23

The brown and white bungalow was a curious shape, custom-made, like a rabbit warren. Up the attic stairs, under the sloping roof, there was one large bedroom for Mummy and Daddy. Downstairs, all rooms led off from a central kitchen – a sitting room, a scullery, the bathroom, the spare room, and a sun room with a tiled roof and a view of the Sperrin mountains. This was where Sarah brought Helen when she found her in the orchard. The farmhouse was closer and cosy, but it was also full of Rent a Crowd using the toilet, the relatives wanting a nice cup of tea, and those who had underestimated the strength of the gooseberry wine, sleeping it off in the upstairs bedrooms.

The sun room was warm and quiet. Helen took off her green chiffon dress and snuggled into a pair of pyjamas. Sarah put fluffy socks on her feet. She covered her lightly with a blanket. She offered her tea or coffee.

'I'd rather have whiskey,' said Helen.

'No way! I have to share a bed with you later and I

don't want you vomiting on me! Your choices are tea or coffee. Or a glass of water, perhaps?'

Helen said. 'Aren't you going to lecture me about the effects of alcohol on unborn babies?'

Sarah shook her head.

'Aren't you going to lecture me for being a stupid, stupid girl for having unprotected sex with a married man?'

'He wasn't married that night,' said Sarah.

Helen's hair was a crazy platinum; her eyes a very dark hazel. She had a light dust of freckles across her nose and her chin was stubborn. Gently she stroked her tummy. Barely two months since conception, and already her clothes were too tight.

Now the initial shock had subsided, she felt remarkably calm. She was going to have a baby and it was going to be OK. It was a small price to pay for one night of passion she would never forget and never regret.

Sarah walked slowly back to the celebrations at the farmyard. How she wished she hadn't insisted on taking Helen to see Dr Hennessey, that morning when she'd arrived from the seaside feeling sick! How she wished she had said what Jennifer had said which was, 'What can you expect when you drink red wine? Coloured drinks always cause hangovers. I'd advise you to stick with white wine in future.'

But instead she had got her an emergency

appointment and had sat quietly waiting for her, reading back copies of medical journals, drumming her fingers and watching her watch, wondering what was taking so long. When Dr Hennessey himself had come to the waiting room and said, 'Sarah, can you come to my surgery please?', she had innocently followed him down the corridor and into his room, to find Helen in floods of tears.

'Cancer!' Sarah had exclaimed in horror. And Helen had looked up and laughed – a hollow, mirthless laugh, and said, 'No, not cancer.'

Of all the days for Helen to discover she was expecting a baby! Sometimes ignorance really was bliss! Dr Hennessey had told them the pregnancy was hardly there – just a few little cells clinging together and multiplying. They both knew what he was suggesting. They could see he was passing no judgement. They could see he was trying to help.

Helen had said robustly, 'Anto, you disappoint me! It's not as bad as it seems. It's just the shock that's making me cry. And pregnancy hormones . . .'

Dr Hennessey said, 'I'm always here if you change your mind.'

'I won't change my mind,' said Helen.

Willie Simpson's yellow camper van was parked up at the front of the hay barn. The Farmers' Club was industriously decorating it with spray foam, a toilet roll and lipstick. Willie was tying tin cans to the exhaust pipe. Upstairs, in their farmhouse bedroom, Mr and Mrs Johnboy Jackson were changing out of their wedding clothes; they were getting ready to leave for the seaside. No one knew, even they didn't know, how long they were going for; their honeymoon depended on the weather. If it rained, they'd be gone for a week; if the sun stayed shining, they'd be back the following afternoon to cut silage. There was talk of a longer, more exotic holiday in the autumn, after the potato gathering.

Sarah joined Rent a Crowd and the relatives to wave them off. She stood beside her mother. Mummy's make-up was still immaculate; there was not a hair out of place. She was chatting to Emma Flood from the village, asking after Emma's husband; it was said he was bad with his nerves.

Emma told her, 'They've changed his medication. It seems to be helping a bit. But I have to tell you, depression is a terrible illness to live with. Every morning the first thing I think is – how is it going to be today? Some days he's good, some days he's bad. Some days he starts good and goes downhill . . .'

Mummy was sympathetic. She said, 'I've heard massage helps stress. I wonder does it help depression? Ruth does a fantastic back massage – you should take him along to try it. And even if you can't get him out of the house, you should try it yourself.'

Emma nodded. 'I'll bear that in mind. Thanks. Sometimes I think if it wasn't for my horse, and my riding, I might go mad living with him . . .'

One of her children called for her and Emma drifted away.

Mummy whispered to Sarah, 'A little birdie tells me Emma is riding more than her horse, to help with the strain of living with a depressed husband.'

Sarah glared at her shameless mother. 'Hush, Mummy, I don't want to hear your filthy gossip!'

Mr and Mrs Johnboy Jackson appeared in the yard through Gran Gran's garden. Daisy was wearing a wrap-over dress; she was carrying her wedding bouquet. She shouted, 'All you single ladies line up. I'm going to throw my bouquet. You know it's the tradition that whoever catches the bouquet gets married next!'

'Where's Helen? Doesn't she want to catch the bouquet?' asked Mummy as every unattached woman, from Laura's little Scarlett, who was two, to the oldest Widow who was eighty, and even Ruth Paisley, lined up for the catch.

Sarah took up position. She said, 'I think Helen has other things to think about.'

'Something more important than catching a husband – what could that possibly be?'

The wedding of the year was over. The newly-weds had driven off in the yellow camper van. Rent a Crowd had gone home to the milking. The ceilidh band was paid. The drunks in the farmhouse had been rounded up and chauffeured home by a designated driver. The bottom tier of the wedding cake was sealed in an airtight box, to wait for the christening party, in the fullness of time, for the first little Jackson Gordon. It was almost six o'clock, time for *Good Evening, Ireland*.

Helen was telling her mother the happy news about the baby.

'What do you mean, you're expecting a baby?'

Mummy's teeth glittered dangerously. She had amazing white teeth for her age, for she was a fan of cosmetic dentistry and regularly visited Curl Up and Dye for bleaching treatments and sodium blasting. She used an electric toothbrush twice a day with whitening toothpaste; she slept in a gum shield of bleach and drank stewed tea through a straw.

Helen concentrated on her mother's brilliant incisors. There wasn't anything else to say. She was expecting a baby, had a bun in the oven, was up the spout, had fallen.

'But you're not married!' said Mummy.

The door into Sarah's bedroom was firmly shut but her mother's voice carried clearly. Sarah tried to concentrate on hanging up her work clothes, play clothes and exercise clothes, and neatly pairing and putting away her work shoes, play shoes and exercise shoes. There was a cardboard box for her toiletries.

She had offered to hold Helen's hand, when she told her mother the happy news, but Helen had said she would do it herself.

'You're very brave,' said Sarah, for they knew Mummy would not take it well. It wasn't the fact of the fornication, for she was a mother who was not coy about sex, who discussed its biology without embarrassment; who freely used the words 'vagina' and 'penis'. What she was, was a woman who emphatically did not approve of unprotected sex; when teaching her daughters the facts of life they had first learned how to unroll a condom and slide it over a cucumber.

Mummy said, 'You'll have to tell him you're pregnant.'

Helen was defiant. 'What makes you think I know who the father is?'

Beyond the closed door there was a silence. Sarah paused in her tidying. She realised she was holding her breath.

Mummy had never cared for Richard Knight. She had always wondered aloud just what it was Helen saw in him. And why it was Richard she wanted when she could have had any other man in the universe. Her voice was resigned when she said, 'The dogs on the street know who the father of your baby is. The cows in the field. The sheep on the mountain.'

Helen's voice was harsh. 'This pregnancy is none of his business. After he married Elisabeth I told him I never wanted to see him again. I told him I never wanted to hear from him again. I told him I did not want to know if he was living or dead.'

Sarah sighed and looked at her watch. It was almost ten past six. If this uncomfortable interview did not soon end she was going to miss *Good Evening, Ireland*. Somehow, it did not seem appropriate to switch on the portable television when there was so much shouting and angst in the bungalow. Sarah tried to think reasonable thoughts. It wasn't the end of the world. Eva was bound to record the programme and she could watch it later, at her leisure. She could use her time usefully while she waited for the storm to pass – she could write Daisy's thank-you letters – that would keep her occupied . . .

'I think that went well!' said Helen when the interview was finally over and she was climbing into bed. She was sharing with Sarah for just one night, before driving back to the seaside and back to work on Monday morning. She was Curator and Keeper of Agriculture at the Wild West Theme Park on the coast; she was responsible for the vegetable gardens, the livestock and pioneer cabins. She had a staff of two, who dressed up as scalping Indians, and took visitors on pony rides round the park. Last summer she'd organised a Bluegrass Festival extravaganza, which was featured on *Good Evening, Ireland*. In the winter she coordinated school trips and taught Key Stage Two primary school children about emigration. It was said she was good at her job.

Sarah watched her snuggle down under the duvet.

She said, 'Have you thought through what you're doing?'

Helen eyes were unnaturally bright. She said, 'I've thought about nothing else since Richard married Elisabeth. I've been thinking about how he made his bed and now he must lie in it. Well, I, too, have made my bed and must lie in it.'

24

Daddy got up at six on Sunday morning to do the milking. He switched on the wireless in the kitchen; religious hymns blared out. Sarah sat straight up in bed, terrified out of the depths of a most bizarre dream where Helen had given birth to a litter of pups, and Mummy, with a tight new face, was barely recognisable. 'I just told Ruth to keep lifting.'

Where was she? What was happening? Had she died and gone to heaven? Then she remembered. Her sister Daisy was married and this was her new life. She was sharing a room with an ironing board; the window looked out on a field of potatoes . . .

Meanwhile, Daddy was slurping at tea and humming along to the hymns; he went out to the yard without switching off the wireless.

Sarah tried to get back to sleep but the hymns were strangely rousing. And Helen, deeply asleep beside her, seemed to find them subconsciously arousing – she rolled over to Sarah's side of the bed and began to stroke Sarah's hair with her fingers;

she murmured 'Richard' in a dangerous voice.

Sarah leapt out of bed. She switched off the wireless in the kitchen. She wanted to sleep for longer – but where? The chair by the Aga smelt horribly of cows; her mother's cream leather sofas were slippy. And because outside was soaking wet, with a gale-force wind and wicked raindrops lashing the windows, the air in the sunroom was frigid. Finally, she took her pillow and climbed into her mother's Jacuzzi. She'd dozed off to the curious thought that if she felt cold she could at least run the hot tap . . .

Daddy came in from the milking at eight, and that's when the bickering started. How could she have forgotten her parents were a volatile couple who liked to argue about everything? And even more so when they had an audience? The high drama of their marriage had always been played out in public.

'What do you mean, there's no food in the house? I've just milked a hundred cows. I'm starving!'

Mummy was dressed in exercise clothes. She was working out to a Pilates video. She was lying on her back on a special foam mat on the wooden floor in her sitting room; a tennis ball was clenched between her knees; she was breathing and counting and circling her arms in time with the music. When the exercise finished she paused the video and shouted: 'Don't come into my sitting room, Kenneth. You'll make it smell of cows!'

Daddy was petulant, demanding. 'I've just done a day's work. I want an Ulster Fry.'

'Then make it yourself.'

'But there's nothing to eat in the house!'

Sarah and Helen exchanged anguished glances. Their father was not exaggerating, for they had both searched the kitchen cupboards and the fridge seeking something to eat. They weren't asking for much – a glass of orange juice, a chunk of wheaten bread, a plate of breakfast cereal. But every cupboard was bare. The only edible item they'd found was one piece of fruit in the bowl: Helen's lemon, which she'd brought with her to make a pot of lemon tea.

Jennifer was now on all fours, one leg extended behind her. She shouted, 'Of course there's no food in the house. Food leads to temptation and after fifty, "temptation turns to fat". If you want an Ulster Fry, you'll have to cook it yourself!'

Kenneth was still dressed in his boiler suit and wellies. His face was unshaven and his teeth were not brushed.

'Come with me, Sarah,' he said, for he was the vainest of men and never left the house until he'd spent half an hour in front of the mirror. Before she had fully grasped what was happening Sarah was bundled into the car and with furious revving and oaths they roared off in a cloud of blue smoke. 'Good riddance,' Mummy shouted after them.

Sarah asked, 'Where are we going?'

'To the shop in the village for food. You'll have to go in to get it. I can't get out of the car, not when I'm dressed like a farmer.'

'But you are a farmer . . .'

They were back within twenty minutes. Sarah was carrying two loaves of bread and the Sunday newspapers, Daddy had a huge plastic bag full of bacon and sausages, potato bread, black pudding, mushrooms and eggs. Still dressed for farming he rolled up his sleeves and began to fry the fry – the Aga plate was far too hot, fat spat everywhere and floated around the house. It slipped into the spare room and up the attic stairs; it snuggled into the beds; it got tangled up in Sarah's hair; it ducked under the fancy glass door that led into Mummy's sitting room and wrapped itself seductively around her disciplined, stretching body.

'I hope you're going to clean up after yourself!' shouted Mummy, but already he'd turned on the wireless and now he turned it up louder. Fresh hymns vibrated round the kitchen; Sarah covered her ears with her hands; Helen rolled her eyes.

'Daddy! You're cooking a heart attack on a plate!'

'I'm frying a tomato, that's healthy.'

They tucked into generous portions – four slices of bacon each. Sarah was burping black pudding and Helen was picking sausage skin from between her teeth when Mummy sidled out of the sitting room, licking her lips, looking greedy. She lifted a slice of bacon off Daddy's plate, put it in her mouth and sucked.

'A moment on the lips, a lifetime on the hips!' she said and she spat the mouthful out into the bin.

Helen packed quickly. Sarah watched her disconsolately. She pressed her lips tightly together to stop the words slipping out: 'Please don't leave me.'

How could she have forgotten this feeling of being out of control? She had only just moved here to live with her parents and already there was no space for her own life; already she had a bit-part in their dramatics and she was still in a supporting role. She was the little girl once again who had watched in panic when Mummy threw Daddy's dinner at him when he came in late from the farm; who had comforted Mummy when she was crying because Daddy wouldn't take her on holiday, who had piously prayed on her knees that Mummy would eventually return when she'd bolted once again to Ruth at Curl Up And Dye.

Helen whispered, 'Why don't you come with me, Sarah? I know it's a long commute every day, but there are only another couple of weeks till the end of the school term, aren't there? Once the holidays start you can come and stay with me permanently – you'll have two whole months of swimming in the sea, walking the beach, eating ice cream on the promenade, spotting people you know, waving to them and chatting . . .'

Sarah smiled with affection at Helen. They had a special empathy for as children they'd been comrades together in the same conflict except then Helen had been the sensible one, who'd mopped up and removed the broken plates of spilt food, who'd prepared strong soothing drinks for her mother, who'd combed and plaited Sarah's hair when Mummy was exiled at Curl Up and Dye.

Mummy called from her sitting room: 'Cooee, Helen, come and say goodbye before you drive away.' A second later a crescendo of noise exploded from the portable television in the kitchen. Daddy was watching *Little House on the Prairie*.

Sarah was tempted to leave with Helen. It would be fun to live with her sister again; she was such a fun person to live with. If only there wasn't so much to do during the last two weeks of term . . . The school reports had gone out and there were parent–teacher meetings every night, right up until nine o'clock to accommodate the commuting parents.

Sarah felt depressed. She said, 'Thank you for asking. I'd love to live with you once the holidays start. Until then I've made my bed and must lie in it.'

25

Sarah's bedroom was white. The walls were white, the ceiling was white, the carpet was white; the curtains were white. There were no pictures on the walls. The only thing of beauty in the white room was Daisy's wedding bouquet – also white: Fleabane daisies, Queen Anne's lace and daylilies. They were artfully arranged in a plain glass vase on the bedside table; because she was taller than everyone else Sarah had caught it effortlessly.

Sarah lay face down on the bed and allowed a few little tears of self-pity to gather at the corners of her eyes. She couldn't think of a thing to do. What did other people who lived with their parents do on Sunday afternoons? It was only two o'clock. The afternoon stretched endlessly and for ever.

When she'd lived in the farmhouse with Daisy there'd been domestic chores in abundance. She'd often spent Sunday with a chainsaw and axe chopping fallen trees to feed the solid-fuel Aga. For unless she kept feeding the Aga there was no hot water for washing and washing up. And the Aga made such a dirty mess when the wind was blowing in the wrong direction – it belched out soot and smoke all over the kitchen surfaces. Unless she kept feeding the Aga there was no hot water for washing and washing up.

It had never before occurred to Sarah that she'd been such a slave to that Aga! Hours and hours of her life had been wasted, every single day, humouring the Draconian tyrant . . . yet, without the drudgery, she was lost.

Her mother's voice floated through from her sitting room: 'Cooee, Sarah, come and watch the Sunday film with me – it's *Gone With the Wind*, my favourite!'

'No, thank you.'

Her father knocked on the bedroom door. 'What about a great big bowl of apple tart and ice cream? Put some meat on your bones!'

'No, thank you.'

She tried not to sound sulky, for this was her life now and she would have to learn to get used to it. Just like the soldiers got used to the trenches during the First World War. And prisoners in jail got used to supervised visiting hours and solitary confinement.

Sarah shut her eyes, she took deep, calming breaths, she tried to think beautiful thoughts. And for the first time since yesterday's wedding she thought about Rupert. Until now all thoughts of Rupert had been lost in the great orchestral symphony crashing through the brown and white bungalow – Helen's pregnancy, her parents' dramatics . . .

She thought about the interview on the sofa in Gran Gran's sitting room, and how she hadn't felt nervous. It hadn't felt like an interview, more like a sociable chat. And it wasn't just him who'd been asking the questions – she'd asked him about the football training on the pitch at Lisglasson on a Saturday morning and why he went to such bother with the little boys from the village and he'd told her somewhat cryptically, 'Same reason, I think, as you teach. Little boys grow into big boys. Big boys grow into men. Show me the boy and I'll show you the man . . .'

She thought about their dance together – his hand in her hand, his cheek on her cheek, their little solo moment . . . she could almost hear the music again and the gentle hubbub of conversation around them; she could almost feel Rupert's hard body against her— Mummy crashed through to the kitchen and switched off *Little House on the Prairie*.

Loudly, she whispered, 'Wake up, Kenneth! Come to bed, darling. I think Sarah's asleep in her room . . .'

Then there was the sound of sniggers and giggles, followed by Jennifer's theatrical whisper, 'Hush, hush, you'll wake up Sarah . . .' There were more sounds – this time of slobbery kisses and little moans of pleasure.

Oh really! Sarah shut her eyes tight. How could she have forgotten the only thing worse than her parents' rowing was when they played 'kiss and make up'? Anything could happen! There had once been a 'kiss and make up' when Mummy permed Daddy's hair to give it a bit of a curl, and a 'kiss and make up' when they'd bounced together on their bed until they broke it.

Sarah slipped out of the bungalow and walked up the lane to the farm. It was raining thin, nasty rain that blew up under her coat, and into her eyes and nostrils. It had been raining steadily now for almost twenty-four hours and overhead the clouds were dark grey and swollen with more rain. The farmyard looked bleak and the house was locked up, but the key to Gran Gran's garden was hanging up in the outside toilet. She took the key and unlocked the green door in the wall. As always, the garden was tranquil; the walls were covered in honeysuckle and dog roses; on the flagstone terrace there were pots of lavender and rosemary in bloom.

When she was a little girl Sarah had loved to sit in this garden, holding her grandmother's hand, looking at the waving green branches of beech trees in the back lane and busy little birds fluttering in and out of them, building nests and having babies and sunlight throwing dappled shadows.

'So peaceful, so perfect,' said Gran Gran. 'So difficult to believe we live on a farm . . .'

The garden had been Gran Gran's hobby and also her consolation, for she'd been married off to Kenneth

Gordon Senior in the 'good old days' when catching a husband was the only thing most girls aspired to. It was an unhappy marriage. She was an elegant woman who liked her shoes to match her handbag; he was the sort of man who preferred his wife to be unadorned. She had despised his rough manners; he'd sneered at her genteel pastimes. He'd criticised her watercolour paintings, and carelessly scratched her gramophone records. He'd refused to eat out in restaurants, and had not allowed her to organise dinner parties. He would not go to the theatre with her; he did not read. All his life he was interested only in farming. When she criticised him for being uncouth, he called her 'Lady Muck'.

Before they got married Daisy and Johnboy had both asked Sarah to stay in the farmhouse. They'd said, 'Derryrose is a huge old barracks. There's loads of room in it for three people. We hate to see you pushed out of your home . . . Please stay. What do you think?'

What Sarah had thought was that Johnboy Jackson was Neanderthal and earthy; working with animals all day he'd turned into a bit of an animal himself. Springing up from the open neck of his shirt was thick, dark, curling hair; it covered his hands and, by five o'clock, there was shadow of it over his face.

What Sarah had thought was that there was only one bathroom in Derryrose and also only one toilet and if she lived there she'd have to share both with Johnboy. At any time of the day or night she might meet him on the landing in his pyjamas, or his boxer shorts, or wrapped only in a towel travelling to or from the bathroom or the toilet . . .

She had been tactful. She'd said, 'Please listen to me, Daisy and Johnboy – I don't mean to cause offence, refusing your kind offer, but I'm really looking forward to moving into the brown and white bungalow! There's central heating at the flick of a switch and hot running water at the push of a button. There's even one of those centralised vacuum cleaner thingies with contact points in all the walls so I won't have to drag a heavy cleaner after me when I'm hoovering . . .' Daisy had been very gentle. She'd said, 'I think you've forgotten what it's like, living with our parents. If you change your mind, you'll always be welcome to move back in with us . . .'

I t was Monday morning. Alexandra lay in bed with her eyes closed, pretending to be asleep. She could hear Ian coming along the landing with her morning cup of tea. Through meshed lashes she watched him hesitate briefly before setting it down and quietly tiptoeing out again. She breathed deeply and slowly. She was trying not to cry, for Ian had not spoken a word to her since Saturday afternoon at the wedding.

How was she supposed to know, when Daisy called for the unattached to come forward to catch her bouquet, that the Widows would up and abandon him, and rush out of the hay barn to join in the fun? How was she supposed to know that by then he'd be so clinically blind he'd been unable to get up from the sofa to follow them? How was she supposed to know he'd be left all alone, in the empty hay barn, disabled and immobile until one of Barney's band, packing up, noticed him and asked him if he needed his stick?

'What stick are you referring to?' asked Ian.

'Your white stick,' said the musician.

How was she supposed to know Ian would be so desperate for his spectacles he would ask a stranger to help him – 'I would be very much obliged if you'd ask my wife to come and fetch me. She's heavily pregnant and she answers to Alexandra.'

Alexandra had been watching the spinsters, the widows and the divorced line up to catch the bouquet. That little chat with her mother, and the Jaffa Cakes in the sunshine, had put her in a good mood. She was laughing and shouting: 'Throw it to Sarah. Sarah needs a husband,' when the musician had interrupted.

'You're Mrs Flemming, aren't you? Your husband is looking for you.'

Dragging her feet she'd followed him back to the hay barn where Ian had blurted out: 'Where are my spectacles? Please may I have my spectacles?'

Reluctantly, she'd handed them over for the fear had come flooding back that now he was going to tell her he was leaving her. But, instead, he'd said: 'I don't understand you. I was *worried* you were unwell. That maybe you'd gone into labour and were whisked away to the hospital without me. But that musician fellow tells me you've been sitting in front of the stage all afternoon. You couldn't have failed to notice me stumbling and desperately looking for you. What sort of a callous woman have I married?'

And he hadn't spoken to her since – not a word all

day Sunday – not even to make himself civil, not even to say 'Goodnight'.

Alexandra carefully pulled herself up into a sitting position; she noticed with surprise that her wrists were not numb. She tried to lift the teacup. She lifted it easily. Gently she drank the tea. She had a curious feeling in her stomach; not nausea, not heartburn . . . What was it? Something vaguely familiar from a long time ago – hunger! She felt hungry. Wow!

She shouted, 'Ian, Ian, it's a miracle. I don't feel sick any more . . .'

There was no answer. She jumped out of bed to look for him. She did not feel dizzy, her legs did not buckle. Rain lashed against the side of the house but she could distinctly hear him whistling in the carport below the bedroom window. She knew he would be attaching his bike to a special frame on the back of his car. The heavens had opened and the rain was not stopping, the roads were lying in puddles; it was too dangerous to cycle, but she knew Ian would be clinging to a vain hope the rain would eventually stop, and he would be able to cycle home later; she knew he would go into withdrawal if he couldn't get out on his bike.

Just for a moment she forgot their stupid row at the wedding. Just for a moment she forgot why they'd had the stupid row.

She opened the window and shouted: 'You're mad, don't you know that? You're mad!'

Filled with fresh energy, she trotted downstairs to the kitchen and stuck two pieces of bread in the toaster. She rummaged in the fridge and brought out butter and milk. She dived into the cupboard and found porridge oats. Suddenly she wasn't just hungry; she was ravenous. She poured milk into a saucepan and turned on the heat, added a teaspoonful of salt and of sugar; she spooned in the porridge oats and began to stir as the milk heated up. Ian loved her porridge. He had always said at the start of their marriage: 'I married her because she makes such delicious porridge.' Once the porridge was ready she poured it into two bowls and left the saucepan in the sink to steep – the only disadvantage of porridge was that the pot needed vigorous scrubbing afterwards.

When Ian came in from the garage she was washed and dressed and wearing make-up. Not looking too bad, all things considered. Even the biting haemorrhoid had relaxed its grip on her bottom.

'I've made you porridge!' she said.

He ran his fingers through his thick thatch of hair; he was frowning.

She chattered on. 'I'm feeling much better this morning! The morning sickness seems to have gone! I've not felt sick *at all* so far. I've made you porridge . . .'

Her voice slipped away. He was still frowning.

He said, 'I, I, I. Is that all you can talk about? I, I, I . . .'

She tried to stand up for herself. Softly she said, 'I made *you* porridge.'

He flopped down at the kitchen table. Suddenly he looked defeated. He said, 'It's always all about you, do you know that? Your career as a teacher. Your career as a gospel singer. Your sickness during your pregnancy . . . Has it ever occurred to you that I might have feelings too? I really don't think it has, or you would never have abandoned me, blind and needy, at the wedding reception on Saturday.'

Not that again! She had never before realised she was married to a man who might bear a grudge. She said, 'I've already apologised. I've already said I'm sorry, maybe fifty times. Can't you forgive me for it? I was desperately, desperately sick. I wasn't thinking straight . . .'

His voice rose. 'I, I, I again. That's all you can ever talk about. Your favourite subject – yourself.'

If he had slapped her across the face he couldn't have shocked her more. He didn't even eat the porridge. He just turned on his heel and walked out the door.

Alexandra felt like weeping, except she couldn't in front of a class of twenty-five little children, or they would start weeping too and come climbing over her wanting to hug her and to 'kiss it better' – whatever was hurting.

What was hurting was that her husband hated her.

What hurt most was she had only herself to blame. She knew now, with startling clarity, that he had married her because he had wanted to be married to her; not because she could sing or because Sarah wouldn't take him.

But she'd been so blinded by insecurity she hadn't been able to see it; it was so pathetic, so textbook, she might have laughed at herself if she was not so close to tears.

Thank goodness, therefore, she had school to focus her attention on and twenty-five children to scold. And a fresh pile of post to read through and answer; the latest batch of letters from the aspirational parents. What could they possibly have thought of this week that they had not already thought of before? But today she was grateful – their tireless enthusiasm was guaranteed to take her mind off her own troubles . . .

The letter from Lord Rupert Glass at *Good Evening, Ireland* lay at the bottom of the pile. Alexandra read it with interest. Rupert wanted to visit the primary school to interview teachers and children. He was researching a project for *Good Evening, Ireland* about primary school education and how families were prepared to uproot from the city and move to rural Ireland to ensure grammar school places for their children. Derryrose Primary School was at the top of the league tables, it was at the forefront of education; it had been inundated with children from the city. It was the ideal school to profile. Would it be in any way possible for him to visit on Tuesday morning to talk to the teachers and children? He would take up as little valuable teaching time as he could. It would be the most informal of interviews . . .

'Knock Knock!'

Alexandra burst into the senior classroom and everyone stood to attention. From the violent flushing on her face, Sarah's first thought was she was just about to have her baby – there was such *energy* about her.

Alexandra said, 'I've had the most wonderful letter. From *Good Evening, Ireland*. Rupert Glass wants to profile Derryrose Primary School! What wonderful publicity! I've phoned him and told him to come first thing tomorrow morning.'

Sarah felt her face flush. Tears sprang into her eyes. She opened her mouth. Then closed it again. A siren was whooping in her head – *I'm going to see him tomorrow morning. I'm going to talk to him tomorrow morning.* She swallowed hard. She smiled.

'My goodness, how exciting,' she said.

27

Rupert had not expected to feel nervous, meeting her again. He certainly had not expected to wake up before his alarm clock, with a fluttering in his tummy, as he had when he was child on Christmas morning. His bedroom was in the new part of his gingerbread house, his bed was enormous, handmade and wooden, bought on a trip to America; it sat in the middle of the bedroom floor and was draped with deceptively simple brown sheets; the purest and most expensive Egyptian cotton. Sometimes he wondered why he bothered, except for his own ascetic pleasure, for he had never yet brought a woman back to this bedroom to share the sheets with him.

Rupert jumped out of bed and walked naked downstairs to the kitchen. He tied an apron round his toned body and switched on the coffeemaker machine. He listened to the farming news on an antique Art Deco wireless set. More torrential rain was predicted for at least another couple of days.

Once the coffee was ready he switched off the

machine, yawned once, and carried his cup back to bed. He imagined for just one second what it would feel like if he was carrying two cups of coffee upstairs; if Sarah was dozing on his sheets; he wondered did she take milk?

Since Saturday at the wedding, Rupert had been suffering from unexpected flashes of Sarah in unexpected places; she'd smiled out of the bathroom mirror at him once when he was shaving, her voice was on a discussion programme on the radio in his car; her scent lingered by the turf pile outside the village shop.

It was disconcerting. It pleased him.

Rupert did not have the morning newspaper – this was the only disadvantage to living in the back of beyond. Instead, he again ran his eye over the week-end supplement with a two-page spread on the Northern Ireland football team. He was trying to remember biographies to go with names and faces. It was the Gala Reception at the Europa Hotel on Friday night, when he'd be expected to know these men intimately, the whole squad including coaches and substitutes, and not just their recent career history, either. He had to remember the schools they'd attended, and the towns they'd grown up in; he had to be able to say, without cog notes or hesitation: 'Well, good evening, Markie McBride! And for those of our viewers who do not recognise the boy made good from Ballymena, Co. Antrim, who was first spotted by a talent scout while kicking a ball against a wall on his housing estate when he was seven and was offered the opportunity of a youth training scholarship with Ballymena United . . .'

Rupert's tummy contracted with excitement when he thought about Friday night. Not the silly-billy football interviews – he could do those standing on his head. It was his date for the evening he was thinking about. He was determined to ask Sarah to go with him. And why wouldn't he? She was a beautiful girl with beautiful manners. The sort of girl he had been looking for all his life . . .

Once his coffee was drunk Rupert dressed carefully in his best suit – the midnight-blue Windsor double-breasted which his grandfather had worn when he lunched with Princess Elizabeth the day she announced her engagement to Philip of Greece in 1947. Somehow, it seemed an appropriate outfit to choose.

The heavily pregnant headmistress could not have been more obliging – or so it seemed to Rupert. She said, 'I don't wish to be interviewed when I'm looking so pregnant. Please allow Ms Gordon to answer the questions instead of me. She knows just as much as I do about aspirational parents moving to live in Derryrose. Please go into the staff room. Help yourself to coffee and biscuits. I'll take all the children into the assembly hall. After you've spoken to Ms Gordon, you can come and talk to them.'

Rupert flicked the switch on the kettle and scooped instant coffee into two shining brand new china cups – the price was still stuck to the bottom of them. He filled the cups with boiling water and was carefully stirring when Sarah joined him in the staff room. The first thing he said to her was, 'Do you take milk in your coffee?'

It was lunch break at Derryrose Primary School.

'Go, go, go,' said Alexandra, and Sarah leapt into her car and screeched out of the school gates and hurtled down the hill to the village, through the unbelievable puddles; they sprayed out in cascades around her. It had now been raining heavily and solidly for four days since the Wedding of the Year, many country roads were impassable, there were flood warnings in low-lying areas, and county councils were buying up sand-bags. The traffic and weather advice on the radio was: 'Only make your journey if it's absolutely necessary.'

Well, this journey was absolutely necessary, for something prodigious had happened and Sarah was going to burst if she couldn't tell her mother about it.

When she'd told Alexandra, Alexandra had said, 'And why wouldn't Lord Rupert Glass ask you to go to the Gala Reception with him? Aren't you a super girl? And as pretty as a picture! Oh Sarah, I'm so very pleased for you! My mother watched you and Rupert dancing together at the wedding and she thought you made a lovely couple . . .'

And Sarah had hesitantly asked, 'So you don't mind if I pop out for ten minutes to tell my mother – she's at the over-fifties morning at Curl Up and Dye in the village . . .'

'Of course I don't mind. Of course you must tell her! Of course I can manage both classes! I'll take them into the assembly hall and sing to them until you come back.' And then, and this was almost impossible to believe, given their track record together, Alexandra had hugged Sarah.

Sarah stopped in front of Curl Up and Dye and carefully stepped out on to the pavement, over the gushing torrent of rainwater running down the street.

From the outside, Curl Up and Dye was shabby in the extreme. There was one large window hung with pink net; the paint on the door was peeling; cigarette butts stained with lipstick lay in the flooded gutter. Most people on their first visit always drove on past looking for a more salubrious establishment.

Sarah pushed open the door and stepped into an ancient old hairdressing salon. The floor was covered in linoleum; there was one sink, two plastic hairdryers, and a pile of stained and dog-eared magazines. It was the sort of place which catered for blue-rinsed pensioners, half price, on a Wednesday. But today was Tuesday and the salon was empty except for Ruth's smiling niece Lucy, who sat at reception, filing her nails.

'Hello, Sarah. Are you booked?'

Sarah shook her head. 'Not yet! But I'm hoping you might fit me in for the Full Works during the rest of the week. I've been invited on a hot date and I'd like to look my best.'

Lucy smiled her dazzling smile.

'The Full Works? Are you serious? Who is he?'

But Sarah shook her head. The news was too enormous to share with Lucy, nice girl that she was. The person she wanted to tell was her mother.

'Is Mummy inside?' asked Sarah.

'Certainly is. She's just finishing up her treatments. I'll buzz you through.'

Sarah opened the plain white door; it looked as if it led to a toilet; she passed into a parallel universe. Curl Up and Dye was a deodorised oasis of fresh flowers, scented candles, and thick carpet on the floor. Sarah turned left into the relaxation suite, where a dozen middle-aged women were reclining in pristine fluffy white bathrobes and eye masks, listening to pan pipes music. A simulated waterfall trickled over some rocks. The lights were tactfully dimmed. She quietly made her way along the rows of reclining ladies. She was trying to recognise her mother from the shape of her feet – she noticed most of the toenails she passed were painted; some had jewels embedded in the nail polish.

Mummy was right at the end. She was lying face down on her stomach and Ruth was astride her, energetically rubbing her back. She was murmuring: 'I always say you can't beat a back massage for stress. I needed a back massage every day that time I thought the tax man had caught me . . . all those frightening letters he sent, wanting to inspect my wee salon. Now relax, Jenny Wren, and let the stress slip away . . .'

Ruth looked up as Sarah approached. She smiled. 'To what do we owe this pleasure?'

'Oh Ruth, the most exciting thing has happened! Lord Rupert Glass has asked me to go with him to the Gala Reception for the Northern Ireland football team on Friday night!'

Ruth's narrow eyebrows shot up. Slowly she climbed down off Mummy who sat bolt upright.

She said: 'He's done what?'

Something was wrong, she could sense it – Ruth and her mother looked so shocked. This was not the reaction she'd been expecting. She attempted a feeble joke, 'He's only asked me to go to the Ball. He's not asked me to marry him!'

Sarah sat in the kitchen with Daddy; they were eating steak and salad. With a baked potato for Daddy who did not feel a meal was complete unless it was served with potatoes. Sarah had wanted to make Spicy Beef Salad, which she always ate on Tuesday, after forty lengths of the swimming pool, but Daddy had taken one look at the recipe in her Thai cookbook and assured her he would not eat 'foreign muck'. So she'd altered the menu accordingly and promised every evening forthwith she'd cook him some recognisable variation of his favourite meat and two veg. 'What a good girl you are!' Daddy had said.

They were watching the headlines on *Good Evening, Ireland* when Mummy came into the kitchen. She'd been out all afternoon, no one knew where she'd been; the house was very quiet without her.

'Do you want steak and salad, Mummy? I grilled you a steak; it's in the bottom of the Aga. The salad is in the fridge. I didn't put a dressing on it, but I've made a one with Roquefort cheese – it's in a glass bowl here on the table . . .'

Mummy pulled out a packet of condoms from her shoulder bag and brandished them.

She said, 'I think we should have a little chat.'

Daddy raised his voice in protest. 'I am trying to eat!'

Mummy ignored him. She said, 'I admit it quite freely, I was taken aback when you told me Rupert had asked you to go to the Gala Reception with him. You may not know this, but Rupert has a terrible reputation with women. He is a notorious philanderer!'

Sarah carefully chewed her steak and swallowed. She tried not to blush or bluster but, really, she had no idea why Mummy thought it was all right to rubbish Rupert at the dinner table.

'I'm only going to a ball with him – eating, drinking, dancing. I think I shall be quite safe,' she said.

Mummy was solemn.

'You're a very innocent girl. Don't apologise for it!

It's quite an achievement in this day and age! But even you must realise there's more to Rupert's invitation than a bit of dancing at a ball?'

She set down the packet of condoms with a flourish on the table beside Sarah's dinner plate. Loudly and dramatically she whispered, 'Ruth and I have both heard, from independent sources, that he is the most chivalrous of lovers. And we think it would be a great pity for you to pass on such an opportunity to get your confidence back, after your disappointment with Ian. We also think, after Helen's happy announcement, that you should be prepared.'

Sarah tried not to feel upset that Mummy had been discussing her love life, or lack of it, with Ruth Paisley. And not just with Ruth. Probably, she had been discussing Sarah's love life, or lack of it, with all the over-fifties ladies in the beauty parlour that morning. Already Sarah could hear their nudge, nudge, wink, wink whispers when they came to collect their grandchildren from school: 'Ms Gordon's got a hot date on Friday night. With Lord Rupert Glass. You know he's a notorious philanderer . . .'

Sarah opened her mouth to protest but then she shut it again. This was her life now and she would have to learn to get used to it.

Mummy sat down to her dinner. She piled salad on to her plate and drenched it with Roquefort dressing. She was looking rather pleased with herself. She had said her piece. Her conscience was clear.

As a final postscript, she added, 'Unfortunately, I'm not going to be here on Friday night. Ruth and I are going to Amsterdam – leaving Thursday, coming back Saturday, one of those cheap city breaks you can take out of Belfast Airport . . . but we'll be thinking about you when we're in the red-light district . . .'

Daddy suddenly spoke up: 'Jennifer, I blame you for Helen's pregnancy. You've always encouraged fornication – you taught her how to use condoms!'

Mummy was defiant. 'If Helen had followed my contraceptive advice, she wouldn't be pregnant!'

28

It was Wednesday evening. Sarah had just finished a gruelling hour with the parents of one of her ten-year-olds. Gruelling, because they'd made it clear they were going to hold her personally responsible if Matilda did not pass the eleven-plus exam in the autumn. In vain, Sarah had tried to explain to them there was more to life than passing exams, but they were not inclined to believe her.

'We've moved from Belfast to this one-horse town to ensure our Matilda gets a grammar school place . . .'

The mother, especially, was very upset Matilda had been awarded only a C grade for reading. Sarah had tried to explain that the grades – A, B and C – were to help identify inherent academic weakness and that now it was clear Matilda was a weak reader, specific help could given.

The mother had been confrontational. 'What are you going to do about it?'

Sarah had calmly suggested Matilda and her

mother read together every day for fifteen minutes – any book would do.

'If Matilda is interested in ponies, I would suggest the Pullein-Thompson novels – my pony-mad sisters loved those when they were her age. If she prefers boarding school stories, as I did, try *Mallory Towers* or the *Chalet School*. You're welcome to borrow a couple of books from our school library to get you started.'

Now the mother looked bewildered. 'But I've never read a book in my life . . .'

Next up was Emma Flood. She was dressed in riding clothes. She said, 'I'm in a terrible hurry. I'm not even going to sit down. Catherine is happy at school and Derryrose Primary is at the top of the league tables. What more is there to say?' She put her riding coat back on, an ankle-length thing with buckles and poppers, and arranged a dashing, waxed hat on her head. 'I still have to ride my horse. I've left him tacked up in the playground. I put a black bin liner bag over his saddle.'

Sarah said, with curiosity, 'You ride even in this weather?'

Emma's eyes twinkled. 'Even in this weather, my horse still needs exercise! I'll hack him up to the windswept graveyard. There are drains cut into the sides of the path. It's the safest place to go in the rain.'

If only there were more parents like Emma, Sarah could easily have got all her beauty treatments fitted in before the Gala Reception. She had particularly wanted to try out Ruth's special oxygenating facial, which plumped and smoothed skin like magic. Unfortunately, she was fully booked up with long-winded, inflexible parents; each had assured her they could not change the allocated time of the parent–teacher interview; each had said the same thing when she asked them: 'My time is just as precious as your time.'

Sarah packed up her things and drove home carefully. She didn't really mind missing the beauty treatments for she was always well groomed, thank goodness. Her most pressing problem was finding something outstanding to wear. She had not had a new evening dress since she'd been at teacher training college and engaged to Ian. Helen had made it for her – it was pink with a flounce, and though perfectly lovely when she was twenty and a virgin, it was not nearly sophisticated enough for a night out with Lord Rupert Glass.

'But what am I going to wear, Mummy?' she asked when she got home.

Mummy said, 'Why don't you drive to Belfast and buy yourself a new dress?'

Sarah shook her head. 'I wish I could, but I'm fully booked up tomorrow. I can't get the parent–teacher interviews changed.'

She texted Helen: *I'm Cinderella. I've nothing to wear to the ball.*

Sarah lay on top of her bed with her fingers in her ears. She was trying not to tune into the sound of two televisions competing against each other. Her mother was watching *Buffy the Vampire Slayer*; her father was riveted to *Animal Planet*. It was only half past eight and she knew from experience that there would be at least another two hours of discordant noise before her parents went to bed. And it wasn't as if she could get away from it; it wasn't as if she could go for a walk, for this was the worst week of weather on record. The only bright side was that Daisy and Johnboy were still on honeymoon; when she said her prayers before bed, Sarah prayed there were no holes in the roof of the camper van.

Because her fingers were plugging her ears, Sarah didn't hear her mobile ringing. It was only the vibration against her leg which alerted her. She switched on the phone: 'Hello.'

Helen said, 'Have you found an evening dress yet?'

'There's not a dress to be found! My pink dress is far too young for me and Mummy says she has nothing suitable, though her cupboards are bursting with clothes . . .'

Helen was firm. 'Mummy has nothing suitable. She buys out of supermarket sales and Oxfam and, fond as I am of the cheap and the cheerful, a gala ball is not the night for making fashion statements. The eyes of Northern Ireland will be upon you!'

Sarah said, 'Mummy has suggested I wear my bridesmaid's dress.'

'Oh no! Now, prepare yourself for some lateral

thinking! I'm phoning because I have an idea. Alexandra has some very nice evening clothes – I remember her wearing lovely stuff at university balls in Dublin when we were students. Not to my taste, of course, they were far too tasteful for me, but there was one in particular I know you would like – a sheer-black dress with long sleeves, ankle length, but it totally leaves nothing to the imagination – big silver buckle at the belly button. Why don't you ask her if you can borrow it?'

Sarah was shocked. 'I couldn't possibly ask Alexandra!'

Helen was clearly grinning. 'I knew you'd say that, so I've taken the liberty of phoning her and asking her myself. She's on her way over, as we speak, not only with the black dress I remember but also with a couple of others she thinks might suit you.'

Sarah was overwhelmed. 'But I thought Alexandra didn't like you!'

'She doesn't. But what's that got to do with finding you a dress?'

Alexandra was not in the least put out to be dragged off her sofa and summoned in lashing rain to Derryrose. Actually, she was thrilled to be getting out of the house. The atmosphere with Ian was awful. He was sulking; he did it so well. How had she never noticed before? This morning her tea was ice-cold.

Alexandra was tempted to tell him not to bother any

more, her sickness had not returned; she was well enough to make her own tea, but with the foul mood he was in, he might twist this information to use it as further evidence of her self-obsession. So she'd chucked the cold tea down the toilet, and made herself a decent cup after he left for work. Maybe, once it stopped raining and he was able to get out on his bike again, his temper might improve.

Alexandra pulled up at the front of the bungalow and Sarah ran out with a large umbrella.

'I'm so very sorry to disturb you,' she said. 'This was all Helen's idea. She didn't tell me what she was doing until she'd spoken to you. It's terribly kind of you to come. I mean, I could have come to your house and saved you having to drive over here in such awful weather.'

'Please stop apologising!' Alexandra replied. 'I'm delighted to help with the loan of a dress. It's not as if I'm going to be able to fit into any of them any time soon.'

The back seat of her car was piled high with gorgeous dresses, in every colour and every fabric, and, from what Sarah could see as she helped carry them into the bungalow, every designer label too.

'What an amazing collection!'

Alexandra was sheepish. 'It's my dirty little secret – buying designer evening wear. But only at discounted prices! I don't know what's wrong with me; I can't walk past a posh shop saying "Sale" without running in and buying something. It didn't matter so much when I was a student in Dublin, for I was constantly going to balls. But none of this recent stuff has ever been worn, for I've nowhere to wear it, except Ian's work party at Christmas, and last year I looked overdressed.'

Kenneth was sitting at the kitchen table, reading the paper and eating an apple; *Animal Planet* was blaring. Jennifer was fully reclined on one of her cream leather sofas. She had an oil-conditioning treatment on her hair and bright yellow goo on her face; she was watching *America's Next Top Model* while massaging thick cream into her hands.

'After you,' said Sarah and they swerved into the spare room. 'I'm afraid there's no room for a chair. Would you mind sitting down on the bed? And I don't have a mirror, either. If I try on the dresses, will you tell me what you think?'

Alexandra graciously reclined on the top of the bed, with her feet tucked up under her bottom.

'Can I get you a cup of tea?' Sarah asked. 'Or maybe a glass of Guinness? My sister Laura always drank Guinness when she was pregnant with the twins. Dr Hennessey recommended it. Full of yeast and vitamin B . . .'

Alexandra said, 'Yes, please, I'd love a glass of Guinness!'

Once Sarah had fetched her a glass, they got down to business together.

'What look are you going for?' asked Alexandra.

'Sophisticated,' said Sarah.

Alexandra said, with authority, 'That cuts out fussy patterns and sparkles. It will have to be that black dress with the buckle. Or this plain sheath of red . . . You could maybe even get away with that simple silver dress cut on the bias . . .'

Sarah's first date with Ian had been like this, years and years before. What to wear had taken days to decide, there'd been a fashion parade of everybody's clothes. Helen had insisted she wear her best black lace knickers for luck, Laura had lent her a pair of earrings, and Daisy had given her a pair of socks with no holes. Jennifer had taken two hours putting rollers in her hair and carefully painting her face so she looked like she wasn't wearing make-up at all and her hair had a natural curl. How ironic that she was now discussing the same sort of things with Ian's wife, for her first date after Ian!

When they had at last agreed the black dress with the buckle was best, Alexandra said, 'I know you're wrapped up from head to foot in material, but can I just recommend you get your legs waxed all the same? The material is very sheer and bristly legs will show through.'

Sarah said doubtfully, 'I haven't time to get to the beauty parlour as I have parent–teacher meetings. I suppose I could always shave them.'

The headmistress of Derryrose Primary School said, 'You can't start shaving your legs! The hair will grow back thicker and stronger! Make an appointment for lunchtime tomorrow. Doesn't it only take ten minutes?'

Alexandra drove home to the Meadows in torrential rain to discover Ian had driven his car into the carport at a careless angle, leaving barely enough room for her car. So either she parked outside in the rain and got wet walking into the house, or she drove into the carport and selfishly parked her car so close to his that she could step out easily, but he wouldn't be able to open his driver's door when he left for work the next morning.

Alexandra's initial impulse was to do neither. Instead, she thought she would telephone Ian and ask him to re-park his car so she could get her car in alongside. She had the phone in her hand and his number flashing on 'speed dial' when she suddenly remembered again his horrible hurtful words: 'I,I,I. That's all you can ever talk about. Your favourite subject – yourself.' And all her guilty feelings about being a self-obsessed harridan, with a tongue as sharp as a rapier, dissolved and disappeared. *It will do him no harm, a bit of a scramble over the passenger's seat to get in behind his steering wheel*, she thought.

She went into the house feeling naughty and used up the rest of the milk in the fridge, making a huge plate of porridge which she did not offer to share with him. He pretended not to notice. He remained slumped on the sofa, watching the news with a sulky expression all over his face, the same sulky expression he had now worn for days.

You'd better be careful the wind doesn't change and your face doesn't stick like that, she thought.

'I'm going to bed,' she told him and went upstairs to their bedroom, got ready for bed in a jiffy, and locked the bedroom door. His pyjamas were ironed and folded in colour-coordinated piles on a shelf in the en-suite dressing room; his toiletries took up a shelf in the en-suite bathroom. She put on a whale music CD to induce relaxation in both herself and the baby. She had tried to play it every night right through the pregnancy, but he'd sneakily waited until she was sleeping and then he'd switched it off.

'Bloody awful racket,' he'd said when she protested.

When he came up to bed she was still wide awake, staring tranquilly into the darkness. He tried the bedroom door, then tried it again, then rattled it. She wondered whether his face was quite so sulky now, as realisation dawned on him that he'd been locked out of the bedroom.

'Alexandra,' he hissed, 'Alexandra, are you awake?'

In spite of herself, she smirked. It was the first time he'd directly addressed her since the wedding. And, of course, she wasn't going to answer him. And she most certainly wasn't going to open the bedroom door. Let him sleep in the spare room. He could pump up the camping mattress and dig out a sleeping bag. He could sleep fully dressed, for all she cared, and he could wash his face with Fairy Liquid.

He had called her 'self-obsessed'. She'd show him self-obsessed.

Rupert drove up the rutted farm lane in his Saab worrying vaguely about the suspension, and his low-profile tyres, listening to Radio Ulster and feeling a little bit like laughing, for it was years since he'd called for a girl at her parents' house wearing a formal dinner jacket and bearing gifts – flowers for the mother, whiskey for the father. He knew he was going to have to go into the parlour where Sarah's parents would solemnly inspect him. They might even ask if his intentions were honourable! Rupert smiled at the thought of it. As he got out of the car, a bullet whizzed past the side of his head.

At first he thought he was mistaken, it was a bumble bee or an insect, the whining drone was the same, but some experiences in life are hard-wired into a man's brain – gut-wrenching sexual attraction is one, and the sound of a bullet whizzing is another. Rupert had heard plenty of bullets whizzing during the civil unrest. He threw himself to the ground even though it was wet and mucky. His arms covered his head for protection;

he rolled up in a ball with his knees to his chest, to protect his vital organs.

Through the roar of adrenalin he heard a man's voice: 'Stand up and take it like a man!'

Then the furious high-pitched sound of Sarah's voice.

'Daddy, that's not Richard Knight. That's my date for the ball. And you've killed him, Daddy. You've killed him!'

There was a scuffling sound and there she was, smelling of citrus and sunlight, her gentle hands running lightly and tenderly up and down his body, feeling for gunshot and blood. Frightened and all as he was, and frankly he was terrified, he could still appreciate the sensual pleasure of being touched by Sarah. She finished her examination right at the top of his thigh; he had an erection in spite of himself. She peeled away his hands from his face and he saw her face radiant and flushed. She gasped with relief when she found him unharmed. He wished he needed mouth-to-mouth resuscitation.

'I'm so sorry, Rupert. It's a case of mistaken identity. My father thinks you're someone else. Get up now and come and meet him. He means no harm, I promise . . .'

She was wearing a modest black dress, made out of some sort of clinging jersey material, with a large silver buckle at her belly. Her hair was knotted low at the back of her head and the simplicity of everything was offset by dazzling diamond chandelier earrings.

In spite of everything he said, 'You look stunning!'

'I thought black was probably best, if you're going to be interviewing the footballers. I'm sure you expect your date to be discreet on your arm. You don't want me hogging the limelight.'

'Is it safe to stand up?' he asked her, for now she was with him he realised he'd rolled in a puddle and the wet had seeped through his clothes and his hair was matted with muck.

She helped him to stand and visibly flinched, for his dinner jacket was filthy. And it ponged. He had rolled in some sort of sticky, stinky green stuff and even with careful sponging she knew it would not come off.

She said, 'I'm so sorry. Your clothes are ruined. Come into the house and borrow Daddy's dinner jacket. I know he's shorter than you, and considerably fatter, but maybe we can find braces or a belt to hold up the trousers.'

Rupert said with dignity. 'I don't believe I'm inclined to meet your father this evening. I think I might postpone that pleasure. If you would care to loan me a towel to sit on I shall drive back to my own house and change.'

Sarah walked slowly back into the bungalow. Her first proper date in two years and her father had tried to shoot him. What did it matter that Daddy was a hopeless shot and could never have hit him except by accident? Rupert didn't know that.

Suddenly she wished her mother had not gone to

Amsterdam for the weekend. Jennifer was just as dangerous as Kenneth but at least she wouldn't have shot at Rupert; instead she might have invited him in for a cup of tea and a chat about condoms!

Sarah took a bath towel out of the hot press and patted her eyes with it. Her father's television was blaring but he was nowhere to be seen; it was one of his little tricks, to go into hiding when he knew he'd gone too far. He would hide until Rupert had driven off. Then he would act defiant.

Already she knew what he'd say: 'He can't have been very interested in you, if I could frighten him off with a few little gunshots . . .'

Sarah watched Rupert carefully drape the bath towel over his driver's seat. She couldn't think of a thing to say. She had already said 'I'm sorry' twice and she did not want to say 'Keep the towel', because she didn't want 'Keep the towel' to be the last thing she ever said to him. And she couldn't bring herself to say 'Goodbye' either. She couldn't bear the thought of 'Goodbye' when she hadn't yet had a chance to properly say 'Hello'.

So she just stood there, soft, serene and silent, waiting for his car to pull away.

Rupert revved up the engine. He said, 'What are you waiting for? Hop in.'

His gingerbread house was even better than she had ever imagined when she'd gazed at it from the outside.

It was cool, clean and bright. The walls were hung with interesting pictures; there were bookcases filled with books; cushions scattered about. It was all brown, taupe, cream and beige, with stripped wooden floorboards and comfortable sofas. Open plan, too, and he didn't seem to be in the least reserved – he stripped off his clothes in front of her, right down to his sodden boxer shorts. Sarah tried to keep her eyes focused on his face, and not to let them wander luxuriously over his very nice body. But it was hard not to notice his muscles and the smoothness of his skin . . . The only other man's body she'd ever really looked at was Ian's – it had not inspired desire. She thought of her mother's words: *Ruth and I have both heard, from independent sources, he is the most chivalrous of lovers*.

Rupert held out his hand and said, 'Come and see my bathroom. I bought the tiles in Marrakesh.'

It had been one of Young Spunky's better ideas when he'd joined *Good Evening, Ireland*, to send Rupert on various city mini-breaks on a direct flight out of Belfast Airport; Rupert had then reported on what the city could offer. In Marrakesh he had found the shopping was good but the bath houses were better. He had bought the colourful tiles, cheap as chips in the market, and lugged them back to Belfast on a small metal trolley which had buckled in Arrivals. And yes, it had cost him a fortune to replicate a Middle Eastern hamman, but Rupert thought it was worth it; these were the solitary pleasures of the single man.

Sarah was silent with admiration. She had never seen anything like it. He switched on the shower and her voice said, 'Would you like me to wash your back?'

Did he ever! Excitement washed over him; drenched him. He had known the very first time he'd seen her, dressed in her frumpy trouser suit, making her little announcement at the Farmers' Club barbecue that she was not like other women. He had known, even before he spoke to her, that there would be no scheming, no games, no playing hard to get . . . She was a woman who knew what she wanted; a rare, uncomplicated woman, who did follow the rule book.

He resisted the urge to kiss her, else they would never get to the Gala Reception. And he had his job to think of. There were footballers waiting to be interviewed.

He said, 'You'll only get wet. Your lovely dress will be ruined. Go and put on some music. Pick whatever you want. The remote control is on top of the stereo . . .'

Rupert washed quickly and shampooed his hair. Then he wrapped a towel round his tidy waist and strode into the living room. Sarah was perched on the edge of the sofa. She was staring into the middle distance, listening to 'Salut D'Amour'.

He took up position in front of her, with his chest inflated and his legs slightly spread, but she didn't seem to be looking any more. This unnerved him slightly and he wondered if she'd changed her mind about him now she'd seen him naked. Perhaps she'd noticed a slackness in his skin or the inescapable ageing process in the folds of his knees and his elbows?

'Are you a fan of Elgar?' he asked.

She smiled an almost-smile which barely reached her eyes. She was holding her mobile at arm's length, as if it was going to bite her. Quietly, she said, 'I like the way Sarah Chang plays it on the violin. Daisy's version on the piano isn't half as pretty . . .'

He was concerned. Five minutes ago she was offering to wash him. Now she was uncomfortably perched and listening to a song of exquisite restraint. He said, abruptly, 'Has something happened?'

'My father has just phoned. He says I have to be home by midnight. He understands you're working and he doesn't expect you to bring me back. He's checked the bus times from Belfast. There's a Derry Express leaving from the bus station at the back of the Europa at twenty minutes past eleven. It swings past the edge of Derryrose village at one minute to midnight. He'll be waiting at the bus stop for me.'

Rupert thought she was joking. He honestly thought she was pulling his leg. He attempted a non-committal question. 'What will happen if you're not on the bus?'

Her voice was steady when she told him. 'Daddy says he will come to Belfast with his shotgun and this time he won't miss when he shoots you.'

At first she thought he was brusque because he was in a hurry – they were running late, thanks to the shooting. So she passed no remarks and made no protest when he quickly changed into a clean dinner jacket, hustled her out of the gingerbread house, leapt into his car and started it up. The only thing he said was: 'Let's go!'

They shot off in flurry of gravel and she opened her mouth to say, 'Steady on! I've not got my seat belt on yet!' but he was busy tuning in the car radio, and she didn't want to distract him. She thought he was trying to get an updated weather report or maybe a traffic report, before deciding the fastest route to Belfast; it was still raining heavily and some roads were closed. She thought he'd turn the volume back down once he'd found what he was looking for. So she politely held her tongue as they shot through the quiet village.

But by the time they reached the motorway, she realised that this was how it was going to be – he was going to listen to the radio the whole way up to Belfast.

Sarah looked out of the window at monotonous wet fields and wet skies. The minutes ticked past, and the silence between them grew denser. She grew colder, inside and out, though the heater was blasting in the car. She was very sorry, of course she was, that her father had tried to shoot him. And sorry, too, that he'd got his clothes dirty. Sorry that they were running late. Sorry that she had to come home early. Sorry. Sorry. Sorry. Sorry.

And sorry, too, that she had not said, 'Stop the car, I'm getting out!' when they'd flashed past the end of her lane. Imperceptible tears built up at the back of Sarah's eyes. They hadn't yet reached the Gala Reception and already she regretted coming with him.

They met Jimmy at the door of the Gala ballroom. He was chatting to a formal waiter bearing a silver tray of champagne.

'Champagne? Sir? Madam?'

'Yes, I'll have a glass,' said Sarah, and she threw it down her throat.

'No, thank you,' said Rupert who drank only water when he was working for he had to keep his wits about him. The room was full of people he'd previously inter-viewed, not just footballers and football supporters, but the great and good of Northern Ireland who would greet him, and expect him to remember their names and everything else about them. Unfortunately, he just couldn't do it. He had an excellent short-term memory and could cram up on background information, fill his head with names, places and dates. He could conduct interviews of searing insight with unexpected and devious questions, but the second the interview was over, it all fell back out of his head. Leaving space for the next set of interviews.

'Good evening. How nice to see you.'

An old fellow in an old dinner jacket, vaguely familiar, was approaching. Rupert knew he ought to know him. He was somebody very famous – that shock of white hair and the ruddy complexion, his broad, outdoor working-man's hands . . . He slotted these pieces into a mental jigsaw and hoped the picture would be clear before he had to speak.

But the old fellow wasn't looking at Rupert. His big friendly smile was for Sarah.

Sarah said, 'Dominick! Good evening! I didn't realise you were a fan of football.'

They kissed with affection. Made chit-chat. Rupert's face was a picture. For the first time in his privileged life, he'd been ignored in favour of his date. The old fellow did not even look in his direction, except to politely say, 'Good evening'. It was Sarah he wanted to speak to and Sarah who stepped forward to speak to him. He kissed her again before drifting off.

'Who was that?'

Sarah straightened her shoulders and smiled serenely. For some unaccountable reason he did not like her lovely smile tonight. It made him uncomfortable; nervous.

She said, 'That was Dominick Dunne. He's a poet from the South Derry area. He's won a lot of literary prizes for his illuminating use of language. I'm surprised you've never heard of him, but I suppose you went to school in England. Alexandra had him in last week to the Primary School to read his poems and talk to the children about the creative process. How they must find their own voice. How everyone's voice is different. I thought him inspirational . . .'

Rupert opened his mouth. Then shut it again. Something was happening. He could feel it. The balance of power was shifting and he couldn't do a thing about it.

Sarah said, 'Actually, I see quite a few people I know, scattered about the place – local heroes, we call them at school. Alexandra thinks it's very important children understand it doesn't matter where you come from – king or countryman – it's where you're going that counts. Look, there's Tony McCoy the jump jockey, he's ridden three thousand winners. And Wendy Houvenaghel, she won a silver medal at the Olympic Games for cycling . . . and that small man over there is Bobby Flood, the lead singer of Achilles' Heel. He bought your father's estate when your father went bankrupt, didn't he? His son Alex is married to Emma. He was a real laugh when he came into the classroom, the children loved him. He sang us his ballad "Enchanting Alice", which went to Number One – he told us the "Alice" in the song is Michael

Temple's daughter Alice – you know your friend Michael Temple? Oh, look, he's blowing me a kiss. I must go over and say hello.'

She turned on her heel and walked away from him, without once hesitating or turning around.

He hissed after her: 'You wouldn't have got here if I hadn't brought you.'

She waved her hand in an elegant movement – too quick for the casual eye. But Rupert saw she was giving him 'the finger' and Jimmy, who'd been quietly watching, saw too.

'That's some wee bridesmaid!' said Jimmy grinning.

They were seated at a table on the edge of the proceedings with other media types. Each place setting had an abundance of complimentary gifts from the sponsors – miniature bottles of perfume, miniature bottles of Bushmills' whiskey, complimentary packets of Tayto crisps, signed photographs of the Northern Ireland football team and a keyring in the shape of Northern Ireland.

Sarah said with delight, 'I'm going to take this photograph with me and pin it up in the classroom on Monday. The children will be thrilled. They'll think I'm the coolest teacher they've ever had in their lives.'

Rupert glowered at her through narrowed eyes. The entire time he'd been interviewing the Northern Ireland football team, she'd spent chatting to Bobby Flood. He hadn't been able to concentrate, or remember who was who, for he'd been able to see her out of the corner of his eye, and she'd seemed to be sparkling from a great distance.

They dined on Northern Ireland produce – smoked salmon, cream of mushroom soup, lamb and new potatoes, brown bread ice cream. Every mouthful was delicious and she ate and smiled and sat pretty while Rupert instigated a deep and impenetrable conversation with the florid, golf-club type on his right. So she chatted to Jimmy instead. She said, 'Don't you bring a date to these dos Jimmy?'

Jimmy was industriously eating everything set down in front of him as if he hadn't been fed for a week and did not expect to be fed for another week. He said, 'After a while they're all the same – monkey suits and rich men talking. Not my scene at all. I'd far rather be down the pub, playing darts with my friends and drinking a pint. Marie's mother says she'll babysit tomorrow night and let us get out together. I'm going to shoot off once I eat. Marie and I will drink the Bushmills and eat the crisps before we go to bed – a complimentary nightcap for us courtesy of the football team!' Once the tea and coffee was cleared away it was almost eleven o'clock. Rupert was now chatting up a woman at the adjacent table – she was in her thirties and very beautiful with voluptuous breasts and tumbling hair. She was just the type he usually went for, the sort he usually had latched to his arm in *Good Evening, Ireland* interviews.

Sarah tried not to care. He'd been so aloof all evening she wasn't sure she even liked him any more. She thought: *How nice that he's been able to find a substitute at such short notice.* She looked around for someone to talk to but the rest of the media table had gathered up their free gifts and gone. The music started; Barney O'Connor was playing 'Haste to the Wedding' and the footballers were energetically jigging on the dance floor. Air-conditioning whipped through the ballroom and she was so cold her face had goose bumps.

She stood up and made for the door. The Derry Express did not leave for another half-hour but she might as well get on it and wait. It couldn't be any more boring than sitting by herself. She briefly thought about saying goodbye to Rupert, but then considered against it. If he was hitting on the voluptuous woman, he wouldn't want her interrupting.

Instead, she scribbled on his napkin: 'It was fun while it lasted. S.'

Sarah's high-heeled shoes clicked noisily down the street. She had thought it was cold in the hotel's Gala ballroom; outside it was freezing. The wet night air blew up under her dress and chilled her naked body. She wrapped her arms tightly around herself and tried to relax her shoulders and to smile. Tensing up in the cold would make her feel colder. She resisted the urge to knock back the complimentary bottle of Bush in her handbag . . .

When she reached the bus station she bought her ticket then quickly retired to the Ladies where she managed to partially warm herself up under the hot air flow of the hand drier. She knew she must have looked mad, contorted at curious angles, but fortunately the bathroom was empty; the Derry Express was the last bus to leave the bus station on Friday night. She stayed in the bathroom until the tannoy announcement: 'Last Call for the Derry Express'.

He was standing by the Derry Express gate, looking ravishing and raging. Her damned pesky nipples leapt to attention through the sheer fabric of her dress. You'd think Alexandra might have warned her!

He said, 'You left without saying goodbye!' She was tired of smiling so this time she didn't bother. Instead, she said, 'I didn't want to disturb you and the woman you were talking to. I left you a note on your napkin. Thanks for the evening. It has been illuminating.'

'Like Dominick Dunne's use of language?'

This time her smile was genuine. 'I'm sorry about that. You didn't deserve it. I can be very brittle when I'm being ignored. You didn't speak a word to me, the whole way up in the car.'

'Because I was listening to the radio! It was an interview with the Northern Ireland football team, just after they won their qualifying game. I needed to make sure I wasn't asking them the same sort of questions when I interviewed them tonight . . .'

So he hadn't been sulking! He'd been silent for a genuine reason!

She said, 'But you ignored me all evening!'

'Because you ignored me all evening!'

The bus driver stuck his head out of the window of the bus. 'Are you pair coming to Derry?'

Rupert said, 'Let me drive you home. I promise I'll talk this time!'

'Thanks, but I've already bought my ticket.'

'The bus is cold and uncomfortable. I can see from the form of your nipples through that frock you're freezing . . .'

'Nice bit of alliteration there, Rupert.'

He was pleased. 'But was it illuminating?'

31

This time as they hurtled down the dark road, conversation flowed.

He said, 'I should have explained myself better when I asked you to the ball. I was actually working tonight – right up until half past ten. It's part of my job description to insinuate myself with the movers and shakers of Ireland. So when a big story breaks they already know me informally and are happy to allow me to interview them formally. That red-faced fellow I was chatting to is part-owner of Dancing Kate, the horse that almost won the Grand National – the horse your friend the jockey was riding . . .'

Sarah felt warm and drowsy. She was wearing his soft cashmere polo neck sweater over the top of her dress and his cashmere socks on her feet. Rather shamefaced, he'd confessed to a pre-booked hotel bedroom and the overnight bag in the boot of his car.

'When you get to my age, you leave nothing to chance. It's a great deal more dignified to cancel a room I don't need, than to realise at midnight I feel too tired to drive home or to realise at midnight my date wants to spend the night with me and then to have to approach Reception and wait while a member of staff trawls through a computer data base to try to find me a room while taking imprints of my credit card.'

Sarah said, 'I'm surprised you don't have a flat in the city.'

Rupert shrugged. 'I tried it once. It was down by the docks in an old redbrick warehouse; fabulous location, amazing building – but I never really liked it. Lisglasson is my home.'

They sat together in companionable silence, both listening to the radio, and this time, when Sarah looked out the car window, the rain seemed to have temporarily abated. She noticed red streaks along the dark sky. It was almost the summer equinox when night did not properly fall until midnight, and the dawn was breaking by three. Those streaks of red in the sky predicted a good day tomorrow. On the farm her father quoted: 'Red sky at night, shepherd's delight.' Was it really going to stop raining at last?

The song on the radio was Helen's favourite song, 'It Should Have Been Me', which she'd played nonstop since Richard married Elisabeth.

Sarah said: 'I should have explained to you sooner why Daddy is being so overprotective. He's not really a psychopath! In general, he's a very modest man. I can't think the last time he tried to shoot somebody – I think it was a Jehovah's Witness come up the lane looking for directions to the motorway – but we had some shocking news this week and he's been over-reacting to everything since.'

She told him about Helen's pregnancy.

'And the father of her child is the man your sister was talking to in the farmhouse kitchen the afternoon of the wedding?'

Sarah nodded. 'His name is Richard Knight. They were friends at university.'

'And lovers at some point?' asked Rupert.

Sarah frowned and looked down at her hands.

'I think we can safely say it was not an immaculate conception.'

It was not in her nature to gossip, and certainly not about Helen. Her pregnancy was still very early, and in Ireland it was considered unlucky to talk about a baby until after the first trimester of gestation. Tempting fate, they called it. Maybe she should have said nothing. Rupert drove on in silence while Helen's song died away in the darkness. Those words he had over-heard Richard say – so heartfelt and moving in their simplicity . . . he was thirty-three and he had never yet been with a woman who might have inspired him to say such things to her. In fact, until tonight, he had never yet been with a woman whom he liked well enough to invite into his house.

Rupert stopped the car in the lay-by by Derryrose roundabout. He was ten minutes ahead of the bus. He said, 'Just because your sister is expecting a baby, it's no reason to lock you up!'

Sarah grinned. 'He didn't lock me up and don't you go telling people he did! He simply lost a run of himself because my mother's not around to keep him under control. She's in Amsterdam until tomorrow . . .'

They sat together in the silent dark. He was deliciously tempted to kiss her. She was so very desirable; she was good enough to eat.

Instead, he said, 'Do you think your father will bring the shotgun when he comes to fetch you?'

The Derry Express roared through the roundabout at eleven fifty-nine, bang on time. Sarah took off the sweater and socks and climbed out of the Saab to wait for her father, but there was no sound of his car, just the distant grumble of the bus as it disappeared up the wide Derry road, red tail lights winking in the half-light.

Rupert rolled down his window. He said, 'Get back in until he turns up.'

'I'm sure he won't be much longer.'

'Then you might as well wait in the car.'

She ducked her head down until it was level with his. She smiled into his eyes. She said, 'Thank you so much for taking me to the ball. I had a wonderful evening. It hasn't turned out exactly the way we might both have liked, but it's midnight now and my time is up.'

He didn't want it to end. 'Why don't I leave you back to the bungalow?'

'He told me to wait for him here.'

'Phone him and tell him I'm leaving you home.'

'I don't want to wake him up if he's sleeping.'

'But if he's already asleep, he's not going to come for you unless you phone him and wake him up!'

There was a small silence between them. Rupert slowly said, 'You're hoping he's fallen asleep. You're hoping he leaves you here all night. You're hoping to be half dead of hypothermia when he wakes up and realises what he has done. You're prepared to stand at this bus stop on a busy main road in a see-through evening dress with scum bags driving past because that's how you're going to punish him – you want him to get such a scare he never gives you a midnight curfew again . . .'

Sarah said, 'I'm unlikely to freeze to death in June, and I can always duck in behind the bus shelter when I see any cars coming from the wrong direction.'

He was appalled by how tough she was. How cunning and how resourceful. Appalled and aroused. He got out of the car in a swift, fluid movement and wrapped his arms round her.

'I'm not letting you do it,' he said and he kissed her.

Only one thought floated through Sarah's head as her lips melted on to his: *It never felt like this when Ian was kissing me.*

After the kiss she said, 'I've been meaning to ask

you, who was the voluptuous woman with tumbling hair you were talking to when I got up to go home?'

He was refreshingly frank. 'I haven't a clue and I couldn't care less. I was only chatting her up in the hope you would be jealous!'

They sat together in the car, with the seats comfortably reclined, playing 'I Spy'.

Sarah said, 'I Spy with my little eye something beginning with S.'

'Sarah?'

'What?'

'*Sarah* begins with S.'

When they grew bored of 'I Spy', Rupert suggested a new game, an adult version of Blind Man's Bluff. They took it in turns to blindfold each other with Rupert's white silk evening scarf; the one who was not blindfolded placed a pound coin on some part of their body, the blindfolded person had to find it. Sarah started by modestly balancing the pound coin in the palm of her hand, but after a few risky locations on Rupert's body, and the provocative 'You're getting hotter' as her blind hands gently groped up his legs and under the folds of his shirt, she placed it on her bit of belly where the buckle lay against her skin. She lay back on her seat and waited as his fingers gently ran over her hair, her ears and her collar bones. He was virtually on top of her; his breath was very soft on her face, almost ticklish.

He murmured: 'I Spy with my little eye . . .'

Her voice was rough with desire. 'You're not supposed to be able to spy anything. You're supposed to be blindfolded . . .'

His nimble fingers traced the hard outline of her nipples and moved with inexorable grace towards the bare skin at the buckle. Sarah hardly dared breathe. She thought she might gasp or cry out . . .

And then she heard her father's car coming, at furious pace, down the road. It was the only car in South Derry that sounded like Concorde taking off.

Bugger!

Rupert slipped off his blindfold and hung it chastely back round his neck. He returned the seats to upright at the push of a button and though they were both sitting primly within seconds his fingers still loitered on the bare skin of her belly.

Daddy screeched to a halt on the main road beside the bus stop.

He leapt out of his car and with the engine running, began to shout, 'Sarah, Sarah, where are you?'

Sarah sighed a very big sigh. She said, 'I suppose I shall have to go and put him out of his misery . . .'

'I'm coming with you,' said Rupert.

Daddy's face was confused and frightened. All week since Daisy had gone on honeymoon he'd been getting up at six for the milking and he was half mad with exhaustion; he'd tried to stay awake to pick up Sarah but had fallen asleep across the kitchen table, with the television blaring and all the lights burning and the doors not locked. He'd only woken up when the television went silent.

She walked out of the lay-by and into the sodium lighting. He grabbed and hugged her. He said: 'Thank God you're still here. I thought you'd been kidnapped.'

Rupert appeared beside her. Solemnly he said: 'She's been sitting in safety in my car for the past two hours. This country is full of weirdos and perverts. I think Sarah has had a lucky escape . . .' As if to prove the point, a speeding car full of carefree teenagers screeched past at a hundred miles an hour.

'Thank you, I suppose,' said Daddy ungraciously.

Rupert chastely shook Sarah's hand. He winked imperceptibly. He said, ' "Parting is such sweet sorrow." It was a privilege to protect you. Keep the socks till I see you again. And I'll keep the scarf somewhere safe . . .'

32

When Sarah got back to the bungalow she steeped Alexandra's dress in a basin and took a long, hot shower. Sometimes there were advantages to hot running water at the flick of a button – in the farmhouse in the middle of the night the water was always freezing. She put on a pair of pyjamas and Rupert's cashmere socks and patiently cuddled up in her little white bed with a hot-water bottle while Daddy heated a small saucepan of milk on the top of the Aga, and stirred in the miniature bottle of Bush.

Daddy seemed to be under the assumption that Sarah had travelled by bus from Belfast just as he had instructed. And that she'd been standing at the bus stop for some time, waiting for him, when Rupert drove past, on his way home from the ball. And that Rupert had conscientiously checked at the bus stop to see if Sarah had been picked up, and had found her cold and abandoned and had rescued her. He also seemed to think, and this time he was accurate in his assumptions, that Mummy was going to be very cross with him when she got back from Amsterdam and found out what he'd done.

'Drink up that milk,' said Daddy. 'You'll not catch a chill with Bushmills whiskey inside you.'

She drank the hot milk to please him and tried to drift off to sleep. But, for the first time in her life, she couldn't sleep. She saw three o'clock and four o'clock and five o'clock on the alarm clock. But she didn't really notice the time passing, except to wonder at it. And to wonder if falling in love was the cause of her insomnia.

At five o'clock she got out of the bed and rummaged in one of her suitcases which she'd stowed under it. This was where she now kept her unused wedding memorabilia from her broken engagement to Ian. The fancy wedding shoes were there, still immaculate, still unworn; her perfect silk stockings were still in their packet; the order of service was there, and the cheerful wedding list that started 'bottles of vodka', 'hundred-pound notes' . . . and the bridal scrapbook she'd spent hours and hours studying, when she'd first got engaged to Ian. Sarah climbed back into bed and flicked through the romantic pages of fairytale frocks, trimmed with diamonds and pearls, floating veils, extravagant bouquets, elegant wedding cakes, satin shoes and ornate engagement rings. Already there was just enough cold morning light flooding in through the curtains to clearly see she'd been more than obsessed with a rose-tinted vision of herself in a fairytale wedding dress, surrounded by bridesmaids and flower girls . . .

Her lusty sisters had tried to tell her. They'd said, 'You've no photos of the husband! You're falling in love with a big white wedding, not with a man.'

And Helen had been right. Except that she hadn't been able to see it. Until now.

It had taken only one shaky date with Rupert for her to finally realise her relationship with Ian should never have been anything more than an innocent adolescent romance; fun while it lasted; first love. And he'd been a very nice boyfriend; she'd loved him, after a fashion. But she'd never felt anything passionate for him. And he'd never felt anything passionate for her. They'd barely touched each other – she'd never wanted to touch him. And as for playing Blind Man's Bluff with him in a cold car after midnight Sarah shuddered at the thought. Thank goodness that her mother had encouraged a premarital sexual test drive, or Sarah might have married Ian and lived unhappily ever after.

At six o'clock Daddy woke up without the assistance of his beeping alarm clock. He padded lightly down the attic stairs in bare feet. There was no wireless fanfare; no blaring television. He didn't slurp his breakfast tea. He slipped like a shadow from the house out into the yard to do the milking.

Daddy needn't have bothered keeping dead quiet

that morning for Sarah's sake, for Sarah had only just fallen asleep clutching her bridal scrapbook.

When Sarah woke up it was lunchtime. She wandered out of the bedroom and found Mummy reclining on her cream leather sofa; her legs were elevated, there were cold teabags on her eyes. She was dressed in travelling clothes.

'Hello there, Mummy. Are you just back?'

'About an hour ago and the flight out of Amsterdam was the worst I have ever endured. Not only has the airline mislaid our bags, but Ruth and I were also squashed in beside a woman breastfeeding a baby – and I'm sorry to sound so politically incorrect, but it was disgusting! Like an animal suckling its young. She was very discreet, the mother, and I'm told breastfeeding is great for one's figure but, for my generation, breasts are sexual objects – your father calls them "fun pillows" . . .'

Sarah smothered a smile. Only her mother could spend two days sightseeing sex-industry workers, yet freely express unjustifiable outrage at a baby latched on to its mother! Mildly she said, 'It's the fashion at the moment to breastfeed. Alexandra says they're pushing it at the antenatal clinic. Once you conceive a child your breasts are no longer sexual objects – they are referred to as mammary glands.'

Mummy lifted a teabag from her eye and stared long and hard at Sarah.

With obvious disappointment she said, 'So you didn't have sex last night.'

'How do you know?'

'Because you sound exactly the same as you did before I left. And you look the same, too. And if my information is correct, and I've no reason to doubt that it isn't – nobody who has had sex with Lord Rupert Glass is ever the same again.'

Sarah perched on the edge of the sofa and stroked her mother's foot with affection.

'Did you have a good trip? Did you visit the coffee houses?'

'Oh, we had a lovely time. Amsterdam is such a pretty city – so much to look at, so much to do – even after the season for tulips is ended! But what happened with Rupert? I thought it was a foregone conclusion you'd spend the night together. I thought you wanted to, darling. Did you get cold feet at the last minute?'

Sarah said, 'I think what happened could be most tactfully described as "circumstances beyond my control".'

Mummy sighed loudly. 'Well, in that case, I'm guessing it's your father's fault. What has the stupid old fool done now? Don't defend him! I know he's done something bad. And he knows it too. He's feeling so guilty he was even on time at the airport, to pick up Ruth and me, and that's a first in five years! And he didn't criticise me for taking a full-size suitcase on a mini-break to Amsterdam and the airline leaving it behind – usually he'd think of a smart-ass remark to make about something like that.'

Sarah said, 'Why don't I get dressed and make us a nice cup of tea? Then I'll tell you what happened.'

Sarah heard the doorbell as she was changing out of her pyjamas and into jeans and a T-shirt. 'Do you want me to answer that?' she shouted to her mother.

Mummy heaved herself off the sofa. 'It's probably the airline with my suitcase. They said it would be on the next flight and they'd send it here in a taxi. I'd better go and confirm it's mine. I hope they didn't open it. I'd be mortified to think of a Customs man examining some of my more kinky purchases.'

Sarah was having another quick flick through her bridal scrapbook when Mummy stuck her head around the bedroom door.

'Are you dressed? It's Rupert! Quickly, put on some make-up before you go out to speak to him. Oh Sarah – he's gorgeous! Far better-looking in the flesh than on the television. He's refusing to come into the house. Just says he wants to check you didn't catch a chill after your foundering at the bus stop. What bus stop?'

Sarah beamed. 'It's a long story!'

She thought he suited short shorts. And he had a nice tan on his legs. She liked the baseball cap that said 'coach'. And the whistle round his neck. She especially noticed he was smiling a huge happy smile which almost split his face in two.

She said, 'Have you been coaching football? What a nice morning for it! I think the rain's finally over. What do you think?'

He thought with her hair down her back she looked very young. He thought her arse was fantastic in jeans. He especially noticed her eyes were shining like stars.

He said, 'Do you want to come over for dinner tonight, or have you something else planned?'

What on earth could she possibly have planned that couldn't be changed for Rupert? Another night in front of her mother's television? Another night in front of her father's television? Another night in her Spartan room, with her fingers jammed in her ears, trying not to tune into her parents playing together with Mummy's new sex toys from Amsterdam?

'I've nothing planned for this evening. I'd love to come over for dinner.'

'Do I need to ask your father's permission?'

She shook her head. 'Not this time.'

'Can you come over around seven o'clock?'

'Do you want me to bring anything?'

'Only yourself.'

33

Mummy was sitting on the edge of the small
white bed in Sarah's room. She was flicking
through Sarah's bridal scrapbook with a funny
expression on her face. If Sarah hadn't known better
she might have thought her frivolous mother was
thinking about something serious. Serious didn't suit
Mummy. She did not wear it well.

Brightly Sarah said, 'Do you remember that old
thing? I spent hours and hours on it when I was
engaged to Ian. There's a photo of your wedding in
there, and Laura's and Jennifer's. I'm going to stick in
a photograph of Daisy's wedding – it's on the cover of
Agriculture Ireland this morning. Helen always said I
should've got a job as a wedding planner not a primary
school teacher . . .'

Abruptly Mummy said, 'He's never going to marry
you.'

Sarah felt herself furiously blushing. The colour
seemed to flare up in her face, and work its way like a
bush fire right into the roots of her hair, then across her

cheeks to her ears. It spread like a stain down her neck and her chest. It caused pain in her heart and a churning in her stomach. She said, 'Who is never going to marry me?' but of course she knew who Mummy was talking about. And Mummy knew she knew.

Quietly Mummy said, 'Put all thoughts of marriage to Rupert out of your head right this instant. Don't even entertain the thought! Lord Rupert Glass will never marry you!'

Sarah had tears in eyes. She said, 'What's wrong with me?'

Mummy was not a mean person. It pained her to pass on bad news. She got no pleasure from telling Sarah: 'I'm so sorry, my darling. I thought you understood or I would never have allowed you to go the Gala Reception with him.'

'You thought I understood what?'

Mummy observed her beautiful daughter with compassion. Sarah's skin was glowing and her eyes were shining; she was falling in love, the first time since Ian; it was such a pity to spoil it. But better she realised now, than two weeks into the relationship, or two months into the relationship, or however long it took for Rupert to come clean with the truth.

Mummy said, 'I thought you understood that Rupert Glass is a notorious philanderer! He only ever has one date with a girl! There's never a second date . . .'

'That's not true!' said Sarah.

'It is true! Please listen! The reason Rupert only ever has one date with a girl is because he has a fiancée, a cousin of his mother's, tucked away waiting to marry him. Like the Russian royal family before the Revolution – they always married their cousins. My source tells me, and I have no reason to doubt her, that their wedding is planned for next summer when Rupert turns thirty-five.'

They say you don't feel the bullet that hits you in the heart, just the numbness that comes with dying. So at first Sarah didn't understand what her mother was telling her. Was she really saying Rupert was already engaged to somebody else? But how could that be? Why hadn't he told her? Why didn't Helen know about this, or Jimmy the cameraman, or somebody else? Why hadn't her mother told her before the Gala Reception?

'I don't believe you,' said Sarah.

Mummy was suddenly very solemn. She said, 'Why don't you believe me? Why would I lie? Have I ever lied to you?'

No, her mother had never lied to her. Never in twenty-four years. Every single question Sarah had ever asked – even about Santa Claus, and the birds and the bees – Mummy had answered her truthfully. And, in some instances, far too truthfully.

Sarah shook her head. She said, 'I'm sorry. I apologise. Of course you've never lied to me. It's just that I can't believe what you're saying. I just can't believe what you're saying.'

*

Sarah lay on top of her bed staring at the white ceiling. Counting the hours and minutes left till she went to Rupert's house and asked him whether or not he was engaged to some cousin of his mother's. For of course she was going to have to confront him with it. She couldn't possibly swallow his dinner, pretending she didn't know or care.

There were five hours and seven minutes remaining until the appointed hour but she couldn't arrive at seven on the dot. In Ireland it was considered rude to arrive for dinner *on time*; she'd have to leave it at least another ten minutes. That made it five hours and seventeen minutes. And even though he'd said to bring only herself, she thought it might be a nice gesture to pull him a bunch of lilac which grew wild in the hedges around Derryrose. Useful too; she could hit him round the head with it when he admitted to being a two-timing cheat.

Mummy was on the phone. From her bedroom Sarah could hear a one-sided conversation: 'I had to tell her, Emma!' and 'I wouldn't have said a thing except he's invited her over for dinner tonight, and I thought it better she knew . . .' and 'No, of course she doesn't believe me!'

Finally, the conversation ended. Jennifer popped her head around the bedroom door. She said, 'Come for a walk with me.'

'Thanks, but no thanks.'

'*Please* come for a walk with me? I've just spent two days smoking and eating, and I think I'm going to burst. You have no idea just how *ravenous* you feel after a little smoke in a coffee shop. I ate a big feed of crispy duck at a Chinese restaurant last night and I had a fried breakfast this morning! I think I've gained half a stone. I really need to go for a walk. Please come with me.' Reluctantly, Sarah rolled off the bed and pulled on her running shoes. She followed her mother out of the house and down the long rutted lane to the road. There was nothing else to do. Alexandra's dress had been hand-washed and was fluttering in a breeze on the washing line. It would be dry when she came back from her walk and she'd take it round to the Meadows. Maybe she'd pull her a bunch of lilac too, to say thank you.

'Where are we going?'

This wasn't their usual route, the route she'd been expecting, up the steep mountain road to the wind-swept graveyard. Today they turned into Lisglasson village and walked up the picturesque main street past the pub and the village Spar. They walked up to the magnificent stone pillars which marked the entrance to the Lisglasson estate, turned left and walked along the demesne wall, half a mile until they reached another gate, not so ostentatious but more frequently used, if the deep tracks cut into the old avenue were anything to go by.

'Nearly there,' said Mummy, and she turned up into

the avenue. Sarah followed. This was the entrance to
Lisglasson Lodge, the dower house on the Lisglasson
estate where Emma Flood lived with her four little
children and her husband Alex who was clinically
depressed. Fond as she was of Emma, Sarah wasn't in
the mood for a social call. She said, 'I'd really rather
not call on Emma.'

Mummy was determined. 'But you must speak to
Emma. She's the reason we've walked all this way. She
has something she wants to show you.'

Emma said, 'Hello, there. Did you walk? God, you've
amazing energy! Please come in and ignore the mess.
I'm hopeless at tidying up. I don't think this place
would be any tidier even if I had a staff of ten, with
nannies for each of the children and a full-time nurse
for Alex.' She led the way through a filthy, cluttered
kitchen into a beautiful hall with elaborate but broken
tiles on the floor and an exquisitely beautiful stained-
glass fan light over the big old front door. Afternoon
sunlight flooded through it, throwing dancing squares
of coloured light.

'How pretty!' said Sarah with admiration.

Emma paused for a second. She said, 'The children
say those are angel kisses on the wall of the staircase.
Sort of makes up for the mess, don't you think?'

In the drawing room she said, 'Pour a drink – over
there on the silver tray. I've got gin and vodka and
probably sherry . . . whiskey too, of course. There's

tonic in the fridge in the kitchen. I'll have a gin and tonic. Would you pour it for me, Mummy? I still haven't found what I'm looking for, but I know for a fact it's in here somewhere. I know I tidied it away. I know it's in *Country Life*, not *Horse and Hound*, though, frankly, once you've seen her, you'll wonder at the mistake. There's a joke down at home that she's never been married because she's waiting for the laws to change, so she can marry her horse.'

Mummy said, ' "Love is blind and lovers cannot see." '

Emma grinned. 'I don't think that's the case in this instance. I think Rupert can see her perfectly clearly. I think that's part of the reason he keeps the engagement so quiet.'

Emma's husband, Alex, came into the drawing room. He was a small, dark man, very intense, very handsome. He was wearing dirty boots, and unwittingly tracking muck everywhere. He said, 'The children have run out on to the road. I was in the little wood at the end of the avenue, looking for foxes, and they ran straight past me.'

There was a brief silence.

Then Mummy said, 'I'll go and get them. You keep on looking, Emma.'

She took Alex gently and firmly by the arm and kindly said, 'Come and show me where the little wood is. I've forgotten where the little wood is.'

He immediately became animated. 'There are foxes

in the little wood. Will I show you the foxes?'

Emma knocked back her gin in one gulp and smiled sadly. She said, 'Your mother is marvellous with him. She took him to Curl Up and Dye for a back massage last week . . .'

'What are you looking for?'

'*Country Life* from five years ago,' Emma replied. 'I remember the date clearly because it arrived in the post on my thirtieth birthday. Angela went to school with me, and she made a point of sending all her school friends a copy when the engagement was officially announced.' Sarah asked, 'Who is Angela?' but of course she had already guessed.

'Angela Churchill-Knox. Rupert's fiancée.'

Sarah sat on the sofa in front of the drawing-room window. *Country Life* lay open on her knee. There was a photograph of Rupert standing beside a plain little thing with a smug smile and the caption: 'Childhood Sweethearts: Lord Rupert Glass, son of Lord Laurence Glass, tenth Baron Glass of Lisglasson in the County of Derry, and Angela Churchill-Knox who have recently announced their engagement . . .'

Emma handed her a drink and sat down beside her. She said, 'I call it life's small sweetener. If it wasn't for Rupert, I'd probably drink a bottle of it every day . . .'

Sarah stared out of the window. She could see her mother with Alex and all the little Flood children. Alex was staring unseeing into the middle distance, while

Catherine held up flowers to his face, in the vain hope he might connect with her.

'What do you mean, "If it wasn't for Rupert"?'

Emma smiled at her kindly. She said, 'Your mother was right. You really are the most innocent girl in Ireland – see no evil, hear no evil, speak no evil – I was like you when I was younger. Before life gave me some bruising. I think you're the only person left who doesn't know about my affair with Rupert.'

She was without shame or apology. She said, 'It's a couple of years now, a casual arrangement. We meet at the windswept graveyard up the side of the mountain, when I hack out my horse for the exercise. It's not an ideal situation, but then my life is not ideal either. I took Alex for better, or for worse, in sickness and in health. I'll never leave him because I promised I wouldn't when I married him.'

Sarah drank her gin. She was surprised she was able to swallow.

Emma continued, 'I know you don't want to believe me that Rupert is charming to all his lady friends. Of course you want to believe his charm is only for you! But why do you think so many women fancy him? Lust after him? Sleep with him? Because he's charming! A man like Rupert, he knows all the lines, and what's best to use with whom. You're not supposed to read anything into it. I don't. I never do.'

34

The first thing Sarah noticed was the silence in and around the Meadows. Utter and absolute silence. It was a sound she had not heard for a while. She knocked on the back door and went into the utility room, with Alexandra's dress floating from a coat hanger.

'Alexandra, where are you?' she called. Her car was parked outside; she couldn't be too far away. Alexandra's tidy house was not so tidy today. The utility room was also her laundry room and it looked as if her laundry had not been done for a fortnight. There were several piles of clothes on the floor in various colour combinations – dark clothing, white clothing, sports clothing and delicates; there was also an overflowing plastic basket of dirty clothing that, to the inexperienced washer, would not have fitted any of the forementioned categories. Yet the washing machine was empty. There was a note sticky-taped to its door in Ian's handwriting, it said: *How can I do the washing when there is no washing powder?*

Clean white cotton work shirts were heaped up on the ironing board. There was another note pinned to the top of the heap. Again Ian's handwriting: *I cannot do the ironing. You have hidden the iron.*

Sarah had wept bitter tears on her walk over to the Meadows. There was a pain in her chest – she was convinced her heart was broken. Her big romance was over before it had even begun. In two hours, fifty-three minutes, she'd be en route to his gingerbread house to tell him so. Until then she might as well have a bit of laugh with Alexandra.

'Alexandra, where are you?'

Pushing on into the kitchen Sarah found dirty dishes piled up on the solid wood island unit and a note that said: *I cannot load up the dishwasher until you have unloaded it.* She found an overflowing, stinking bin and the slate floor needed brushing. The windows were tightly shut, the blinds were still drawn and the air was stale.

There was nowhere to hang up the dress where it wouldn't get dirty or stained, so she pushed on through to the hall. She went on up the stairs (they needed hoovering) and past the guest room, where she saw a sleeping bag and a blow-up camping mattress. Clearly all was not well in paradise.

'Alexandra, are you in the house?'

The master bedroom was immaculate as always. The bed was made with fragrant, fresh sheets. The mirrored slide robes were shining and fingerprint-free.

Sarah slid one back and hung up the dress on a rail. Concealed in the wardrobe was a large bag of washing powder, the iron and the vacuum cleaner. There were various other things, too – toilet roll, toothpaste, car keys, a pair of men's sunglasses, socks, an iPod, a mobile phone, a packet of biscuits. What on earth was going on?

Then she spotted Alexandra lying outside in the garden, on a striped sun lounger in her bra and knickers. Sarah opened the bedroom window and shouted: 'Are you living or dead?'

Alexandra sat up and looked round her. She spotted Sarah. She waved. She shouted: 'This is the first blink of sun in a week and I'm sunbathing. Sure, nobody can see me from the road . . . I love the feel of hot sun on my bump. They say babies born in the summer are of a sunnier disposition than those who are born in the winter. Come and join me! And bring the key to the bedroom door with you. Lock it before you come down.'

When Sarah joined her in the garden she was pouring the last of a can of Guinness into a glass. She crushed the can and said, 'I'm happy to say that since I was round at your house last Wednesday night, I've acquired a fresh taste for Guinness. Oh my, it's delicious, especially with ham sandwiches, how could I ever have forgotten? It was my favourite lunchtime snack when I was a student. But for years now, since I left Dublin, I've been a total teetotaller to please that ungrateful husband of mine. You know he has an unhealthy obsession about the evils of alcohol? I think, myself, it's because he has addiction problems. I think he's afraid to take a drink in case he becomes addicted. Was he like that when he was with you?'

Sarah sat down on the grass and lifted her face to the sun. She said, 'Yes, he was. We'd go out with my sisters to the Chinese restaurant and they'd all be throwing the drink down their throats and I would be sitting there sober and diligent – and jealous, too, I have to admit. They seemed to be having such fun, and I always felt so bored.'

It was her most bitter regret that she had not been blind drunk the night she and Ian had first tried to make love. She had always thought that it might have been less of a traumatic memory if only she'd passed out, unconscious, during it.

Alexandra opened a cool box and pulled out another can. She whispered, 'I have to hide them in here. He'd empty them down the sink if he found them in the house! Will you share this one with me? I can't really drink two whole cans when I'm so heavily pregnant. In case I go into labour and when I get to the hospital they refuse to give me pain relief because I'm already half anaesthetised. Run in and get yourself a clean glass out of the cupboard above the fridge. And listen, I must apologise for the disgusting state of the house.'

Alexandra lay back on the sun lounger and

stretched luxuriously. She said, 'We're having a power struggle, Ian and me, and it's to the death. I'm as hard as nails and I'm not giving in. I'm teaching him a lesson about sulking he will never forget.'

In the kitchen, Sarah remembered again the reason why she'd come to visit Alexandra – to take her mind off her impending dinner date. Only two hours and thirty-three minutes left to go. From the pocket of her jeans she pulled out the page from *Country Life*. Emma had told her to keep it, to use as evidence when she went to see Rupert.

She had practised with Emma what she would say. She repeated it once again: 'You're a two-timing cheat and I never want to see you again.'

If only it was as easy as that to switch off last night's beautiful feelings with one simple, hard-boiled sentence. And even though the evidence of his engagement to Angela Churchill-Knox was in black and white in front of her but she couldn't help wishing it was all a mistake, a broken engagement that was part of his history, not part of his future with her. Emma had said this Angela one was 'suitable' – suitable for what? And why more suitable than her?

'You're crying,' said Alexandra.

Sarah handed her the page from *Country Life*. She poured the Guinness into the glass and drank it while Alexandra silently read the caption beneath the photograph. Then Alexandra said, 'It's a cliché, but it's true – all men are bastards! Aristocrats, accountants, they're all the same! They'll say anything to get into your knickers. They'll tell you any lie. How lovely they seem at the start, and how loveable! Then you fall in love with them and discover too late they're all sulkers or two-timing cheats. I'm starting to feel like Tammy Wynette, giving all my love to just one man . . .'

She began to sing at the top of her voice.

Sarah laughed in spite of herself. She said, 'Are you quite sure you've had only one can of Guinness?'

Alexandra took another quick drink, then flung herself back on the sun lounger.

'I have to be frank with you. I always thought your sister Helen was a terrible tart, the way she used and abused the men who swarmed around her like flies. At university in Dublin she had at least ten boyfriends on the go at once. Sometimes I wondered how she remembered their names. You know how she oozes sex appeal, she only has to look at a man with that sidelong, smouldering glance she has . . . and don't pretend she doesn't know the effect she has on all of them! Even Ian was in love with her for five minutes once when she smiled in his direction. What a two-timing tart, I used to think, but I'm starting to think she was just right to use them and abuse them – to treat them mean and keep them keen . . .'

Sarah walked home from Alexandra's house slowly. And not just because she had now drunk two gins and half a can of Guinness and everything was mellow.

There was something profound inside her head which she desperately needed to think about. If only her head wasn't so woolly! She was remembering the words Richard had said in the farmhouse kitchen to Helen, the afternoon of the wedding. He'd said, 'I didn't want you to use me like you used everybody else. You'd never have stayed with me, I'm not very interesting. I've nothing to offer out of the ordinary. We might have lasted a month. Then you would have dumped me and we wouldn't even have been friends any more. Friendship with you is better than nothing. So I always kept you at arm's length . . .'

Bloody Richard Knight, Sarah's sisters called him. Bloody Richard who had broken Helen's heart. Bloody Richard who'd slept with Helen the night before he married her friend. Bloody Richard who was the father of her baby. But what had Richard ever done wrong except fall in love with a two-timing cheat?

It was as simple and as complicated as that.

35

Sarah spent a whole hour getting ready, longer even than for the Gala Reception. She prepared with as much care and attention as she had when she'd had her interview for the job at Derryrose Primary School.

'Right, I'm off now! I don't expect to be late.'

Mummy admired her beautiful daughter. She'd put rollers in her silky blond hair while Sarah carefully painted her fingernails and toenails an iridescent silver. Sarah was wearing a draped silver top, held together with diamond clips, it left little to the imagination, and her very best pair of white jeans and her mother's diamond chandelier earrings. Mummy said, 'I know you won't believe this, but you're the picture of me when I was your age. Do you want me to drive you over there?'

But Sarah preferred to walk. It was only a mile and a half, maybe not even that; it was a beautiful evening with long summer shadows, and there were still fifty-five minutes before she could politely appear on Rupert's threshold, confront him with *Country Life*, and dump him with the words: 'You're a two-timing cheat and I never want to see you again.'

He had said seven o'clock and she would not be earlier than seven.

She had a pair of amusing old Crocs on her feet and her wedding shoes in a plastic bag. She would throw the Crocs into Rupert's hedge and change into her wedding shoes before she confronted Rupert. An elevation of five foolish inches would give her the necessary confidence to say what she had to say: 'You're a two-timing cheat and I never want to see you again.'

Sarah strolled along the road swinging a plastic carrier bag. She sang little snatches of Tammy Wynette and thought about Alexandra. Drunk, half naked, heavily pregnant and sunbathing in the garden . . . Was that what marriage to Ian did to you? She'd had a lucky escape!

In the blink of an eye she reached Rupert's house, and she was still twenty minutes too early. There were cars parked on his pea gravel – a Range Rover, a Jag, and a Volvo V70. Whoever was visiting Rupert did not have cash-flow problems! Quietly she watched from the footpath as another car pulled in through his gate, over the cattle grid. Another large luxury vehicle – was it a Rolls Royce? A middle-aged couple leapt out and the doors banged. Sarah watched a slender blonde woman in a stunning dress open the boot and remove an armful of brightly wrapped gifts. Her voice was awfully posh when she shouted: 'Here, Jonty, you carry something!'

Realisation broke like a horrible sweat. She had not been invited to Rupert's house for a simple meal; she'd been invited to a proper dinner party, maybe even a birthday party, if those wrapped-up gifts were anything to go by!

Rupert's front door opened and out tumbled the rest of the dinner-party guests, kissing and gaily greeting the newcomers. The women were much older than Sarah but expensively and elegantly ageless, each would have easily given Mummy a run for her money. Their clothes screeched 'I'm very rich!' Who were these people? Certainly not farming friends of her parents, or neighbours from round Derryrose . . .

When her mobile rang she expected it to be Mummy – checking up that she'd got there safely, that she hadn't fallen into a ditch or been run over by a tractor. Offering a few last little words of useless reassurance, probably: *The course of true love never did run smooth*.

No, it most certainly did not run smooth once you found out the fellow you fancied was a two-timing cheat who was already engaged to a suitable girl.

Sarah groped for the phone – if this was her mother she was going to beg her to jump into her car and come and snatch her off the side of the road. And drive her to safety far away. A confrontation with Rupert was impossible if he was hosting a dinner party. It would be better if he thought she hadn't turned up; better if she walked away.

But it wasn't Mummy on the phone, it was Rupert. He said, 'I can see you on the road. I'm watching you from the bathroom window. You look beautiful from where I'm standing. Don't hesitate. Come in.'

She felt pleased and shy. Until she remembered what Emma had told her: 'A man like Rupert, he knows all the lines and what's best to use with whom.'

She stroked the page from *Country Life* to give her the confidence. She said, 'I didn't realise you were having a dinner party. And that all your friends would be here . . .'

His voice was very reassuring. He said, 'They're not my friends, they're my sisters. I've four sisters just like you, and they come once a year on my birthday to have dinner with me and to boss me about. I want you to meet them – that's why I invited you over. Come on in and meet them.'

How she wished her mother had not taken her to speak to Emma! How she wished she had never seen his engagement photograph in *Country Life*. How she wished the most difficult thing she had to do was to put on her high heels and walk into the Gamekeeper's Cottage and meet Rupert's sisters!

Except that when she got in there, and was being introduced to his sisters, what was she supposed to say? There was nothing left for her to say except:

'You're a two-timing cheat and I never want to see you again.'

Sarah switched off her phone and stuck it back into the hip pocket of her jeans. She turned to walk away. It would take her only twenty minutes to walk back home to Derryrose. First thing she'd do when she got there was stick Rupert's engagement photograph to Angela Churchill-Knox into the bridal scrapbook. Then she'd retreat to her little white bedroom and have a really long cry.

'Where are you going?'

He'd come up behind her, running, swift and silent in his earth-warrior sandals. His dark hair was wet from the shower and he was wearing jeans and an open-necked shirt – he was as informally dressed as she was. She wondered fleetingly if these were the clothes he had planned to wear, or if he'd dressed in them to make her feel better when he saw her out on the road, in her flimsy silver top and white jeans.

She said, 'I'm going home.'

'But my sisters are waiting to meet you! They've dressed up in their very best dresses to impress you. They've talked of nothing else since I told them you were coming. "When is she arriving? When are we going to meet her?" Why are you running out on me?'

She took *County Life* from her bag and showed him the engagement photograph.

'I wasn't planning to dine with you, even before I saw it was a dinner party. I came only to show you this.'

What was it she'd planned to say to him? What was the line she'd practised? Why couldn't she remember? Tears of frustration built up in her eyes. Ah, yes, she remembered now – 'You're a two-timing cheat and I never want to see you again.'

Rupert's face was very angry. 'Who showed you this magazine? I bet it was Emma. She's the only person you know who knows about this . . . Angela's parents *insisted* they announce it formally somewhere and at the time I thought – oh well, what does it matter what I thought – I thought nobody reads this type of magazine any more except Angela and her time-warp cronies . . . It was the only announcement I allowed them to make – I wouldn't allow it in *The Irish Times*, too many people would see it. I thought I was getting off lightly having it announced only in *Country Life*.'

She didn't know what he was talking about. She didn't really care. It seemed to her he was attaching a ridiculous significance to the insignificant.

She said, 'Why didn't you tell me you were engaged?'

But he wasn't listening to her. He was too busy raging about Emma. 'That nasty, spiteful, unkind girl . . . I told Emma it was over between us. I even told her why. On Wednesday night, before the Gala Reception, I met her up at the windswept graveyard. I told her I was taking you to the Gala Reception. I told her this time was different . . .'

She began to walk away from him. He ran after her.

He said, 'Please come back. I can explain everything. Please come back and let me explain.'

What was it Richard had said to Helen in the farmhouse kitchen at the wedding? Loudly and clearly Sarah repeated the chilling, thrilling words.

She said: 'I will not share you.'

She left him standing on the side of the road. She went on walking away from him. Away from the Gamekeeper's Cottage and his sisters and his dinner party and his birthday. She felt curiously light; liberated.

After the big, long cry, that she was planning for her little white bedroom, she was going to have a really long think about what she should do with her life. First thing she was going to do was move out of her parents' bungalow and establish her independence. Grow up. Take charge of her life. When Daisy and Johnboy came back from their honeymoon she'd tell them she'd reconsidered. She'd tell them, 'Thank you very much. I'd love to live with you in the farmhouse.' Maybe she'd even find a proper boyfriend who was not a two-timing cheat.

Sarah's bedroom window was open and her bedroom door was firmly shut. She was listening for the distinctive sound of the yellow camper van. There had been no rain since the previous evening and the ground was finally dry again. Daisy's and Johnboy's honeymoon could not last for much longer; there was silage ready for cutting.

Sarah knew her mother and father were taking it in turns to listen for her. Sometimes she heard her father's rasping breath above the noise of the twin televisions; sometimes she smelt her mother's musky perfume. Sometimes they spoke to her through the door:

'Open the door. We've brought you fish and chips.'

'Open the door. We've brought ice cream from Maud's in the village.'

'Open the door. We've brought you a glass of gooseberry wine.'

Please go away and leave me alone!!

Finally she heard the camper van chugging up the long rutted lane. Sarah did not hesitate. She leapt off the bed, flung open the door, rushed out of the bungalow and chased it. It did not travel at speed. In her Crocs she had caught it up by the time it reached the farmyard. The engine was still running when she banged on the driver's side window.

She shouted: 'Please help me, Johnboy and Daisy. I can't live with my parents any longer!'

Johnboy opened his door and jumped down. He said, 'What on earth has happened?'

Sarah threw herself on him weeping. How comforting Johnboy Jackson was. How pleasant to be around. How could she ever have dismissed him as a Neanderthal? He was solid and reassuring and she'd missed him as much as she'd missed Daisy. She'd missed them both. How happy she was they were back!

Daisy stepped down from the passenger seat. She said, 'Something has happened! You look totally different! What on earth has happened?'

'Rupert asked me out, Daddy tried to shoot Rupert, I had a hot date with Rupert. Mummy gave me condoms. I fell in love with Rupert and discovered he was a two-timing cheat with a secret fiancée down the country . . .'

Daisy looked bewildered. She said: 'How long have we been away for? I thought it was less than a week.'

36

E va woke up with a start. She'd been having a curious dream, something about bunny rabbits. She picked up the photograph of John on her bedside table and told him: 'I have a curious feeling our first grandchild is coming today . . . I can't tell you how I know this. It's just the most curious feeling. Will I phone Alexandra and tell her, or do you think it will spoil the surprise?'

Eva hopped out of bed and crossed over the landing to the small room which had been Alexandra's but was now redecorated in soothing shades of traditional cream. The ladies from the Widows' Group had painted a pastoral scene along the side of one wall. There were fluffy sheep and fluffy clouds, bunny rabbits and beautiful flowers; a sky of palest azure and a smiling sun. This was where Alexandra's baby was going to sleep when Eva was looking after it, him or her, they didn't know yet, while Alexandra was teaching. She had all the baby stuff bought and a book called *Routines for Baby* had been dug out of the attic and dusted down. It was almost thirty years since there was a baby at Muff and Eva was taking no chances with modern ideas about child rearing – there was so much conflicting advice nowadays about where and how babies should sleep – let Baby sleep in the bed beside you, don't let Baby sleep in the bed beside you, allow Baby to cry down to sleep, rock Baby over to sleep . . .

Young mums didn't know what was for the best any more. They'd been told the old ways were wrong but in Eva's opinion the modern ways were worse. And it was the children who were suffering. In thirty years' teaching she'd noticed a gradual decline in concentration in the classroom and an increasing abundance of sleepy heads in the morning.

When she'd tackled the mothers about it, they always said the same thing: 'I can't get him to go to bed. I send him to his room, but he keeps coming back down the stairs. We never established a proper bedtime when he was a baby because the health visitor said he would sleep when he was tired. But he just doesn't seem to get tired until half past ten every night. And then, of course, he wants to sleep in until half past ten every morning.'

Eva lovingly stroked the frill along the pale green curtains. Half past ten! She'd never heard worse. Alexandra and Johnboy had always gone to bed at seven. And they'd always had a lovely nap for an hour every day after school. The secret of Eva's success at establishing nap time and bedtime was simple – she had an uncompromising attitude and black-out linings sewn into the back of the bedroom curtains. Children slept so much better in a darkened room! For this little baby she'd tested the room by pulling the curtains in the middle of the day and when she'd discovered a small bright gap under the bedroom door she'd plugged it with a draught excluder. Now the room was ready and all they were waiting for was Baby.

Eva slipped into her dress of startling green that she'd worn at the wedding of the year. She was going with the ladies of the Widows' Group to support Mary Murphy in the final of the All-Ireland Scone-Baking Contest. The final was being held in the Ulster Hall; Mary was up against stiff competition. Because she was a nervous wee woman, who lived alone, with no family to speak of, the Widows were travelling with her, in the Derryrose school minibus – and afterwards, win or lose, they were going to take her out for a feed, to a restaurant which did not serve scones. Eva was driving the minibus and she'd instructed the Widows to rendezvous at Derryrose Primary School car park at nine o'clock on the dot. The Widows were all exceedingly punctual, having nothing better to think about and only themselves to get organised. Eva was also a punctual person who timed everything to the last second and by the time she'd finished fussing with her hair she knew she was running late. She had wanted to swing past the Meadows to warn Ian to keep a close eye on his wife, and not to go gallivanting off on his bicycle, but she wasn't going to have time now. She would have to phone him instead. There was something funny going on in that house; the atmosphere was very uncomfortable. Last weekend she'd found a cryptic note on the fridge in Alexandra's tidy teacher's handwriting: *Stop putting the butter back in the fridge. It will not spread when it's hard.*

Eva trotted out to the car with her mobile in her hand. She would call on the way to the school.

The number was ringing and Eva was hurtling down the country road. It was against the law to talk into a mobile while driving, the police came down heavy on those they caught at it, and Eva was in general a law-abiding driver, who always slowed down to the speed limit, and dipped her lights at on-coming traffic. She found it difficult to do bad things, things she knew were illegal, and it was only because she so desperately wanted to speak to Ian before he cycled off into the wide blue yonder that she didn't switch it off and tidy it away into its black leather holster as she usually did.

She swung off the country road and on to the big main road which ran from Belfast to Derry. The phone was still ringing unanswered when she saw the traffic police squad car tucked into the lay-by behind the bus shelter at the Derryrose roundabout. It was a crafty place for the traffic police to lurk, for speeding drivers could not see them until it was too late to slow down;

those with out-of date tax discs could not swerve away into the village and mobile abusers were always caught red-handed and fined on the spot – one thousand pounds, pay up and argue about it later. Eva's telephone-holding hand did not move away from the side of her head but with one desperate movement she managed to let the phone drop while vigorously scratching at the back of her ear. She continued to hear the phone ringing, even after it was dropped, and that pleased her for she thought she had managed to drop it into her handbag. She vigorously continued to scratch the back of her ear until she was safely past the policemen. When the phone rang off she made a mental note that in future she must try not to make illegal manoeuvres. As it said in the Bible – behold, your sins will always find you out!

Alexandra heard the phone ringing but decided not to answer it. Why should she drag herself out of her lovely comfortable bed and dash downstairs *in her condition* when Ian was off work and in the house somewhere and could answer it just as well as she could? This was the start of his holiday leave, and it was best to establish the precedent now, that she wouldn't be getting out of bed to answer telephones or doorbells.

Alexandra had pillows heaped up behind her and a decent cup of tea at her elbow. She was so much better rested now Ian was sleeping in the spare room. She was no longer too hot in bed, and she was able to get up and go to the toilet at least twice every night without feeling she had to apologise to him that their baby was compressing her bladder. And his breathing had always annoyed her, even before conception.

Alexandra lay back on her pillows and flicked through the first of her magazines. It was the one Sarah had given her with a feature on the benefits of reflexology for pregnant ladies. Once Sarah had read it she'd booked Alexandra a one-hour session at Curl Up and Dye; they were going together at midday. While Ruth massaged Alexandra's feet, Sarah was going to have a pedicure – what a fun, girly way to spend the first day of the school summer holidays . . . Alexandra ran her hands over the swell of her bump. How could she have been so wrong about Sarah? It was astonishing to think she'd judged her so harshly just because she had once been engaged to Ian . . .

At first Alexandra thought she had peed herself again. Things had been leaking steadily out of that end for a couple of days, little dribbles; she assumed it was because the baby was lying so heavy on her bladder. It was still another fortnight until the baby was due; at her next antenatal appointment she would mention it to the midwife; until then she was wearing a sanitary towel in her pants and washing a lot to keep fresh.

She climbed out of bed to go to the bathroom. There was a funny little pop somewhere beneath her bump, then a gush that saturated the sanitary towel and ran down her legs and on to the bedroom carpet. Her first thought was of the mess, *I hope it doesn't leave a stain*, and the second was for her mother, *I want my mother. Where is she?*

She knew Eva had gone to the Ulster Hall with the ladies from the Widows' Group. She tried Eva's number and when the phone kept ringing and ringing she assumed she must have switched it off when she was driving the minibus. But it was already after eleven. If she'd left the primary school car park at nine o'clock as per arrangements, she'd have been in Belfast an hour ago. Oh well, she'd just have to keep on trying.

It never occurred to Alexandra that Eva might not have her phone with her. That she might have dropped it in her car and it might have slipped down the side of the seat. Such twists of fate never happened to Eva. She was not a mother who made silly mistakes.

37

When Sarah pulled up at the house, Alexandra was already in a lot of pain. She was trying to be brave about it, and do sensible things like take deep, calming breaths, but each time a contraction squeezed her guts she wanted to cry out a swear word. How strange that primordial pain should have this effect on a good-living woman who sang gospel songs in church and who scolded the children in her class when they used such profanities as 'Jeepers!'

Sarah walked round to the back of the house and knocked on the kitchen door. A roar of obscenity and counting greeted her. She listened with bemusement.

'Thirty-two, feck it, thirty-four, feck it . . .'

She shouted: 'Alexandra? Are you all right in there?'

Alexandra opened the door. From the outside she looked normal – a woman not long out of bed, still wrapped in her robe, putting on make-up. There was eye shadow on one eye, and her hair was rolled up in heated rollers. She said, 'Hello, there. I've been waiting for you! Yes, I'm all right just now, but that one was huge, it lasted nearly forty seconds. I was timing it on the kitchen clock, it's the only clock in the house with a second hand. The counting helps me to concentrate. Amazing how quickly the pain goes away. Now, from my calculations, and the pattern over the past half-hour, I've got about ten minutes before the next one. That should give us enough time for a nice cup of tea . . .'

Sarah said, 'Has your baby started to come? How exciting! Where's Ian? Where's your mother?'

Alexandra's make-up was scattered across the kitchen table and a full-length, free-standing mirror was positioned beside it. Maternity outfits were hanging over the back of the kitchen chairs, shoes neatly paired on the floor. She might have been getting ready for school. She flicked the switch on the kettle, then selected a pencil and began to draw a careful green line along her left eye.

She said, 'I'm really sorry about our reflexology date. I'm going to have to cancel. I've a feeling I might be otherwise occupied for the next couple of hours. And for the rest of my life after that.'

Sarah repeated, 'Where's Ian? Where's your mother?'

'Mother has gone to the Ulster Hall, in the school minibus, if you care to remember? She's taking the Widows' Group out for the day, to a scone-baking competition. Ironic, really, when you think she's never baked a scone in her life! She wouldn't know where to start! She was always far too busy working when Johnboy and I were growing up. Daddy did all the baking. And all the cooking, too. She can't boil water—'

'Please, Alexandra, where's Ian?'

A contraction came on her like a roaring banshee. It seemed to Sarah it grabbed her roughly in the guts and as it squeezed, she buckled. She grabbed the side of the table and the back of a chair, her face was contorted with agony. She started to count. By the time she'd reached twenty-five her eyes were popping, her breathing was laboured and her language was out of control. Thirty-two, frig sake, thirty-four, frig sake.'

At forty-four it suddenly stopped, as quickly as it had started. She resumed her upright position, checked her notebook, and said, 'That was a little sooner than I was expecting. It's only eight minutes since the last contraction. I think I've gone up a gear. Is the tea ready? Oh goody, I'm desperate for a cup of tea.'

'At what stage do you go to the hospital?' asked Sarah.

Alexandra replied, 'Well, actually, I've decided not to go to the hospital, not while this foul sewer is coming out of my mouth. I can't seem to stop it, either! Earlier on there, before you arrived, I tried to use civilised language – "Oh dear" and "That hurts!" Unfortunately, when I'm in the grip of the contraction, some dark part of my brain takes over. And you know, the pain is only going to get worse. It's still quite manageable at the minute, but when the contractions are coming faster and stronger with no break between them, I just know my language will be X-rated in its awfulness . . .'

Sarah's voice came out in a squeak. She said, 'What do you mean, you've decided not to go to the hospital? Of course you must go to the hospital!'

Alexandra filled her lips with a lipstick in a nice shade of apricot. She carefully blotted with a piece of kitchen roll. She admired herself in the mirror and firmly shook her head.

She said, 'It's a pity, for I was looking forward to some pain relief! But I can't possibly go now. One of the children in my class – his mum is a midwife . . . I don't want her thinking I use such language on a regular basis. She might complain to the Department of Education and have me removed from my teaching position. OK, that's my face finished. I'll just take out the rollers then I'm going for a little walk. Do you want to come with me? I thought it might be relaxing to walk up the road and back down again, especially when the weather's so pleasant. And I must try Mother's number again. I'm really surprised I can't get through to her. She must have switched the phone to "silent", or maybe she switched it off when she was driving the minibus and has forgotten to switch it back on.'

It was one of those rare occasions in life when Sarah was truly lost for words.

Finally she said, 'You still haven't told me where Ian is.'

Alexandra pointed to a note on the door of the fridge. It was in Ian's handwriting. It said: *Bike ride to Derry, back 6 p.m.*

A bubble of panic rose in Sarah. Six p.m. was hours away. Even if she had his number and phoned him, it would still be at least a couple of hours before he got home. And Eva had switched off her phone. Sarah was all alone with a crazy woman in labour, who was refusing medical help because of a few little swear words.

Sarah whispered the worst swear word she could think of. There. She felt better already.

Sarah had planned to take Rupert's mobile number off her speed dial. She'd meant to delete it; she meant to delete him. But not just yet. Not until she'd forgotten how it felt to dance in his arms at the Wedding of the Year. And all the other bits too. How it had felt to sit in his car beside him at Derryrose roundabout, when they'd played their funny little game of Blind Man's Bluff. Not until she'd forgotten the crease between his eyes when he smiled and how it made her heart skip a beat. Yes, she knew it was over, before it had even begun, and the reasons why it was over were wise. He was a two-timing cheat and she never wanted to see him again.

But she wasn't quite ready to delete him.

Well, today, thank goodness for her indecision and for this week's programming schedule on the

GoodEveningIreland.com website. Thanks to the fact that she still fancied him rotten, she knew he was at the Ulster Hall with the crew from *Good Evening, Ireland*, reporting on the scone-baking championship. Himself and Jimmy – and, no doubt, Jimmy would be offering to sample the scones. And Rupert's face would be inscrutable – how she longed to kiss his inscrutable face. While Alexandra was lost in the middle of another contraction – 'forty-two, damnation, forty-four, damnation . . .' – she phoned him.

He answered immediately.

'Sarah, is that you?'

Was it normal to feel weak at the knees just at the sound of a voice? She wanted to smile and to savour it. She could picture him as clearly as if he was standing in front of her, in a spotless shirt and sober tie, his shoes polished till they were gleaming.

'Sarah, is that you?'

She said, 'I'm sorry to disturb you when you're working. I believe you're at the Ulster Hall for the scone-baking competition?'

'Yes, you're right,' said Rupert softly. He could hear her voice was shaking. She sounded nervous. He hoped she wasn't nervous because she was talking to him.

He had phoned her every day since his birthday dinner at the Gamekeeper's Cottage but she hadn't picked up to speak to him. He'd even called round to the brown and white bungalow in the hope he might speak to her there. But her mother had answered the door and said, 'You've got a cheek coming here! And who would have thought it of you – on the TV you act like a gentleman! I suppose it would spoil your image as Ireland's most eligible bachelor if it was common knowledge that you're already engaged! And what an ugly potato of a girl to choose – when you could have had my lovely Sarah! It was a pity Kenneth didn't shoot you when he had the opportunity!'

Sarah said, 'I have an emergency situation. I'm with Alexandra – the headmistress at Derryrose Primary School. You met her when you came to interview us – she's in active labour and she's alone. I'm here, but it's not me she wants. She wants her mother. Do you remember Eva from my sister's wedding, the mother of the bridegroom? You wanted to interview her, but I couldn't find her . . . she's somewhere in the Ulster Hall. She went up with a group in a minibus . . . Is there any way you could find her for me and tell her what has happened? We can't reach her on her own phone . . .'

Her voice fizzled to a stop. It felt pushy and rude to have phoned him. She felt she had taken advantage of his celebrity. She felt she was using him.

'I'm sorry to have bothered you,' she said.

'Where are you?' he asked, but she had already hung up.

Rupert drove the mother to the Meadows even though he had a lunch date arranged in Belfast with his parents and Angela.

'It's no bother at all,' he insisted. 'Get into my car, Mrs Jackson.'

When she saw him, Sarah said, 'Thank you', and the way she looked at him when she was saying it, with her eyes shining like stars, he thought maybe she wasn't so furious with him any more. He hazarded a smile and she smiled back. Rupert's spirits lifted, for wasn't this the only reason he'd put himself out, and tracked down the mother and driven her back to the Meadows? So Sarah might think of him favourably? Perhaps she might even listen to what he had to say to her . . .

Politely he asked Alexandra: 'Where is your husband? Can I fetch him?'

Alexandra shook her head. 'And don't waste your time looking for him. It's my own fault he's not got his phone. I hid it from him last week. Whether he's here or not, it'll all be the same in a hundred years. I've got

Sarah and my mother. I'm going to be all right now.'

Rupert felt a sense of relief, for it was forty miles to Derry along a winding mountain road with a dozen different places for stopping – small town hotels, country pubs – it might take him all day to find Ian. And already he was running late for his lunch date with his parents and Angela. He was careful to keep his voice neutral. 'Well, if you're very sure. I must say your mother and Sarah seem like a competent couple of midwives . . .'

Alexandra gave him a watery smile. 'Even if you did find my husband, he might not want to come home with you! He's not spoken to me since the Wedding of the Year. We've been having a stupid row. That's why he's miles away on his bike – to get away from me!'

Rupert decided to leave. There was still time to reschedule lunch; he could meet his parents and Angela at three o'clock, not at two. He held out his hand for shaking. He smiled into Alexandra's eyes.

He said, 'Best of luck with the baby.'

Alexandra took his hand just as the contraction caught her. Her grip tightened and tightened, her eyes filled with pain. She squeezed them tight shut and she breathed through her nose, counting loudly and clearly. But this time when she reached thirty and the pain had built to a crescendo, she began to scream for Ian: 'Thirty-five, Ian Flemming where are you?, thirty-seven, Ian Flemming, I need you, thirty-nine, O Ian, Ian! Wherefore art thou, Ian?'

Sarah's eyes met Rupert's over the top of Alexandra's head. He could read what her eyes were asking. They were asking him to drive up the mountain and to please, please, please find Ian.

Rupert drove down the road towards Derry – slowly, in case he missed Ian. First he drove through Derryrose village and past Phase Two of Bluebell Orchard. The outside shell of the houses was finished, the roofs were on; the internal fittings were going in. Flemming's Fitted Bathrooms had the contract for three bathrooms each and a shower room in every house – normally Ian would be on this site, in a hard hat and polished black shoes, overseeing installation and calculating his profit, but it was the builders' holidays and the site was deserted. Rupert paused briefly to admire the houses – they were large with large gardens around them, perfect for young energetic families; when he'd interviewed Sarah, she'd told him every house had been bought by a family and every family had applied for places at Derryrose Primary School in the autumn. It was generally believed that the next building work in the village would be an extension to the primary school.

Then Rupert drove along the wide paved road to Derryrose roundabout. He turned left on to the main road that ran between Belfast and Derry. There was a small mountain range between Derryrose and Derry but the first part of the journey was in the wetlands where the road was flat and fast and wide. Lorries and buses whizzed past; you needed nerves of steel to ride a bike on that part of the road.

Rupert drove quickly. He would easily be able to see if Ian was coming towards him, but he didn't really expect to see him so close to Derryrose, not if he wasn't due home until six. After seven miles the road reached the foot of the mountain. It had to be very tough on your legs, the straight ten miles to the top; there was a crawler lane for slow-moving vehicles. Rupert drove up, up, up, past small, bleak homesteads, and cold-looking sheep. As he got closer to the top of the mountain, the farmland changed from grassy fields to mountain pasture, scattered with yellow gorse and purple heather. Finally he reached the top, and parked up at the View Point picnic tables. On one side of the road the mountain fell away a thousand feet to a rushing stream on the valley floor, on the other side the mountain rose a thousand feet to its summit. There was a footpath to the very top, five hundreds steps, they said, and at the top, on a clear day, you could see the whole way to Derry. If Rupert climbed to the top he'd have a panoramic view of perhaps twenty miles of mountain road. His feet and the bottom of his trousers would get dirty but he might be able to see Ian. Anyway, he wanted to climb and to breathe in the brisk mountain air. He wanted space to think about Sarah.

All those unanswered phone calls, and the visit to the brown and white bungalow – he wanted to explain to Sarah that his engagement to Angela was an arranged engagement, and his marriage to Angela would be an arranged marriage.

But he worried Sarah would not believe him for he could hardly believe it himself that he'd been pressurised into something so antiquated and so unfair. This was the twenty-first century. People did not have arranged marriages any more. Even the royal families of Europe were allowed to pick and choose whom they wanted to marry – *Hello!* magazine was constantly running happy-ever-after stories of royal princes marrying commoner girls; wasn't the Crown Prince of Spain married to a girl who used to the read the news, and wasn't the Crown Prince of Denmark married to an Australian he'd met in a pub at the Olympic Games? And Mr Pin-up, Prince William of England . . . his lovely long-term girlfriend was the daughter of a businessman, not an aristocrat.

It was the clever work of his clever mother to dress up a barbaric, old-fashioned marriage contract arrangement and pretend he had a choice in the matter. 'Your father and I are very tolerant, but if you're not married by thirty-five, we expect you to marry Angela . . .'

His sisters had been horrified.

'Don't agree to it!' they'd said. 'Refuse point blank,' they'd said.

But it hadn't seemed like such a big deal at the time. He'd been young and optimistic when he'd agreed to the terms of the contract. Thirty-five had seemed like a lifetime away. Ireland was full of attractive, well-educated, interesting, suitable girls – some day he would meet one, and this ridiculous promise he'd made, to marry dull Angela when he was thirty-five, would be conveniently forgotten about. Except the years had floated past, and he'd never met anybody he really liked, not until he met Sarah. That first night he'd seen her in the pub dressed in her trouser suit he'd been interested and attracted, same as with all the other girls he'd wined and dined and wooed and abandoned in fifteen years of philandering.

Then he'd met her again at the wedding and he'd started to really like her – her serenity and her common sense, the crooked tooth at the front of her smile. She was beautiful and she was wise, how often did you get that together?

Rupert kept climbing to the top of the mountain. Left foot, right foot, left foot, right foot. His legs were exhausted and his ears were freezing. The sun was shining but the air was bitter. At the top there was a thicket of gorse. He threw himself down beside it, he was sheltered now from the wind.

Today he was going to tell his parents and Angela he was breaking off his arranged engagement. He was taking them all out for a very fine lunch in a public place to tell them. He was rather hoping the dignified splendour of the hushed and upmarket restaurant would keep them from behaving badly when he broke the news. His mother was much too civilised to squeal at him in a public place. He hoped.

To be honest, he felt a bit sorry for Angela; she was as much a victim of circumstance as he was. And she wasn't a bad-looking girl. A course of radical electrolysis treatments, a careful diet, a decent hairdresser – God forbid, and he laughed when he thought of it, but if she'd had Sarah's mother rearing her she might have been almost a good-looking girl!

Without this ridiculous marriage contract arrangement she might motivate herself to catch the eye of some other man. Perhaps not a peer with a title, but the country was full of shy farmers who'd be grateful for a bit of attention.

Rupert phoned Sarah's number as his eyes swept twenty miles of green and brown blustery valley. Somewhere, in a dip, or behind a rock, or climbing upwards, was Ian on his road bike. Sarah answered the phone.

'How's it progressing?' he asked her.

Sarah said, 'We're on "fuck" now. It can't be much longer. I don't think she has any more swear words left in her repertoire. She's already been through all the French ones we know. I don't suppose you know any in those dead languages you learned at school?'

He spotted him, Ian Flemming, an eejit on a road bike, climbing up and up.

'I think I see him! Praise God, I think I see him. Tell Alexandra I've found him. Tell her the next time the pains come on she must sing "Hallelujah".'

At first Ian thought it was a joke when Lord Rupert Glass from the television flagged him down and told him his wife was in labour. Some sort of candid camera moment. He looked around; he was expecting to see a camera poking out of a gorse bush.

He said, 'She was all right this morning when I left her.'

He was still feeling angry with Alexandra, for the mean way she'd been treating him; for hiding his spectacles at the Wedding of the Year, and closing him out of the bedroom; for refusing to do his washing and ironing, for hiding his phone and his iPod.

Rupert said, 'You *are* Ian Flemming, aren't you? You're married to Alexandra. The baby is coming, just now. Get into the car. I'll drive you to her.'

Rupert tried to stick the road bike into the boot of his car, but the bike didn't fold, and the boot was too small, it was an impossible task. Ian watched him, frowning. He said, 'That bike cost a lot of money. Please be careful with it.'

Little Lord Rupert looked at him strangely. 'I can see now why Sarah jilted you. And why she's been in no hurry to find a replacement. No woman deserves to be married to such a selfish, self-centred man! What are you doing out here on a road bike, miles from civilisation, with no way of anyone contacting you, when you know your wife is about to have a baby?'

'My wife's huffing with me,' said Ian.

Rupert carried the road bike to the side of the mountain which dropped for a thousand feet. Evenly he said, 'Get into the car, please, before I throw your silly bike over the edge of the mountain.'

They drove in silence. Ian stared out of the window. He was trying not to hear what Rupert was telling him – something about how lucky he was to be married to a woman who loved him so much she was screaming for him during the pains of labour.

Ian said, 'Screaming?' and a tiny knot of panic began to build in his belly. 'Why is she screaming? Has she not taken pain relief? There are epidurals available at the hospital. Has she not had an epidural?'

'She's not at the hospital. She's at home. She's had no pain relief. I don't know how she's managing to stay upright. She held my hand during one contraction and she almost crushed all the bones in it.'

'She held *your* hand?'

Alexandra was suffering the transition phase of her labour. She was bathed in sweat and her careful make-up had run in streams down her face. Her hair hung in limp rat's tails round her face. She was wearing one of Ian's unwashed shirts from out of the laundry basket. Her contractions were less than two minutes apart and were lasting longer than a minute. She had barely managed to catch her breath after one contraction, before the next marched in. But she was no longer swearing and counting. Instead she was chanting 'Ian, Ian, Ian', and when she was fit to move, she paced forwards and backwards from the kitchen to the utility-room door and watched for Sarah who was out on the road, looking for Rupert's car. She was waiting for Sarah to wave when she saw it.

When the pain was indescribable she lay down on her side on the camping mattress Eva had brought from the guest room; it was positioned cosily beside the Aga. She took deep, calming breaths and thought about Ian.

Her mother said, 'Can't be much longer now. It's nearly ten minutes since Rupert called Sarah. He's bound to be down the mountain by now.'

But Alexandra was beyond hearing Eva. She was thinking of Ian and herself on honeymoon, rubbing suntan lotion into sunburnt, naked skin and the salty taste of his kisses. She was remembering how he'd jumped up from his beach towel and run off to fetch her anything she'd asked for. 'Glass of water? No problem!' 'Your novel lying on the bed in our room? No problem!' 'You've forgotten your sunglasses, let me get them for you . . .'

She'd laughed at the time at his enthusiasm. She'd said, 'Why are you being so kind to me?'

'Because I love you.'

This time when she walked to the utility-room door Sarah was waving frantically.

'I can see the car coming! I can see the car coming!'

The car screeched up to the side of the house. Ian leapt out and ran to his wife. There were tears streaming down his face. He was calling, 'Alexandra, I'm coming. Alexandra, I'm here for you . . .'

Sarah said to Rupert, 'Could I trouble you to phone Dr Hennessey's surgery? Can you tell him the baby has come in a rush? I know Alexandra is refusing to go to the hospital, but once the baby is born, a doctor really ought to come and check everything is all right. I think they give babies drops at birth – is it Vitamin K? I'm not sure!'

Rupert said, 'I'll do better than phone. I shall drive there directly and tell him. I shall emphasise the urgency. You can depend on me.'

Sarah had been rather hoping he might stay. It was a week since she'd seen him. She'd missed him. 'Leaving so soon?' she said, and she couldn't keep the disappointment out of her voice.

Sarah stood in a queue in the village shop. She was waiting to pay for a bunch of tired pink carnations, and a card that said: 'Congratulations, it's a Girl'. It was after six o'clock and all the bigger, better shops, with bigger, better bouquets, were shut. Alexandra would have to wait to get something professional out of a florist's.

How amazing the baby was born, and how effortless it had been after Ian arrived! Rupert had just pulled off down the road, and she'd been staring after his car, wondering if he was watching her in his rearview mirror, wondering if she should blow him a kiss, when Eva had shouted, 'Sarah, Sarah, Sarah', and she'd dashed into the house to find Ian supporting Alexandra's full body weight, talking to her calmly and quietly, while Eva was down at the business end with a towel and a bowl of hot water.

And then suddenly the baby was born. It shot out of its mother with an elegant twist and there it was, in the real world. And suddenly Alexandra and Ian were the parents of the newest little girl in the whole wide world. She was the most beautiful human being Sarah had ever seen and tears welled up in her eyes again when she thought about it.

They'd wrapped her in a navy-blue bath towel, and put her on Alexandra's chest. Alexandra had said, 'Let's call her Sarah. Sarah Flemming. Isn't that a beautiful name?'

'We missed you last week, Sarah.'

Sarah had not noticed Jane Temple standing behind her in the queue with a net of lemons in her basket. She knew Jane was married to Michael who was best friends with Rupert.

'Missed me where?' asked Sarah.

Jane's long dark hair was tied back off her lovely face and she was wearing a dress of pink linen and gorgeous pink shoes with a long pointed toe and embroidered pink flowers.

She said, 'At Rupert's birthday party! He told us you were coming – we were all so excited to meet you properly! You know he's never before invited a girl into his Gamekeeper's Cottage? You're the very first. His sisters were beside themselves – they thought he was going to announce his engagement!'

Sarah's mouth opened. Then closed. She stared at Jane. Jane stared back.

Sarah said quietly, 'But Rupert is already engaged to a girl called Angela Churchill-Knox. I found out only last Saturday, or I'd never have agreed to come to the birthday party . . .' It was her turn to pay. She fumbled in her purse for a ten-pound note, grabbed her change, and shot out of the shop. She started up her car and was about to pull out of the street when Jane came running after her. Her pretty pink shoes were holding her back, so she took them off and ran barefoot. Sarah deliberated as to whether or not she should drive off and pretend she hadn't seen her.

'Wait a minute!'

Sarah wound down her window. She composed her features into something noncommittal and pleasant.

Jane emphatically said, 'I don't know who told you

about Rupert's engagement, but I think whoever it was told you only half the story. And not the nice half, either! I'm sure he can explain it better than me, if you'd only give him a chance! The important thing is that Rupert was gutted when you didn't come into his party . . . I actually thought he was going to cry . . .'

Dr Hennessey had checked Baby Sarah and pronounced her perfect. He'd checked Alexandra and pronounced her perfect. Mother and baby had been bathed and were now tucked up together, fast asleep, in the master bedroom at the Meadows. Ian was sitting on the edge of the bed, alternately stroking his wife and his daughter. He was still wearing his cycling clothes, but had removed his helmet.

Before she'd fallen asleep he'd tried to tell Alexandra how sorry he was for acting so sulky the last few weeks of her pregnancy, but she'd stopped him mid flow.

'Ahh stop. There's nothing to forgive. Isn't that the whole point of being in love? There's nothing to forgive. Anyways, I've been a bit of a sulky cow myself . . .'

Sarah knocked on the bedroom door and brought in her bunch of flowers.

She whispered, 'Is Alexandra asleep? She must be exhausted! I can see now why they call it labour! And you were magnificent too, the way you were able to support her, and calm her down and help her to focus. You make a great team . . .'

Ian smiled at his ex-fiancée with affection. She was

still the prettiest girl he had ever seen, with her long blond hair, stunning figure and sweet, serene, smiling face. She was the sort of girl any man would be proud of . . . but she wasn't Alexandra.

He said, 'Is Rupert Glass in love with you?'

'What makes you say that?' asked Sarah.

'I can't think of one other reason why he'd have spent an hour up a mountain road looking for me except that you asked him to do it.'

Sarah drove to the Gamekeeper's Cottage. It was almost eight o'clock and just starting to get dark. Rupert's car was there, he was home. She rang the doorbell and the jingle-jangle noise sounded faintly through the house. She wondered if maybe she should walk round to the glass box at the back, where all the light was coming from.

Eventually he opened the door. He was wearing jeans and an open necked shirt. He was barefoot, his feet were beautiful.

'I didn't give you a chance to explain the photograph in *Country Life*,' she said. 'I'm sorry. Please will you tell me what you wanted to say?'

He led the way silently through the old house which he used as an office. There were photographs all over the walls of Rupert with famous people – Rupert and the United States President, Rupert with the Rolling Stones; Rupert and the squad of the Northern Ireland football team. They crossed the glass bridge to his private quarters. She could hear something surreal behind the closed door – was it her voice she could hear?

He was watching her on the television: Sarah in front of the church; Sarah in the walled garden; dancing with Sarah to 'The Blue Danube'. She looked at the television. She looked at Rupert.

He said, 'Jimmy made it for me, the afternoon of your sister's wedding. He put it on a loop. I can watch you for hours, if I want.'

Then, quietly, he explained about his engagement to Angela – and how he'd never thought of it as cheating when he went out with other girls, because he hadn't considered his engagement to Angela as anything more than a casual arrangement, a contractual agreement, a way to stop his mother nagging him . . .

He told her how that afternoon he'd met with his parents and Angela and told them he would not be marrying Angela on his thirty-fifth birthday. He was not love with her and she was not in love with him, and they would not be getting married.

He said, 'So I'm no longer a two-timing cheat. Just a man with a broken engagement.'

Sarah smiled, 'A broken engagement is nothing to boast about . . .'

He smiled too. He said, 'In that case, do you think you might like to see me again, now that I'm no longer a two-timing cheat?'

It had always been Gran Gran's ambition to create for herself a self-contained apartment within the walls of Derryrose. During the hard years with Kenneth she'd even had plans drawn up, for it was her little fantasy that she might live in her apartment, while he lived in the rest of the house. And she hadn't been asking for so very much. Upstairs, she'd wanted a bedroom and bathroom; downstairs, a small kitchen and sitting room. The entrance would be through the green-painted door in the high stone wall of her garden and all other access routes to the rest of farmhouse would be bricked up.

'It will be my little kingdom,' said Gran Gran. 'Somewhere I can play records and invite friends over for drinks.'

But Kenneth hadn't allowed her to do it. He'd said, 'A divorce would be cheaper, Lady Muck.'

So they'd struggled on together, each year less happy than the last, making each other more miserable, and everyone else around them. At regular intervals she'd presented to him the plans and asked him to reconsider and every time he'd said, 'A divorce would be cheaper, Lady Muck.'

It was the happiest day of her life, the day he dropped dead of a heart attack.

It took only a month to build the self-contained apartment Gran Gran had always dreamed of. Sarah followed her plans but more than her plans it was the hard work and goodwill of everybody involved that got the job done so quickly.

Johnboy and Daisy carried out the 1970s furniture from the sitting room to the hay barn across the yard. There it sat in state while Sarah and Rupert pulled up the swirly green carpets and took down the dense, green, tasselled curtains. They burnt everything on a bonfire. Then Sarah hired a steam stripper and spent three solid days stripping off green swirly wallpaper; Rupert hired a sanding machine and spent two days sanding down old floorboards. A plumbing company, recommended by Ian, installed oil-fired central heating with a timer device for hot water. Sarah painted ceilings, shutters, skirting boards and walls.

'The colour of primroses,' said Daisy.

Sarah and Rupert then carried a selection of furniture back into the sitting room: the coffee tables, the piano, the sheepskin rug and the gramophone. Gran Gran's tatty sofas were donated to the East Belfast Mission. Sarah bought new sofas in the summer sales.

Sarah sketched and measured the old panelled gun room in the hall beside Gran Gran's sitting room. She took these sketches to Kitchen City and a member of staff designed, free of charge, a fabulous, compact kitchen, full of *all mod cons*. Sarah chose aluminium kitchen units; Kitchen City delivered and Johnboy screwed them in – he was a whizz with an electric screwdriver. Ian insisted on giving her, free of charge, a fitted bathroom from the instore collection – to say 'thank you' for helping Alexandra while she was in labour, and for sending Rupert to find him, making it possible for him to be present at the birth of their baby daughter. The bathroom was installed in the dressing room of the bedroom she'd shared with Daisy since she was a teenager.

A joiner and a plasterer spent a day erecting a stud wall between Sarah's bedroom and the rest of the upstairs landing. Downstairs they erected another stud wall between the sitting room, the gun room and the rest of the house. Once the plaster dried Sarah painted it primrose.

She graciously declined the offer of a television set from her parents' brown and white bungalow.

'But how are you going to watch Rupert Glass on *Good Evening, Ireland*?' asked Mummy.

'I'm not going to watch him on *Good Evening, Ireland*.'

During the renovations Mummy worried that perhaps Sarah was playing gooseberry to the newly-weds.

She said, 'Daisy and Johnboy are awfully sweet and I know they won't say anything, but don't you think perhaps you should sleep here in the bungalow, with your father and me?'

Sarah declined this kind offer. 'Thank you, but I've found somewhere very suitable to sleep.'

Helen drove up one Saturday morning at the end of July. She'd been invited for lunch. Then she was taking Sarah back with her to spend August by the sea. This was her first trip back to Derryrose since the Wedding of the Year and her first chance to see Sarah's apartment. She was very impressed with the renovations.

She said, 'I can't smell turf any more! It must have been impregnated in the green swirly carpet and the old tasselled curtains.'

Sarah was cleaning windows. She said, 'That's the curse of this cold, damp climate. Gran Gran was always freezing, poor thing. She had the fire blazing day and night to keep this room warm. Now I have central heating at the flick of a switch I don't think I'll bother with curtains or a rug, not during the summer months, anyway. Curtains would only block the view to the garden.'

Helen sat down on the edge of the window sill; she unwrapped a Bounty Bar.

She said, 'When you come to stay with me at the villa, you will do no housework! I absolutely forbid it. I have a cleaning lady who leaves the place spotless and will be very offended if you usurp her authority! And as for cooking, it's out of the question. We're going to live on chips and ice cream, and cups of tea in beach-front cafés.'

Sarah laughed. After all this hard work she was looking forward to waking up to the sound of waves crashing on rocks, and the salty smell of the sea. And to swimming and walking on the beach, to eating ice cream and spotting people she knew, waving to them and chatting.

She said, 'I'm really looking forward to it. But I shall insist you eat better than what you're suggesting – a lady in your condition needs a nutritious diet! Are you feeling quite well? You still don't look pregnant!'

Helen gently rubbed her tummy. She'd just been to an appointment at the hospital on the coast. She was twelve weeks' pregnant exactly. They'd taken samples of urine and blood; they were calm and kind; efficient. They'd asked her if she would have a husband or partner with her when she was delivering her baby and she'd told them, 'I've got my sister Sarah. She's had loads of experience with home birth and delivering babies . . .'

Helen said, 'I may not look pregnant, but I have to say, it is the most extraordinary feeling, to have Richard's baby inside me. No doubt you think I'm barking mad, but it's almost as if he's with me. We may not be married, but we couldn't be closer . . .'

*

Last night Rupert had offered to hunt down Richard and tell him, man to man, that Helen was expecting his baby. He'd said, 'I'm sure his wife is related to Angela, it's such an unusual name . . . Why don't I ask Angela if she's related to Elisabeth? I could find out, then, where Richard lives and go and see him without Helen ever knowing . . .'

And Sarah had frostily enquired, 'Are you referring to Angela Churchill-Knox, the woman you were once engaged to marry?'

Rupert liked it when she was jealous. Sparks flashed from her serene grey eyes and her voice became cold and brittle. Even though he had never felt anything for Angela, except perhaps compassion, it amused him enormously that Sarah was jealous of the history between them. (And if he was being honest with himself, he had to admit to similar feelings when he saw her chatting to Ian.)

He'd run his hand over the top of her silky hair and said, 'I don't know anyone else called Angela, do you?'

Sarah had kissed his stroking hand.

She said, 'It's not difficult to get in contact with Richard, if we ever need him! He's been phoning the farmhouse every day since the Wedding of the Year, and each time he phones I dial one four seven one and write down the number he's calling from. So, if we ever need him, he's at the end of one of those numbers . . . But I honestly don't think she wants him to know about the baby. I think we should mind our own business.'

*

Sarah jumped lightly down from the window.

She said, 'Please can I have a bite of your Bounty Bar?'

Helen could hardly recognise her sister – because she was so happy. Sarah's hair was no longer scraped back; it hung in a gentle plait down her back. Her clothing was no longer scary and rigid. Today she was pretty and fresh in a thin summer dress and bare feet.

She said, 'How are you managing to shift Rupert Glass without our mother interfering?'

Sarah laughed. 'Because she doesn't know anything about it! He walks across the fields to see me, he never uses the lane. I walk across the fields to see him, and when it's raining I drive across the fields in the Landrover. Sometimes Mummy says to me – "Oh darling, wasn't it a pity you never got your night with Rupert . . ." and I just have to laugh.'

'So, when am I going to meet him?' asked Helen.

'He's coming in half an hour. He says he's bringing lunch with him. He's really looking forward to meeting you . . .'

Helen wiped a small smudge of dirt from the end of Sarah's nose and, arm in arm, they walked together out of the French doors, into the garden. She plucked a piece of rosemary between her fingers, rubbed it, and sniffed.

'I feel quite nervous about meeting Lord Rupert!

Do you think he'll like me? Do you think I'll like him?'

Sarah was robust. 'Of course you'll like him. I promise. I know you have a soft spot for toffs!'

Pick up a *little black dress* – it's a girl thing.

ITALIAN FOR BEGINNERS
Kristin Harmel
PBO £5.99

Despairing of finding love, Cat Connelly takes up an invitation to go to Italy, where an unexpected friendship, a whirlwind tour of the Eternal City and a surprise encounter show her that the best things in life (and love) are always unexpected . . .

Say '*arrivederci*, lonely hearts' with another fabulous page-turner from Kristin Harmel.

978 0 7553 4743 8

THE GIRL MOST LIKELY TO . . .
Susan Donovan
PBO £5.99

Years after walking out of her small town in West Virginia, Kat Cavanaugh's back and looking for apologies – especially from Riley Bohland, the man who broke her heart. But soon Kat's questioning everything she thought she knew about her past . . . and about her future.

A red-hot tale of getting mad, getting even – and getting everything you want!

978 0 7553 5144 2

Pick up a *little black dress* – it's a girl thing.

THE FARMER NEEDS A WIFE
Janet Gover
PBO £5.99

Rural romances become all the rage when editor Helen Woodley starts a new magazine column profiling Australia's lovelorn farmers. But a lot of people (and Helen herself) are about to find out that the course of true love ain't ever smooth . . .

978 0 7553 4715 5

It's not all haystacks and pitchforks, ladies – get ready for a scorching outback read!

HIDE YOUR EYES
Alison Gaylin
PBO £5.99

Samantha Leiffer's in big trouble: the chest she saw a sinister man dumping into the Hudson river contained a dead body, meaning she's now a witness in a murder case. It's just as well hot, hardline detective John Krull is by her side . . .

978 0 7553 4802 2

'Alison Gaylin is my new mustread' Harlen Coben

Pick up a *little black dress* – it's a girl thing.

978 0 7553 4731 5

HANDBAGS AND HOMICIDE
Dorothy Howell
PBO £4.99

Haley didn't actually mean *murder* when she said she'd 'kill for' the latest fashions. But when her department store boss is discovered dead in the store room, fingers are pointed firmly at her! Will gorgeous Ty Cameron believe in her innocence?

A sharp, comic debut combining mystery, romance and shopping – what more could a girl want!

TRULY MADLY YOURS
Rachel Gibson
PBO £4.99

Delaney Shaw has to stay put in the town of Truly, Idaho for an entire year to claim her three-million-dollar inheritance ... At least the other condition of her stepfather's will, that she has nothing to do with sexy bad-boy Nick Allegrezza, sounds more manageable ... doesn't it?

Fall in love with Rachel Gibson and her fabulous, sexy romantic reads!

978 0 7553 3744 6

You can buy any of these other
Little Black Dress titles from your
bookshop or *direct from the publisher*.

FREE P&P AND UK DELIVERY
(Overseas and Ireland £3.50 per book)

TO ORDER SIMPLY CALL THIS NUMBER

01235 400 414

or visit our website: www.headline.co.uk

Prices and availability subject to change without notice.